GOD'S
LITTLE ACRE

GOD'S
LITTLE ACRE
Clerical Tales of the Countryside

EDITED BY MARK BRYANT

Hodder & Stoughton
LONDON SYDNEY AUCKLAND

First published in Great Britain in 1998

10 9 8 7 6 5 4 3

British Library Cataloguing in Publication Data
A record for this book is available from the British Library

ISBN 0 340 72178 2

Typeset by Avon Dataset Ltd, Bidford-on-Avon, Warks

Printed and bound in Great Britain by
The Guernsey Press Co. Ltd, Channel Isles

Hodder and Stoughton
A Division of Hodder Headline
338 Euston Road
London NW1 3BH

For Dena and Terry

Contents

Introduction

Far away from the noise and bustle of the urban metropolis, deep in the peaceful heartland of rural Britain, the centre of village life has always been the ancient stone church. Set in 'God's little acre' – that small, walled garden of hallowed ground which separates it from the patchwork of farms and fields, mountains and pastures – the scene seems to have remained unchanged since time immemorial. Custodian of the churchyard as well as the souls of his flock is the genial country parson, a pillar of the local community and a respected minister of God. Whether surrounded by apples, marrows and plaited bread at Harvest Festival or leading carols by candlelight at Christmas, whether christening babies in the font or drinking tea with elderly parishioners, and whether marrying farmhands or burying the local gentry, the village priest has been the traditional figurehead and unifying force among country folk for generations.

This book is an anthology of some of the very best and most evocative clerical stories of the countryside and contains tales by some of the greatest short-story-writers of all time, from the early nineteenth century to the present day, and both male and female. I have tried to make the collection as balanced as the limitations of length and copyright availability have allowed, and, for ease of reading, have generally avoided stories written entirely in regional dialects. The tales themselves range from comedy and romance to mystery and crime, and take place at all seasons of the year and in locations varying from the West Country, Wales and East Anglia, to Yorkshire, the Scottish Highlands and Ireland. In addition, whether Roman Catholic or Protestant, High Church or Low, all kinds of rural clergymen are represented here, from shy curates to headstrong vicars and from fire-and-brimstone preachers to doddery old rectors.

So turn off the distractions of TV and radio, find a quiet room away from street traffic and aircraft noises, take the phone off the hook and draw the curtains to shut out the scaffolding and construction-workers outside. Then, as you settle down in an easy chair and start to turn the pages, let your mind drift away to the sound of horse-drawn carts, birdsong and church bells, and let your imagination unlock the lych-gate to 'God's little acre', that old stone church and its kindly country parson . . .

Mark Bryant

The Rival Pastors

T. F. Powys

It is always a dangerous thing to allow churches to be built too near to each other, for, like old Devon bulls in the same field, they do not often agree. Whenever two churches are but a mile apart their bells are sure to clang angrily and their pastors are as prone to fight, and to be as jealous of one another, as two Dartmoor stags.

Everyone knows that, in political matters, those who hold nearly the same opinions quarrel over them the most, and though High and Low Church ministers are both Catholic Christians, yet either would address themselves more politely to an atheist or papist than to each other.

It is certainly fortunate for the quiet and peace of the modest layman that each church, however near, is set in its own parish, for if two churches – so near as Shelton and Maids Madder – had no legal boundary there would be sure to be murder.

The towers of these two churches were in full view of one another and looked resentful, and their respective ministers were certainly not behindhand in the battle of tongues.

Mr Hayhoe of Maids Madder belonged to the evangelical persuasion – a persuasion that was, alas! scarce enough in those moving times, when faith hid in the hollow trees and when so many had gone over to the scarlet lady of Rome. Mr Hayhoe was all the more bitter in heart for being left so lonely.

Mr Dirdoe of Shelton, though wearing the same kind of cloth

– the deepest black that could be purchased for money – held views that Mr Hayhoe abhorred. Mr Dirdoe believed in ritualism, and held that any pastor who was too lazy to turn to the east when the creed was being said must be little less than a man of Belial.

Mr Hayhoe was at heart and in conversation a Calvinist, Mr Dirdoe a disciple of Dr Keble. Mr Hayhoe was married, Mr Dirdoe was a single man. Each gentleman kept to his own parish, and so terrified his people with threats of everlasting damnation if they entered the church of his rival that no one either in Shelton or Maids Madder ever thought of doing so – except Lily Topp.

Whether it was the Devil's doing or no, it is not possible to tell, but unfortunately the parish boundary that divided Maids Madder from Shelton went through the middle of Daisy Cottage which was owned by John Topp, though his cottage was but a hundred yards from Maids Madder Church.

When John Topp sat down at his table for tea he took up the knife and cut the loaf of bread in Shelton, and Mrs Topp, when she filled his cup, was in Maids Madder, while Lily Topp more often than not had a foot in both the parishes.

'Maiden,' Mr Topp would observe with a great laugh, 'be in two places at once.'

When Mr Hayhoe came home from the evening service, Mrs Hayhoe would anxiously watch her husband, who was in the habit, because his own beard was so rough, of calling her a poor weak woman. If Mr Hayhoe looked sadly at the cold pork that his wife had provided for supper, Mrs Hayhoe knew that Lily Topp had not been in her pew beside her mother, and so must have committed the crime of visiting Shelton Church, where even incense was used for evensong.

Mr Hayhoe preached in a black gown – the year was 1880 – he was short and thick-set, but with the mildest eyes that any troubled sinner could wish to see. Though he used rough words in his sermons, his acts were the kindest; 'but with damnation knocking at one's door,' he would say, ' 'tis best to speak plain.'

Mr Dirdoe, on the other hand, was thin and saintly and extremely nice in all that he did or said. His eyes were kind, too, though melancholy, his fingers were long, and his hands as white as a maid's. He, too, as well as Mr Hayhoe, would be sure to notice whether Lily Topp visited Shelton Church, where the child would sit in a pew in front of the boys, who would throw nuts at her.

As is often the case with men whose thoughts ever dwell in the imagination and seek both their delight and sorrow in religion, neither of the rival pastors ever paid much heed to the earthly or carnal affairs of their people. These pastors were only concerned with the souls of their flocks, and each believed that the soul of Lily Topp was in jeopardy.

No doctor is more courteous in matters of etiquette than a country minister, for to trespass upon another's preserves – even to hunt a soul – is considered a very dreadful crime. Mr Dirdoe dared not call at Daisy Cottage, neither dared Mr Hayhoe, for neither knew in which village they would find the occupants. But, alas for Mr Dirdoe! the manners and warmth of the church at Maids Madder and the fierce pulpit cries of Mr Hayhoe had captured John Topp and his wife, Alice, who remained safe in the evangelical fold. Only Lily was the sometime wanderer.

In both the reverend gentlemen's minds there was the awful thought – 'What if Lily should be damned?'

Just as Daisy Cottage was in the two parishes so also were John Topp's fields, for though they were both very little fields one was in Maids Madder and one in Shelton. The fields were high up upon the down, and when John was at plough he could be easily seen from the Rectory windows at Maids Madder or from the Shelton Vicarage garden.

Though so separate in ideas that each believed the other's doctrine to be most damnable and capable of leading any who listened to it to perdition, yet, besides possessing the same loving-kindness in his eyes, each of the ministers had the same favourite hymn. And they never sang it without thinking of Lily Topp, for the hymn was 'There were Ninety and Nine'. No pastors of religion could be more humble either than these two good men, though they never met one another for fear they might say too much. But neither, for one moment, would allow himself to think that the simple peasants under his charge were not quite as interested in matters of religion as he.

When two good men seek so lovingly to save a sinner, one can easily conceive that the same idea might come to both at the same moment.

Mr Dirdoe was an early riser, and so was Mr Hayhoe, and after breakfast each would walk in his parish, visit the sick, talk to any old hedger he might meet, and then return, to write his sermon. One summer morning, when all the fowls of the air were singing their matins, Mr Dirdoe took a turn in his garden. No one, unless it were Mr Hayhoe, had more honourable ideas than he. He would have thrust his right hand into the fire and burnt it to the stump sooner than have harmed any by word, thought, or deed. He believed as strongly as his rival in the soundness of family life, and would never think of addressing Lily Topp upon the subject of religion without asking her father's leave.

Mr Dirdoe, as it happened that morning, looked up at the hills and saw John Topp at plough. Mr Dirdoe knew every field in his parish, and John Topp was ploughing in Shelton.

Mr Dirdoe returned to his house. A tramp was resting upon the doorstep, and the pastor asked him politely if he would mind moving for one moment. The tramp moved sullenly, and Mr Dirdoe fetched his hat and began to climb the downs. As he climbed Mr Dirdoe sang his favourite hymn . . .

Although John Topp's horses were old, they were happy with their master, for John never hurried them, and when they had a mind to rest he permitted them. John liked the horses to stop when he was alone, but he never wished anyone to notice that he was resting them, for he always affirmed at home that his horses worked as fast as the best and, if they rested at all, it was because they broke their traces with their vigorous motion.

John heard the hymn. He saw Mr Dirdoe approach him, and his horses stopped. John called out to them, but they remained still. He gave the reins a shake, but that did no good.

'Maybe 'e won't notice that they bain't moving,' said John, eyeing the approaching minister with much concern, 'but, all-same, 'tis best for I to give they horses their bait.' John had provided a nosebag for each horse, though for himself he had taken nothing. He now permitted them to eat.

Mr Dirdoe was not a man, as some are, who is afraid to name the master in whose employment he lived.

'I ask,' he said, 'in the name of God, to have a word with you, John.'

But John shook his head.

'Thik bain't a name to speak in these fields,' he said.

'And why?' asked Mr Dirdoe.

'Because they horses bain't churchgoers,' replied John.

'I wish to ask you,' said Mr Dirdoe, without heeding John's reply, 'if I may speak of the Eucharist, auricular confession, and the penitentiary to your daughter, Lily.'

John Topp laughed loudly.

'Oh!' he said, 'thee won't catch our Lil wi' they sprats!'

'You give me permission to try?' enquired Mr Dirdoe eagerly.

'Thee may try what thee like,' replied John, 'but our Lil bain't born yesterday, and that I do know.'

Mr Dirdoe strode down the hill. In his mind's eye he saw Lily Topp. A young creature, with round legs, running like a fawn, whose black eyes were merry, and whose cheeks might have been jealous of her lips that were like cherries, had not they themselves resembled rosy apples. That was but the carnal child of the flesh. Mr Dirdoe saw her soul, too – a white virgin pearl hidden in her heart . . .

Mr John Topp had been ploughing the last furrow in his Shelton field when Mr Dirdoe visited him, and upon the very next day he commenced to plough his other field, that was situated in Maids Madder. He had not been there but half an hour – and had already rested his horses four times, and was driving away his own troubles with a whiff of tobacco, at one end of the field – when he saw Mr Hayhoe approaching from the direction of Maids Madder Rectory.

Mr Hayhoe, who regarded the field a little contemptuously because it was not a page of the Scriptures, at once began to speak of salvation by faith, how few were predestined to be saved and how many were to be damned. 'And if,' said Mr Hayhoe, raising his voice so that even one of John's horses raised its head, 'Lily continues to go to Shelton Church she will be damned too.'

'No one bain't damned,' said Mr Topp, 'for doing what they be minded, and she who do bide most times in two parishes do like to visit two churches.'

'But there is only one God,' replied Mr Hayhoe.

'So folk do say,' replied Mr Topp calmly.

'And Him only shalt thou serve,' said Mr Hayhoe.

' 'Twould insult our Lil to tell she so,' answered Mr Topp, 'for she do say she'll marry a squire, and do go to Shelton Church to see what folk do wear at weddings.'

'You must permit me to reason with her,' pleaded Mr Hayhoe. 'Would you allow your daughter to call at the Rectory every Saturday afternoon at four o'clock?'

'Which door be she to knock at?' enquired Mr Topp.

'The front door,' replied Mr Hayhoe, 'and I will open it myself.'

John Topp looked at the minister a little suspiciously.

'Our Lil bain't one who do fancy any nonsense,' he said.

'Then she cannot like sacerdotalism,' observed Mr Hayhoe gladly.

'No, she don't,' said Mr Topp. 'She don't like none of they matters, for she be a good maid.'

If the poor weak woman, who had married Mr Hayhoe because he came as a missionary to her father's village, had one idea left of her own, it was about her sofa-covers. These she liked to keep clean. But when she heard that her husband had invited Lily Topp to have a talk with him on Saturday afternoons she was sure that he would invite Lily to sit upon the study sofa.

'And her clothes are so dirty,' Mrs Hayhoe said with a sigh.

'If she goes to Hell they will be dirtier,' remarked Mr Hayhoe.

Mrs Hayhoe had only just time to take away the cushion that she feared Lily might lean her head upon, when a quick knock came at the front door, and a young child with a skipping-rope in her hand and a merry look in her eyes was invited to enter by Mr Hayhoe and conducted to his study.

Had Lily regarded anything else but the furniture she might have been a little alarmed at the extreme deference shown to her by the pastor, who, indeed, treated every man, woman and child with the same polite consideration, for he saw them all – sinners though all of them were – as children of God. Mr Hayhoe handed Lily, with a bow, to the sofa.

'You must pardon me,' he said, 'for taking you from your pastimes, but my excuse and warrant is that you have a soul to be saved.'

'Oh, I wasn't doing nothing important,' replied Lily. 'I was only skipping alone. I weren't playing wi' Tommy.'

'Lily,' said Mr Hayhoe, 'I long to call you a child of grace and to keep you in our fold.'

''Tain't nor child of grace that our Daddy do call I, nor Tommy neither,' replied Lily, 'for 'tis little Devil wi' both one and t' other.'

'Lily,' said Mr Hayhoe, 'do not listen to vain talkers who set snares for your feet.'

'Why,' exclaimed Lily, jumping up with a laugh and skipping across the room, 'that's just what Mr Dirdoe do say!'

'I hope you do not listen to him,' said Mr Hayhoe, turning a little pale.

'Oh no,' replied Lily. 'I don't take no notice of they men.'

'But you will listen to me, Lily?'

'If thee do talk nice,' answered Lily.

'Mr Dirdoe promised you Heaven, I suppose,' enquired Mr Hayhoe sadly, 'if you curtsyed to the Altar?'

'He promised I a packet of bull's-eyes,' laughed Lily.

'I will give you two packets if you stay with us,' said Mr Hayhoe.

Lily laughed, kicked up her heels in the air and brought them down upon the sofa-cover. The poor weak woman opened the study door . . .

Though Mr Dirdoe hadn't succeeded in catching Lily Topp when he spoke to her in the lane before she visited Mr Hayhoe, yet he did not despair of her. Every Saturday afternoon, as soon as she had eaten her dinner, Lily would skip along the Shelton road to meet him, and he would first explain and then condemn the evangelical dogma, while Lily waited patiently and watched the birds in the sky. Presently Mr Dirdoe would give her, as a reward for her patient listening, a packet of sweets.

Never in his life before had Mr Dirdoe been so happy, and he secretly began to dread the day when Lily would no more divide her favours between Maids Madder Church and Shelton, but come entirely to Shelton, for then he would only think it proper to preach to her from the pulpit. But all means now appeared to be right in his eyes for so good an end, and soon it became a common thing to see Mr Dirdoe on Saturday afternoons skipping himself – his heels up, his coat-tails flying – or else holding one end of a rope while Tommy held the other as Lily skipped.

Sometimes Lily met Mr Dirdoe alone, for Tommy would often prefer to go with the other boys to stone the seagulls upon the cliffs, and then Mr Dirdoe would sit beside Lily upon a log of wood in Shelton Lane, hold her hand in his and tell her a number of exciting stories all about what happened to him when he was a child. Now and again Lily, as well as Tommy, had occupations at Madder that amused her more than listening to Mr Dirdoe's stories, and then Mr Dirdoe would sit upon the log and wait for her in vain, looking so sad and melancholy that everyone who saw him there laughed loudly.

One Saturday Lily, who had taken a little longer than usual over her dinner – for she had the bones of a fresh herring to pick at with her fingers – found Mr Dirdoe with his face hidden in his hands, looking so disconsolate that she felt pity for him.

'Our Dad do say,' remarked Lily, 'that thee'd be happier if 'ee had a young girl to mind out to, an' 'tis a pity I bain't a little older to be thee's bride.'

'I am seeking you, Lily, as a bride for God,' replied Mr Dirdoe.

'Be God very old?' asked Lily.

'He is immortal,' answered Mr Dirdoe.

'Our Dad do say,' continued Lily, 'that thee mid kiss me if thee's mouth do itch, for 'tain't worth while to destroy theeself for want of a kiss.'

Mr Dirdoe sat Lily beside him and stroked her hand.

'I am seeking your soul,' he said, 'so that I may give it, blameless, to the angels.'

'Why, that's just what Mr Hayhoe do say,' laughed Lily.

After Lily Topp had been for an hour or two with Mr Dirdoe she would, as a rule, visit Mr Hayhoe at Madder Rectory, where he had been wont to condemn strongly all ceremonial. While he talked he permitted Lily to pull out the drawers of a cabinet that was in the study and lay their contents upon the sofa-cover. This Lily was pleased enough to do, for in each drawer there were a number of curious things – shells and coins, beads and amber charms – that had all been collected by Mr Hayhoe's great-grandmother.

Seeing her so happy with these toys, Mr Hayhoe would leave his talk and tell her the same tales that his grandmother had told him about all her travels. They would both be as happy as possible, until the poor weak woman would knock at the door and say that it was high time that Lily went home.

' 'Tis a pity old women be so interfering,' Lily would observe, as she helped Mr Hayhoe to put back the drawers, 'for when 'tain't their sofa-covers, 'tis their chairs they do think of – and 'tain't we two who be crabbed.'

Since Ben Jonson wrote these pretty lines:

> *Weep with me, all you that read*
> *This little story;*
> *And know, for whom a tear you shed*
> *Death's self is sorry.*

some of those whose years have numbered scarce thirteen finish all too early their happy play in the day-time sun, and so a day arrived when Mr Dirdoe sat waiting sadly and no Lily came. A carriage, that he knew to be the doctor's, went by him towards Madder, though Mr Dirdoe did not heed it.

Mr Dirdoe had decided to make one final effort that afternoon to save Lily Topp from the error of her Madder ways. He would not meet her again, for the people of Shelton were already beginning to talk about him and to say untrue things.

Mr Dirdoe, upon one of his short holidays, had seen in a jeweller's window at Weyminster a golden chain with a crucifix attached. This he had purchased as a gift for Lily, hoping that with this little cross upon her bosom she would always wish to worship before the more splendid one upon the Shelton altar.

Mr Dirdoe waited. The same carriage that had passed him, going to Madder, returned again. The doctor's bald head was inside.

Mr Dirdoe wondered what could have happened to Lily. Perhaps, he thought, Mr Hayhoe has beguiled her earlier than usual to Madder Rectory, in order to read Spurgeon's *Sermons*.

Mr Dirdoe jumped up excitedly; a sudden idea came to him. He would go and take the lamb out of the very jaws of the lion.

Madder was unusually silent, as if a cloud of gloom had fallen upon it, when Mr Dirdoe walked boldly through the village on his way to the Rectory. As he walked he overtook the Madder sexton, Mr Endor, whom he knew by sight. He walked with him, though neither of the two spoke one word, as far as the churchyard gates.

For all the righteous zeal that burned in Mr Dirdoe's heart, his hand trembled when he knocked at the Rectory door. The door was opened by the poor weak woman, who looked extremely surprised to see the visitor. Mrs Hayhoe held in her hand a new sofa-cover. She conducted Mr Dirdoe at once to the study.

During his walk Mr Dirdoe had prepared a torrent of words that he felt must totally destroy all that Martin Luther or Jack Calvin had ever put into Mr Hayhoe's head, and after refuting his rival he would offer his gift to Lily and lead her away to the right fold.

But all Mr Dirdoe's wonderful arguments were forgotten when he saw his rival, for Mr Hayhoe, with his arms thrown out before him and his head resting upon the great Bible, was weeping bitterly.

He recovered himself as Mr Dirdoe entered and, grasping the rival pastor's hand, nodded to a picture upon the wall that showed the lost lamb being carried to its fold in the loving arms of the Good Shepherd.

The church bell tolled.

The rival pastors, weeping together, embraced one another.

For the Duration of the War

Saki

The Rev. Wilfrid Gaspilton, in one of those clerical migrations inconsequent-seeming to the lay mind, had removed from the moderately fashionable parish of St Luke's, Kensingate, to the immoderately rural parish of St Chuddock's, somewhere in Yondershire. There were doubtless substantial advantages connected with the move, but there were certainly some very obvious drawbacks. Neither the migratory clergyman nor his wife were able to adapt themselves naturally and comfortably to the conditions of country life. Beryl, Mrs Gaspilton, had always looked indulgently on the country as a place where people of irreproachable income and hospitable instincts cultivated tennis-lawns and rose-gardens and Jacobean pleasaunces, wherein selected gatherings of interested weekend guests might disport themselves. Mrs Gaspilton considered herself as distinctly an interesting personality, and from a limited standpoint she was doubtless right. She had indolent dark eyes and a comfortable chin, which belied the slightly plaintive inflection which she threw into her voice at suitable intervals. She was tolerably well satisfied with the smaller advantages of life, but she regretted that Fate had not seen its way to reserve for her some of the ampler successes for which she felt herself well qualified. She would have liked to be the centre of a literary, slightly political salon, where discerning satellites might have recognized the breadth of her outlook on human affairs and the undoubted smallness of her feet. As it was, Destiny had chosen for her that she should be the wife of a rector, and had now further decreed that a country rectory should be the background to her existence. She rapidly made up her mind that her surroundings did not call for exploration: Noah had predicted the Flood, but no one expected him to swim about in it. Digging in a wet garden or trudging through muddy lanes were exertions which she did not propose to undertake. As long as the garden produced asparagus and carnations at pleasingly frequent intervals Mrs Gaspilton was content to approve of its expense and otherwise ignore its existence. She would fold herself up, so to speak, in an elegant, indolent little world of her own, enjoying the minor recreations of being gently rude to the doctor's wife and continuing the leisurely production of her one literary effort, *The Forbidden Horsepond*, a translation of Baptiste Lepoy's *L'Abreuvoir interdit*. It was a labour which had already been so long drawn-out that it seemed probable that Baptiste Lepoy would drop out of vogue before her translation of his temporarily famous novel was finished. However, the languid prosecution of the work had invested Mrs Gaspilton with a certain literary dignity, even in Kensingate circles, and would place her on a pinnacle in St Chuddock's, where hardly anyone read French, and assuredly no one had heard of *L'Abreuvoir interdit*.

The Rector's wife might be content to turn her back complacently on the country; it was the Rector's tragedy that the country turned its back on him. With the best intention in the world and the immortal example of Gilbert White before him, the Rev. Wilfrid found himself as bored and ill at ease in his new surroundings as Charles II would have been at a modern Wesleyan Conference. The birds that hopped across his lawn hopped across it as though it were their lawn, and not his, and gave him plainly to understand that in their eyes he was infinitely less interesting than a garden worm or the rectory cat. The hedgeside and meadow flowers were equally uninspiring; the lesser celandine seemed particularly unworthy of the attention that English poets had bestowed on it, and the Rector knew that he would be utterly miserable if left alone for a quarter of an hour in its company. With the human inhabitants of his parish he was no better off; to know them was merely to know their ailments, and the ailments were almost invariably rheumatism. Some, of course, had other bodily infirmities, but they always had rheumatism as well. The Rector had not yet grasped the fact that in rural cottage life not to have rheumatism is as glaring an omission as not to have been presented at Court would be in more ambitious circles. And with all this dearth of local interest there was Beryl shutting herself off with her ridiculous labours on *The Forbidden Horsepond*.

'I don't see why you should suppose that anyone wants to read Baptiste Lepoy in English,' the Reverend Wilfrid remarked to his wife one morning, finding her surrounded with her usual elegant litter of dictionaries, fountain pens, and scribbling paper; 'hardly anyone bothers to read him now in France.'

'My dear,' said Beryl, with an intonation of gentle weariness, 'haven't two or three leading London publishers told me they wondered no one had ever translated *L'Abreuvoir interdit*, and begged me –'

'Publishers always clamour for the books that no one has ever written, and turn a cold shoulder on them as soon as they're written. If St Paul were living now they would pester him to write an Epistle to the Esquimaux, but no London publisher would dream of reading his Epistle to the Ephesians.'

'Is there any asparagus anywhere in the garden?' asked Beryl; 'because I've told cook –'

'Not anywhere in the garden,' snapped the Rector, 'but there's no doubt plenty in the asparagus-bed, which is the usual place for it.'

And he walked away into the region of fruit trees and vegetable beds to exchange irritation for boredom. It was there, among the gooseberry bushes and beneath the medlar trees, that the temptation to the perpetration of a great literary fraud came to him.

Some weeks later the *Bi-Monthly Review* gave to the world, under the guarantee of the Rev. Wilfrid Gaspilton, some fragments of Persian verse, alleged to have been unearthed and translated by a nephew who was at present compaigning somewhere in the Tigris valley. The Rev. Wilfrid possessed a host of nephews, and it was, of course, quite possible that one or more of them might be in military employ in Mesopotamia, though no one could call to mind any particular nephew who could have been suspected of being a Persian scholar.

The verses were attributed to one Ghurab, a hunter, or, according to other accounts, warden of the royal fishponds, who lived, in some unspecified century, in the neighbourhood of Karmanshah. They breathed a spirit of comfortable, even-tempered satire and philosophy, disclosing a mockery that did not trouble to be bitter, a joy in Life that was not passionate to the verge of being troublesome.

> A Mouse that prayed for Allah's aid
> Blasphemed when no such aid befell:
> A Cat, who feasted on that mouse,
> Thought Allah managed vastly well.

> Pray not for aid to One who made
> A set of never-changing Laws,
> But in your need remember well
> He gave you speed, or guile – or claws.

> Some laud a life of mild content:
> Content may fall, as well as Pride.
> The Frog who hugged his lowly Ditch
> Was much disgruntled when it dried.

You are not on the Road to Hell,
    You tell me with fanatic glee:
Vain boaster, what shall that avail
    If Hell is on the road to thee?

A Poet praised the Evening Star,
    Another praised the Parrot's hue:
A Merchant praised his merchandise
    And he, at least, praised what he knew.

It was this verse which gave the critics and commentators some
clue as to the probable date of the composition; the parrot, they
reminded the public, was in high vogue as a type of elegance in
the days of Hafiz of Shiraz; in the quatrains of Omar it makes no
appearance.

The next verse, it was pointed out, would apply to the political
conditions of the present day as strikingly as to the region and
era for which it was written –

A Sultan dreamed day-long of Peace,
    The while his Rivals' armies grew:
They changed his Day-dreams into sleep
– The Peace, methinks, he never knew.

Woman appeared little, and wine not at all in the verse of the
hunter-poet, but there was at least one contribution to the love-
philosophy of the East –

O Moon-faced Charmer, with Star-drownèd Eyes,
    And cheeks of soft delight, exhaling musk,
They tell me that thy charm will fade; ah well,
    The Rose itself grows hue-less in the Dusk.

Finally, there was a recognition of the Inevitable, a chill breath blowing across the poet's comfortable estimate of life –

> There is a sadness in each Dawn,
>   A sadness that you cannot rede,
> The joyous Day brings in its train
>   The Feast, the Loved One, and the Steed.
>
> Ah, there shall come a Dawn at last
>   That brings no life-stir to your ken,
> A long, cold Dawn without a Day,
>   And ye shall rede its sadness then.

The verses of Ghurab came on the public at a moment when a comfortable, slightly quizzical philosophy was certain to be welcome, and their reception was enthusiastic. Elderly colonels, who had outlived the love of truth, wrote to the papers to say that they had been familiar with the works of Ghurab in Afghanistan, and Aden, and other suitable localities a quarter of a century ago. A Ghurab-of-Karmanshah Club sprang into existence, the members of which alluded to each other as Brother Ghurabians on the slightest provocation. And to the flood of enquiries, criticisms, and requests for information, which naturally poured in on the discoverer, or rather the discloser, of this long-hidden poet, the Rev. Wilfrid made one effectual reply: military considerations forbade any disclosures which might throw unnecessary light on his nephew's movements.

After the war the Rector's position will be one of unthinkable embarrassment, but for the moment, at any rate, he has driven *The Forbidden Horsepond* out of the field.

A Fisher of Men

John Galsworthy

Long ago it is, now, that I used to see him issue from the rectory, followed by his dogs, an Irish and a fox-terrier. He would cross to the churchyard, and, at the gate, stand looking over the Cornish upland of his cure of souls, towards the sea, distant nearly a mile. About his black thin figure there was one bright spot, a little gold cross, dangling on his vest. His eyes at such moments were like the eyes of fishermen watching from the cliffs for pilchards to come by; but as this fisher of men marked the grey roofs covered with yellow lichen where his human fishes dwelt, red stains would come into his meagre cheeks. His lips would move, and he would turn abruptly in at the gate over which was written: 'This is the Gate of Heaven.'

A certain green spot within that churchyard was kept clear of grave-stones, which thickly covered all the rest of the ground. He never – I believe – failed to look at it, and think: 'I will keep that corner free. I will not be buried amongst men who refuse their God!'

For this was his misfortune, which, like a creeping fate, had come on him year by year throughout his twenty years of rectorship. It had eaten into his heart, as is the way with troubles which a man cannot understand. In plain words, his catch of souls had dwindled season by season till, from three hundred when he was first presented to the living, it barely numbered forty. Sunday after Sunday he had conducted his three services.

18

Twice a week from the old pulpit, scanning through the church twilight that ever scantier flock of faces, he had in his dry, spasmodic voice – whose harsh tones, no doubt, were music to himself – pronounced this conduct blessed, and that accursed, in accordance with his creed. Week after week he had told us all the sinfulness of not attending God's House, of not observing the Lord's Day. He had respected every proper ritual and ceremony; never refusing baptism even to the illegitimate, nor burial to any but such as took their own lives; joining in marriage with a certain exceptional alacrity those whose conduct had caused scandal in the village. His face had been set, too, against irreverence; no one, I remember, might come to his church in flannel trousers.

Yet his flock had slowly diminished! Living, unmarried, in the neglected rectory, with his dogs, an old housekeeper, and a canary, he seemed to have no interests, such as shooting, or fishing, to take him away from his parish duties; he asked nothing better than to enter the houses and lives of his parishioners; and as he passed their doors – spare, black, and clean-shaven – he could often be seen to stop, make, as it were, a minatory gesture, and walk on with his hungry eyes fixed straight before him. Year by year, to encourage them, he printed privately and distributed documents containing phrases such as these: 'It were better for him that a mill-stone were hanged about his neck, and he were cast into the sea.' 'But the fearful and unbelieving shall have their part in the lake which burneth with fire and brimstone.' When he wrote them, his eyes – I fancy – flared, as though watching such penalties in process of infliction. Had not his parishioners in justice merited those fates?

If, in his walks, he came across a truant, some fisherman or farmer, he would always stop, with his eyes fastened on the culprit's face:

'You don't come to church now; how's that?'

Like true Cornishmen, hoping to avoid unpleasantness, they

would offer some polite excuse: They didn't knaw ezactly, zur – the missus 'ad been ailin'; there was always somethin' – like – that! This temporizing with the devil never failed to make the rector's eyes blaze, or to elicit from him a short dry laugh: 'You don't know what you're saying, man! You must be mad to think you can save your soul that way! This is a Christian country!'

Yet never after one of these encounters did he see the face of that parishioner in his church again. 'Let un wait!' they would murmur, 'tidden likely we'm gwine to his church t'be spoke to like dogs!'

But, indeed, had they been dogs, the rector would not have spoken to them like that. To dogs his conduct was invariably gentle. He might be seen sometimes beside a field of standing corn, where the heads of his two terriers could be marked spasmodically emerging above the golden stalks, as they hunted a covey of partridges or brood of young pheasants which they had scented. His harsh voice could be heard calling them: 'Jim, Jim! Pat, Pat! To heel, you rascals!' But when they came out, their tongues lolling ecstatically, he only stopped and shook his finger at them, and they would lick his hand, or rub themselves against his trousers, confident that he would never strike them. With every animal, with every bird and insect he was like this, so gentle that they trusted him completely. He could often be surprised sitting on a high slate stile, or standing in a dip of the wide road between banks of gorse and bramble, with his head, in its wide hat, rather to one side, while a bullfinch or hedge-sparrow on a branch, not three feet off, would be telling him its little tale. Before going for a walk he would sweep his field-glass over the pale-gold landscape of cornfield, scorched pasturage and sand-dune, to see if any horse seemed needing water, or sheep were lying on its back. He was an avowed enemy, too, of traps and gins, and whenever he met with one, took pains to ensure its catching nothing. Such consistent tenderness to dumb animals was perhaps due to a desire to take their side against farmers who would not come to church; but more, I think, to the feeling that the poor things had no souls, that they were here today and gone tomorrow – they could not be saved and must be treated with compassion, unlike those men with immortal spirits entrusted by God specially to his care, for whose wanton disobedience no punishment, perhaps, could be too harsh. It was as if, by endowing him with her authority over other men, the Church had divided him into two.

For the view he took of life was very simple, undisturbed by any sense of irony, unspoiled by curiosity, or desire to link effect with cause, or, indeed, to admit the necessity of cause at all. At some fixed date God had made the earth of matter; this matter He had divided into the inanimate and the animate, unconnected with each other; animate matter He had again divided into men, and animals; in men He had placed souls, making them in His own image. Men again He had divided into the Church and other men; and for the government and improvement of these other men, God had passed Himself into His Church. That Church again had passed herself into her ministers. Thus, on the Church's minister – placed by Providence beyond the fear of being in the wrong – there had been enjoined the bounden duty of instructing, ruling, and saving at all costs the souls of men.

This was why, I think, when he encountered in the simple folk committed to his charge a strange dumb democratic spirit, a wayward feeling that the universe was indivisible, that power had not developed, but had evolved, that things were relative, not absolute, and so forth – expressed in their simple way, he had experienced from the first a gnawing irritation which, like a worm, seemed to have cankered his heart. Gradually one had seen this canker stealing out into his face and body, into his eyes and voice, into the very gestures of his lean arms and hands. His whole form gave the impression of a dark tree withered and eaten by some desiccating wind, like the stiff oaks of his Cornish

21

upland, gnarled and riven by the Atlantic gales.

Night and day in the worn old rectory, with its red conservatory, he must have brooded over the wrong done him by his people, in depriving him of his just due, the power to save their souls. It was as though an officer, gagged and bound at the head of his company, should have been forced to watch them manoeuvring without him. He was like a schoolmaster tied to his desk amongst the pandemonium of his scholars. His failure was a fact strange and intolerable to him, inexplicable, tragic – a fact mured up in the mystery which each man's blindness to the nature of his own spirit wraps round his relations with his fellow beings. He could not doubt that, bereaved by their own wilful conduct of his ministrations, of the Church in fact, and, through the Church, of God, his parishioners were given up to damnation. If they were thus given up to damnation, he, their proper pastor – their rightful leader, the symbol of the Church, that is of God – was but a barren, withered thing. This thought he could not bear. Unable to see himself as others saw him, he searched to find excuses for them. He found none; for he knew that he had preached no narrow doctrines cursed with the bigotry which he recognized in the Romish or Nonconformist faiths. The doctrines and dogmas he was appointed to administer were of the due and necessary breadth, no more, no less. He was scrupulous, even against his own personal feeling, to observe the letter of the encyclicals. Thus, nothing in the matter of his teaching could account for the gradual defection of his flock. Nor in the manner of it could he detect anything that seemed to himself unjustified. Yet, as the tide ebbed from the base of the grey cliffs, so, without haste, with deadly certainty, the tide ebbed from his church. What could he, then, believe but that his parishioners meant to be personally offensive to himself?

In the school-house, at the post office, on the green, at choir practice, or on the way to service, wherever he met them, one could see that he was perpetually detecting small slights or incivilities. He had come, I think, almost to imagine that these people, who never came to church, fixed the hours of their births and deaths and marriages maliciously, that they might mock at the inconvenience caused to one who neither could, nor would, refuse to do his duty. It was blasphemy they were committing. In avoiding God's church, yet requiring such services of His minister, they were making God their servant.

One could find him any evening in his study, his chin resting on his hand, the oil-lamp flaring slightly, his dogs curled up beside him, and the cloth cover drawn over the cage of his canary so that the little creature should not suffer from the light. Almost the first words he spoke would show how ceaselessly he brooded. 'Nothing,' he would say, 'ever prospers in this village; I've started this and that! Look at the football club, look at the Bible class – all no good! With people such as these, wanting in all reverence, humility, and love of discipline! You have not had the dealings with them that I have!'

In truth his dealings with them had become notorious throughout the district. A petition, privately subscribed, and presented to the Bishop for his removal, had, of course, met with failure. A rector could not be removed from his living for any reason – it had been purchased for him by his father. Nor could his position as minister be interfered with on any such excuse as that of the mere personal dislike of his parishioners – as well, indeed, seek by petition to remove the Church herself. The knowledge of his unassailable position found expression among his parishioners in dogged looks, and the words: 'Well, we don't trouble!'

It was in the twentieth year of his rectorship that a slight collision with the parish council drew from him this letter: 'It is my duty to record my intention to attend no more meetings, for I cannot, as a Christian, continue to meet those who obstinately refuse to come to church.'

It was then late September, and the harvest festival had been appointed for the following Sunday. The week passed, but the farmers had provided no offerings for the decoration of the church; the fishermen, too, accustomed by an old tradition in that parish to supply some purchased fruit in lieu of their shining fishes, sent nothing. The boycott had obviously been preconcerted.

But when the rector stepped that Sunday into the pulpit the church was fuller than it had been for many years. Men and women who had long ceased to attend had come, possessed evidently by an itch to see how 'th' old man' would take it. The eyes of the farmers and fishermen, hardened by the elements, had in them a grim humorous curiosity, such as one may remark in the eyes of a ring of men round some poor wretch, whom, moved by a crude sense of justice, they have baited into the loss of dignity. Their faces, with hardly an exception, seemed to say: 'Sir, we were given neither hand nor voice in the choosing of you. From the first day you showed us the cloven hoof. We have never wanted you. If we must have you, let us at all events get some sport out of you!'

The rector's white figure rising from the dark pulpit received without movement the shafts of all our glances; his own deep-set hungering eyes were fixed on the Bible in his hand. He gave out his text: 'The kindly fruits of the earth, in due season –'

His voice – strangely smooth and low that morning, I remember – began discoursing of the beneficence and kindliness of God, who had allowed the earth to provide men year by year with food, according to their needs. It was as though the mellow sentiment of that season of fruition had fallen on his exiled spirit. But presently he paused, and, leaning forward, looked man by man, woman by woman, at us all. Those eyes now had in them the peculiar flare which we knew so well. His voice rose again: 'And how have you met this benefaction, my brethren, how have you shown your gratitude to God, embodied in His Church and in me, her appointed representative? Do you think, then, that God will let you insult Him with impunity? Do you think in your foolish pride that God will suffer you unpunished to place this conspired slight on Him? If you imagine this, you are woefully mistaken. I know the depths of your rebellious hearts; I read them like this Book. You seek, you have always sought, to set my authority at defiance – a wayward and disobedient generation. But let me tell you: God, who has set His Holy Church over you, is a just and strong God; as a kind master chastises his dogs for their own good, so will He chastise you. You have sought to drive me out from among you' – and from his pale twisting lips, through the hush, there came a sound like a laugh – 'to drive the Church, to drive God Himself, away! You could not have made a grosser error. Do you think that we, in solemn charge of your salvation, are to be moved by such puerile rebellion? Not so! God has appointed us – to God alone we are accountable. Not if every man and woman in the parish, aye, and every child, deserted this church, would I recoil one step from my duty, or resign my charge! As well imagine, forsooth, that your great Church is some poor man-elected leader, subject to your whims, and to be deposed as the fancy takes you! Do you conceive the nature of the Church and of my office to be so mean and petty that I am to feed you with the food you wish me to feed you with, to lead you into such fields as you dictate? No! my brethren, you have not that power! Is the shepherd elected by the sheep? Listen, then, to the truth, or to your peril be it! The Church is a rock set up by God amongst the shifting sands of life. It comes from Heaven, not from this miserable earth. Its mission is to command, yours to obey. If the last man in this Christian country proved a rebel and a traitor, the Church and her ministers would stand immovable, as I stand here, firm in my sacred resolve to save your souls. Go down on your knees, and beg God to forgive you for the wanton insult you have offered Him! ... Hymn 266: "Lead, kindly Light, amid the encircling gloom." '

Through the grey aisles, where so great a silence reigned, the notes of the organ rose. The first verse of that hymn was sung only by the choir and a few women's voices; then one by one the men joined in. Our voices swelled into a shout louder than we had ever heard in the little church before – a mutinous, harsh, roaring sound, as though, in the words of that gentle hymn, each one of this grim congregation were pouring out all the resentment in his heart. The roar emerging through the open door must have startled the passing tourists, and the geese in the neighbouring farmyard. It ended with a groan like the long-drawn sob of a wave sucking back.

In the village all the next week little except this sermon was discussed. Farmers and fishermen are men of the world. The conditions of their lives, which are guarded only by their own unremitting efforts, which are backed by no authority save their own courage in the long struggle with land and sea, gives them a certain deep philosophy. Amongst the fishermen there was one white-bearded old fellow who even seemed to see a deep significance in the rector's sermon.

'Mun putts hissel' above us, like the Czar o' Roossia,' he said, '`tes the sperrit o' the thing that's wrong. Talk o' lovin' kindness, there's none 'bout the Church, 'sfar's I can see, 'tes all: "Du this, or ye'll be blasted!" This man – he's a regular chip o' the old block!' He spoke, indeed, as though the rector's attitude towards them were a symbol of the Church's attitude to men. Among the farmers such analogies were veiled by the expression of simpler thoughts:

'Yu med tak' a 'arse to the watter, yu can't mak' un drink!'

'Whu wants mun, savin' our souls! Let mun save's own!'

'We'm not gude enough to listen to his prachin', I rackon!'

It was before a congregation consisting of his clerk, two tourists, three old women, one of them stone deaf, and four little girls, that the unfortunate man stood next Sunday morning.

Late that same wild and windy afternoon a jeering rumour

spread down in the village: 'Th' old man's up to Tresellyn 'Igh Cliff, talkin' to the watters!'

A crowd soon gathered, eager for the least sensation that should break monotony. Beyond the combe, above the grey roofs of the fishing village, Tresellyn High Cliff rises abruptly. At the top, on the very edge, the tiny black shape of a man could be seen standing with his arms raised above his head. Now he kneeled, then stood motionless for many minutes with hands outstretched; while behind him the white and brown specks of his two terriers were visible, couched along the short grass. Suddenly he could be seen gesticulating wildly, and the speck shapes of the dogs leaping up, and cowering again as if terrified at their master's conduct.

For two hours this fantastic show was witnessed by the villagers with gloating gravity. The general verdict was: 'Th' old man's carryin' on praaperly.' But very gradually the sight of that tiny black figure appealing to his God – the God of his Church militant which lived by domination – roused the superstition of men who themselves were living in primitive conflict with the elements. They could not but appreciate what was so in keeping with the vengeful spirit of a fighting race. One could see that they even began to be afraid. Then a great burst of rain, sweeping from the sea, smothered all sight of him.

Early next morning the news spread that the rector had been found in his armchair, the two dogs at his feet, and the canary perched on his dead hand. His clothes were unchanged and wet, as if he had sunk into that chair, and passed away, from sheer exhaustion. The body of 'the poor unfortunate gentleman' – the old housekeeper told me – was huddled and shrunk together; his chin rested on the little gold cross dangling on his vest.

They buried him in that green spot, apart from his parishioners, which he had selected for his grave, placing on the tombstone these words:

> HIC JACET
> P——W——
> PASTOR ECCLESIÆ BRITANNICÆ
> 'GOD IS LOVE'

An Elixir of Love

W. S. Gilbert

I

Ploverleigh was a picturesque little village in Dorsetshire, ten miles from anywhere. It lay in a pretty valley nestling amid clumps of elm trees, and a pleasant little trout stream ran right through it from end to end. The vicar of Ploverleigh was the Hon. and Rev. Mortimer De Becheville, third son of the 48th Earl of Caramel. He was an excellent gentleman, and his living was worth £1,200 a year. He was a graduate of Cambridge, and held a College Fellowship, besides which his father allowed him £500 a year. So he was very comfortably 'off'.

Mr De Becheville had a very easy time of it, for he spent eleven-twelfths of the year away from the parish, delegating his duties to the Rev. Stanley Gay, an admirable young curate to whom he paid a stipend of £120 a year, pocketing by this means a clear annual profit of £1,080. It was said by unkind and ungenerous people, that, as Mr De Becheville had (presumably) been selected for his sacred duties at a high salary on account of his special and exceptional qualifications for their discharge, it was hardly fair to delegate them to a wholly inexperienced young gentleman of two-and-twenty. It was argued that if a colonel, or a stipendiary magistrate, or a superintendent of a country lunatic asylum, or any other person holding a responsible office (outside the Church of England), for which he was handsomely paid,

29

were to do his work by cheap deputy, such a responsible official would be looked upon as a swindler. But this line of reasoning is only applied to the cure of souls by uncharitable and narrow-minded people who never go to church, and consequently can't know anything about it. Besides, who cares what people who never go to church think? If it comes to that, Mr De Becheville was *not* selected (as it happens) on account of his special and exceptional fitness for the cure of souls inasmuch as the living was a family one, and went to De Becheville because his two elder brothers preferred the Guards. So that argument falls to the ground.

The Rev. Stanley Gay was a Leveller. I don't mean to say that he was a mere I'm-as-good-as-you Radical spouter, who advocated a redistribution of property from mere sordid motives. Mr Gay was an aesthetic Leveller. He held that as Love is the great bond of union between man and woman, no arbitrary obstacle should be allowed to interfere with its progress. He did not desire to abolish rank, but he *did* desire that a mere difference in rank should not be an obstacle in the way of making two young people happy. He could prove to you by figures (for he was a famous mathematician) that, rank notwithstanding, all men are equal, and this is how he did it.

He began, as a matter of course, with x, because, as he said, x, whether it represents one or one hundred thousand, is always x, and do what you will, you cannot make w or y of it by any known process.

Having made this quite clear to you, he carried on his argument by means of algebra, until he got right through algebra to the 'cases' at the end of the book, and then he slid by gentle and imperceptible degrees into conic sections, where x, although you found it masquerading as the equation to the parabola, was still as much x as ever. Then if you were not too tired to follow him, you found yourself up to the eyes in plane and spherical trigonometry, where x again turned up in a variety of assumed characters, sometimes as 'cos α', sometimes as 'cos β', but generally with a $\sqrt[3]{}$ over it, and none the less x on that account. This singular character then made its appearance in a quaint binomial disguise, and was eventually run to earth in the very heart of differential and integral calculus, looking less like x, but being, in point of fact, more like x than ever. The force of his argument went to show that, do what you would, you could not stamp x out, and therefore it was better and wiser and more straightforward to call him x at once than to invest him with complicated sham dignities which meant nothing, and only served to bother and perplex people who met him for the first time. It's a very easy problem – anybody can do it.

Mr Gay was, as a matter of course, engaged to be married. He loved a pretty little girl of eighteen, with soft brown eyes, and bright silky brown hair. Her name was Jessie Lightly, and she was the only daughter of Sir Caractacus Lightly, a wealthy baronet who had a large place in the neighbourhood of Ploverleigh. Sir Caractacus was a very dignified old gentleman, whose wife had died two years after Jessie's birth. A well-bred, courtly old gentleman, too, with a keen sense of honour. He was very fond of Mr Gay, though he had no sympathy with his levelling views.

One beautiful moonlit evening Mr Gay and Jessie were sitting together on Sir Caractacus's lawn. Everything around them was pure and calm and still, so they grew sentimental.

'Stanley,' said Jessie, 'we are very, very happy, are we not?'

'Unspeakably happy,' said Gay. 'So happy that when I look around me, and see how many there are whose lives are embittered by disappointment – by envy, by hatred, and by malice' (when he grew oratorical he generally lapsed into the Litany) 'I turn to the tranquil and unruffled calm of my own pure and happy love for you with gratitude unspeakable.'

He really meant all this, though he expressed himself in rather flatulent periods.

'I wish with all my heart,' said Jessie, 'that every soul on earth were as happy as we two.'

'And why are they not?' asked Gay, who hopped on to his hobby whenever it was, so to speak, brought round to the front door. 'And why are they not, Jessie? I will tell you why they are not. Because –'

'Yes, darling,' said Jessie, who had often heard his argument before. 'I know why. It's dreadful.'

'It's as simple as possible,' said Gay. 'Take x to represent the abstract human being –'

'Certainly, dear,' said Jessie, who agreed with his argument heart and soul, but didn't want to hear it again. 'We took it last night.'

'Then,' said Gay, not heeding the interruption, 'let $x + 1$, $x + 2$, $x + 3$, represent three grades of high rank.'

'Exactly, it's contemptible,' said Jessie. 'How softly the wind sighs among the trees.'

'What is a duke?' asked Gay – not for information, but oratorically, with a view to making a point.

'A mere $x + 3$,' said Jessie. 'Could anything be more hollow. What a lovely evening!'

'The Duke of Buckingham and Chandos – it sounds well, I grant you,' continued Gay, 'but call him the $x + 3$ of Buckingham and Chandos, and you reduce him at once to –'

'I know,' said Jessie, 'to his lowest common denominator,' and her little upper lip curled with contempt.

'Nothing of the kind,' said Gay, turning red. 'Either hear me out, or let me drop the subject. At all events don't make ridiculous suggestions.'

'I'm very sorry, dear,' said Jessie, humbly. 'Go on, I'm listening, and I won't interrupt any more.'

But Gay was annoyed and wouldn't go on. So they returned to the house together. It was their first tiff.

II

In St Martin's Lane lived Baylis and Culpepper, magicians,
astrologers, and professors of the Black Art. Baylis had sold
himself to the Devil at a very early age, and had become
remarkably proficient in all kinds of enchantment. Culpepper
had been his apprentice, and having also acquired considerable
skill as a necromancer, was taken into partnership by the genial
old magician, who from the first had taken a liking to the frank
and fair-haired boy. Ten years ago (the date of my story) the firm
of Baylis & Culpepper stood at the very head of the London
family magicians. They did what is known as a pushing trade,
but although they advertised largely, and never neglected a
chance, it was admitted even by their rivals, that the goods they
supplied could be relied on as sound useful articles. They had a
special reputation for a class of serviceable family nativity, and
they did a very large and increasing business in love philtres –
'The Patent Oxy-Hydrogen Love-at-First-Sight Draught'
in bottles at 1*s*. 1½*d*. and 2*s*. 3*d*. ('our leading article', as
Baylis called it) was strong enough in itself to keep the firm
going, had all its other resources failed them. But the establishment in St Martin's Lane was also a 'Noted House for Amulets',
and if you wanted a neat, well-finished divining-rod, I don't
know any place to which I would sooner recommend you. Their
Curses at a shilling per dozen were the cheapest things in the
trade, and they sold thousands of them in the course of the year.
Their Blessings – also very cheap indeed, and quite effective –
were not much asked for. 'We always keep a few on hand as
curiosities and for completeness, but we don't sell two in the
twelvemonth,' said Mr Baylis. 'A gentleman bought one last
week to send to his mother-in-law, but it turned out that he
was afflicted in the head, and the persons who had charge of
him declined to pay for it, and it's been returned to us. But the
sale of penny curses, especially on Saturday nights, is

tremendous. We can't turn 'em out fast enough.'

As Baylis and Culpepper were making up their books one evening, just at closing time, a gentle young clergyman with large violet eyes, and a beautiful girl of eighteen, with soft brown hair, and a Madonna-like purity of expression, entered the warehouse. These were Stanley Gay and Jessie Lightly. And this is how it came to pass that they found themselves in London, and in the warehouse of the worthy magicians.

As the reader knows, Stanley Gay and Jessie had for many months given themselves up to the conviction that it was their duty to do all in their power to bring their fellow men and women together in holy matrimony, without regard to distinctions of age or rank. Stanley gave lectures on the subject at mechanics' institutes, and the mechanics were unanimous in their approval of his views. He preached his doctrine in workhouses, in beer-shops, and in lunatic asylums, and his listeners supported him with enthusiasm. He addressed navvies at the roadside on the humanizing advantages that would accrue to them if they married refined and wealthy ladies of rank, and not a navvy dissented. In short, he felt more and more convinced every day that he had at last discovered the secret of human happiness. Still he had a formidable battle to fight with class prejudice, and he and Jessie pondered gravely on the difficulties that were before them, and on the best means of overcoming them.

'It's no use disguising the fact, Jessie,' said Mr Gay, 'that the Countesses won't like it.' And little Jessie gave a sigh, and owned that she expected some difficulty with the Countesses. 'We must look these things in the face, Jessie, it won't do to ignore them. We have convinced the humble mechanics and artisans, but the aristocracy hold aloof.'

'The working-man is the true Intelligence after all,' said Jessie.

'He is a noble creature when he is quite sober,' said Gay. 'God bless him.'

Stanley Gay and Jessie were in this frame of mind when they

came across Baylis & Culpepper's advertisement in the *Connubial Chronicle*.

'My dear Jessie,' said Gay, 'I see a way out of our difficulty.'

And dear little Jessie's face beamed with hope.

'These Love Philtres that Baylis & Culpepper advertise – they are very cheap indeed, and if we may judge by the testimonials, they are very effective. Listen, darling.'

And Stanley Gay read as follows:

'From the Earl of Market Harborough. – "I am a hideous old man of eighty, and everyone avoided me. I took a family bottle of your philtre, immediately on my accession to the title and estates a fortnight ago, and I can't keep the young women off. Please send me a pipe of it to lay down."

'From Amelia Orange Blossom. – "I am a very pretty girl of fifteen. For upwards of fourteen years past I have been without a definitely declared admirer. I took a large bottle of your philtre yesterday, and within fourteen hours a young nobleman winked at me in church. Send me a couple of dozen." '

'What can the girl want with a couple of dozen young noblemen, darling?' asked Jessie.

'I don't know – perhaps she took it too strong. Now these men,' said Gay, laying down the paper, 'are benefactors indeed, if they can accomplish all they undertake. I would ennoble these men. They should have statues. I would enthrone them in high places. They would be $x + 3$.'

'My generous darling,' said Jessie, gazing into his eyes in a fervid ecstasy.

'Not at all,' replied Gay. 'They deserve it. We confer peerages on generals who plunge half a nation into mourning – shall we deny them to men who bring a life's happiness home to every door? Always supposing,' added the cautious clergyman, 'that they can really do what they profess.'

The upshot of this conversation was that Gay determined to lay in a stock of philtres for general use among his parishioners.

If the effect upon them was satisfactory he would extend the sphere of their operations. So when Sir Caractacus and his daughter went to town for the season, Stanley Gay spent a fortnight with them, and thus it came to pass that he and Jessie went together to Baylis & Culpepper's.

'Have you any fresh Love Philtres today?' said Gay.

'Plenty, sir,' said Mr Culpepper. 'How many would you like?'

'Well – let me see,' said Gay. 'There are a hundred and forty souls in my parish – say twelve dozen.'

'I think, dear,' said little Jessie, 'you are better to take a few more than you really want, in case of accidents.'

'In purchasing a large quantity, sir,' said Mr Culpepper, 'we would strongly advise you taking it in the wood, and drawing it off as you happen to want it. We have it in four-and-a-half and nine-gallon casks, and we deduct ten per cent, for cash payments.'

'Then, Mr Culpepper, be good enough to let me have a nine-gallon cask of Love Philtre as soon as possible. Send it to the Rev. Stanley Gay, Ploverleigh.'

He wrote a cheque for the amount, and so the transaction ended.

'Is there any other article?' said Mr Culpepper.

'Nothing today. Good afternoon.'

'Have you seen our new Wishing-caps? They are lined with silk and very chastely quilted, sir. We sold one to the Archbishop of Canterbury not an hour ago. Allow me to put you up a Wishing-cap.'

'I tell you that I want nothing more,' said Gay, going.

'Our Flying Carpets are quite the talk of the town, sir,' said Culpepper, producing a very handsome piece of Persian tapestry. 'You spread it on the ground and sit on it, and then you think of a place and you find yourself there before you can count ten. Our Abudah Chests, sir, each chest containing a patent Hag, who comes out and prophesies disasters whenever you touch this spring, are highly spoken of. We can sell the Abudah Chest complete for fifteen guineas.'

'I think you tradespeople make a great mistake in worrying people to buy things they don't want,' said Gay.

'You'd be surprised if you knew the quantity of things we get rid of by this means, sir.'

'No doubt, but I think you keep a great many people out of your shop. If x represents the amount you gain by it, and y the amount you lose by it, then if $\frac{x}{2} = y$ you are clearly out of pocket by it at the end of the year. Think this over. Good evening.'

And Mr Gay left the shop with Jessie.

'Stanley,' said she, 'what a blessing you are to mankind. You do good wherever you go.'

'My dear Jessie,' replied Gay, 'I have had a magnificent education, and if I can show these worthy but half-educated tradesmen that their ignorance of the profounder mathematics is misleading them, I am only dealing as I should deal with the blessings that have been entrusted to my care.'

As Messrs Baylis & Culpepper have nothing more to do with this story, it may be stated at once that Stanley Gay's words had a marked effect upon them. They determined never to push an article again, and within two years of this resolve they retired on ample fortunes, Baylis to a beautiful detached house on Clapham Common, and Culpepper to a handsome château on the Mediterranean, about four miles from Nice.

III

We are once more at Ploverleigh, but this time at the Vicarage. The scene is Mr Gay's handsome library, and in this library three persons are assembled – Mr Gay, Jessie, and old Zorah Clarke. It should be explained that Zorah is Mr Gay's cook and housekeeper, and it is understood between him and Sir

Caractacus Lightly that Jessie may call on the curate whenever she likes, on condition that Zorah is present during the whole time of the visit. Zorah is stone deaf and has to be communicated with through the medium of pantomime, so that while she is really no impediment whatever to the free flow of conversation, the chastening influence of her presence would suffice of itself to silence ill-natured comments, if such articles had an existence among the primitive and innocent inhabitants of Ploverleigh.

The nine-gallon cask of Love Philtre had arrived in due course, and Mr Gay had decided that it should be locked up in a cupboard in his library, as he thought it would scarcely be prudent to trust it to Zorah, whose curiosity might get the better of her discretion. Zorah (who believed that the cask contained sherry) was much scandalized at her master's action in keeping it in his library, and looked upon it as an evident and unmistakable sign that he had deliberately made up his mind to take a steady course of drinking. However, Mr Gay partly reassured the good old lady by informing her in pantomime (an art of expression in which long practice had made him singularly expert) that the liquid was not intoxicating in the ordinary sense of the word, but that it was a cunning and subtle essence, concocted from innocent herbs by learned gentlemen who had devoted a lifetime to the study of its properties. He added (still in pantomime) that he did not propose to drink a single drop of it himself, but that he intended to distribute it among his parishioners, whom it would benefit socially, mentally and morally to a considerable extent. Master as he was of the art of expression by gesture, it took two days' hard work to make this clear to her, and even then she had acquired but a faint and feeble idea of its properties, for she always referred to it as sarsaparilla.

'Jessie,' said Gay, 'the question now arises – How shall we most effectually dispense the great boon we have at our command? Shall we give a party to our friends, and put the Love

Philtre on the table in decanters, and allow them to help themselves?'

'We must be very careful, dear,' said Jessie, 'not to allow any married people to taste it.'

'True,' said Gay, 'quite true. I never thought of that. It wouldn't do at all. I am much obliged to you for the suggestion. It would be terrible – quite terrible.'

And Stanley Gay turned quite pale and faint at the very thought of such a *contretemps*.

'Then,' said Jessie, 'there are the engaged couples. I don't think we ought to do anything to interfere with the prospects of those who have already plighted their troth.'

'Quite true,' said Gay, 'we have no right, as you say, to interfere with the arrangements of engaged couples. That narrows our sphere of action very considerably.'

'Then the widows and the widowers of less than one year's standing should be exempted from its influence.'

'Certainly, most certainly. That reflection did not occur to me, I confess. It is clear that the dispensing of the philtre will be a very delicate operation: it will have to be conducted with the utmost tact. Can you think of any more exceptions?'

'Let me see,' said Jessie. 'There's Tibbits, our gardener, who has fits; and there's Williamson, Papa's second groom, who drinks, oughtn't to be allowed to marry; and Major Crump, who uses dreadful language before ladies; and Dame Parboy, who is bedridden; and the old ladies in the almshouses – and little Tommy, the idiot – and, indeed, all children under – under what age shall we say?'

'All children who have not been confirmed,' said Gay. 'Yes, these exceptions never occurred to me.'

'I don't think we shall ever use the nine gallons, dear,' said Jessie. 'One tablespoonful is a dose.'

'I have just thought of another exception,' said Gay. 'Your Papa.'

'Oh! Papa *must* marry again! Poor dear old Papa! Oh! You *must* let *him* marry.'

'My dear Jessie,' said Gay, 'Heaven has offered me the chance of entering into the married state unencumbered with a mother-in-law. And I am content to accept the blessing as I find it. Indeed, I prefer it so.'

'Papa *does* so want to marry – he is always talking of it,' replied the poor little woman, with a pretty pout. 'O indeed, *indeed*, my new Mamma, whoever she may be, shall never interfere with us. Why, how thankless you are! My Papa is about to confer upon you the most inestimable treasure in the world, a young, beautiful and devoted wife, and you withhold from him a priceless blessing that you are ready to confer on the very meanest of your parishioners.'

'Jessie,' said Gay, 'you have said enough. Sir Caractacus *shall* marry. I was wrong. If a certain burden to which I will not more particularly refer is to descend upon my shoulders, I will endeavour to bear it without repining.'

It was finally determined that there was only one way in which the philtre could be safely and properly distributed. Mr Gay was to give out that he was much interested in the sale of a very peculiar and curious old Amontillado, and small sample bottles of the wine were to be circulated among such of his parishioners as were decently eligible as brides and bridegrooms. The scheme was put into operation as soon as it was decided upon. Mr Gay sent to the nearest market-town for a gross of two-ounce phials, and Jessie and he spent a long afternoon bottling the elixir into these convenient receptacles. They then rolled them up in papers, and addressed them to the persons who were destined to be operated upon. And when all this was done Jessie returned to her Papa, and Mr Gay sat up all night explaining in pantomime to Zorah that a widowed aunt of his, in somewhat straitened circumstances, who resided in a small but picturesque villa in the suburbs of Montilla, and had been compelled to take a large quantity of the very finest sherry from a bankrupt wine-merchant, in satisfaction of a year's rent of her second floor, and that he had undertaken to push its sale in Ploverleigh in consideration of a commission of two-and-a-half per cent on the sales effected – which commission was to be added to the fund for the restoration of the church steeple. He began his explanation at 9 p.m. and at 6 a.m. Zorah thought she began to understand him, and Stanley Gay, quite exhausted with his pantomime exertions, retired, dead beat, to his chamber.

IV

The next morning as Sir Caractacus Lightly sat at breakfast with Jessie, the footman informed him that Mr Gay's housekeeper wished to speak to him on very particular business. The courtly old Baronet directed that she should be shown into the library, and at once proceeded to ask what she wanted.

'If you please, Sir Caractacus, and beggin' your pardon,' said Zorah as he entered, 'I've come with a message from my master.'

'Pray be seated,' said Sir Caractacus. But the poor old lady could not hear him, so he explained his meaning to her in the best dumb show he could command. He pointed to a chair – walked to it – sat down in it – leant back, crossed his legs cosily, got up, and waved his hand to her in a manner that clearly conveyed to her that she was expected to do as he had done.

'My master's compliments and he's gone into the wine trade, and would you accept a sample?'

After all, Mr Gay's exertions had failed to convey his exact meaning to the deaf old lady.

'You astonish me,' said Sir Caractacus; then, finding that she did not understand him, he rumpled his hair, opened his mouth, strained his eye-balls, and threw himself into an attitude of the most horror-struck amazement. Having made his state of mind quite clear to her, he smiled pleasantly, and nodded to her to proceed.

'If you'll kindly taste it, sir, I'll take back any orders with which you may favour me.'

Sir Caractacus rang for a wineglass and proceeded to taste the sample.

'I don't know what it is, but it's not Amontillado,' said he, smacking his lips; 'still it is a pleasant cordial. Taste it.'

The old lady seemed to gather his meaning at once. She nodded, bobbed a curtsey, and emptied the glass.

Baylis & Culpepper had not over-stated the singular effects of the 'Patent Oxy-Hydrogen Love-at-First-Sight Draught'. Sir Caractacus's hard and firmly-set features gradually relaxed as the old lady sipped the contents of her glass. Zorah set it down when she had quite emptied it, and as she did so her eyes met those of the good old Baronet. She blushed under the ardour of his gaze, and a tear trembled on her old eyelid.

'You're a remarkably fine woman,' said Sir Caractacus, 'and singularly well preserved for your age.'

'Alas, kind sir,' said Zorah, 'I am that hard of hearin' that cannons is whispers.'

Sir Caractacus stood up, stroked his face significantly, smacked his hands together, slapped them both upon his heart, and sank on one knee at her feet. He then got up and nodded smilingly at her to imply that he really meant it.

Zorah turned aside and trembled.

'I ain't no scollard, Sir Caractacus, and I don't rightly know how a poor old 'ooman like me did ought to own her likings for a lordly barrownight – but a true 'art is more precious than diamonds they do say, and a lovin' wife is a crown of gold to her husband. I ain't fashionable, but I'm a respectable old party, and can make you comfortable if nothing else.'

'Zorah, you are the very jewel of my hopes. My dear daughter will soon be taken from me. It lies with you to brighten my desolate old age. Will you be Lady Lightly?'

And he pointed to a picture of his late wife, and went through the pantomime of putting a ring on Zorah's finger. He then indicated the despair that would possess him if she refused to accept his offer. Having achieved these feats of silent eloquence, he smiled and nodded at her reassuringly, and waited for a reply with an interrogative expression of countenance.

'Yes, dearie,' murmured Zorah, as she sank into the Baronet's arms.

After a happy half-hour Zorah felt it was her duty to return to her master, so the lovers took a fond farewell of each other, and Sir Caractacus returned to the breakfast-room.

'Jessie,' said Sir Caractacus, 'I think you really love your poor old father?'

'Indeed, Papa, I do.'

'Then you will, I trust, be pleased to hear that my declining years are not unlikely to be solaced by the companionship of a good, virtuous, and companionable woman.'

'My dear Papa,' said Jessie, 'do you really mean that – that you are likely to be married?'

'Indeed, Jessie, I think it is more than probable! You know you are going to leave me very soon, and my dear little nurse must be replaced, or what will become of me?'

Jessie's eyes filled with tears – but they were tears of joy.

'I cannot tell you Papa – dear, dear, Papa – how happy you have made me.'

'And you will, I am sure, accept your new Mamma with every feeling of respect and affection.'

'Any wife of yours is a Mamma of mine,' said Jessie.

'My darling! Yes, Jessie, before very long I hope to lead to the altar a bride who will love and honour me as I deserve. She is no light and giddy girl, Jessie. She is a woman of sober age and staid demeanour, yet easy and comfortable in her ways. I am going to marry Mr Gay's cook, Zorah.'

'Zorah,' cried Jessie, 'dear, dear old Zorah! Oh, indeed, I am very, very glad and happy!'

'Bless you, my child,' said the Baronet. 'I knew my pet would not blame her poor old father for acting on the impulse of a heart that has never misled him. Yes, I think – nay, I am sure – that I have taken a wise and prudent step. Zorah is not what the world calls beautiful.'

'Zorah is very good, and very clean and honest, and quite, quite sober in her habits,' said Jessie warmly, 'and that is worth more – far more than beauty, dear Papa. Beauty will fade and perish, but personal cleanliness is practically undying, for it can be renewed whenever it discovers symptoms of decay. Oh, I am sure you will be happy!' And Jessie hurried off to tell Stanley Gay how nobly the potion had done its work.

'Stanley, dear Stanley,' said she, 'I have such news – Papa and Zorah are engaged!'

'I am very glad to hear it. She will make him an excellent wife; it is a very auspicious beginning.'

'And have *you* any news to tell me?'

'None, except that all the bottles are distributed, and I am now waiting to see their effect. By the way, the Bishop has arrived unexpectedly, and is stopping at the Rectory, and I have sent him a bottle. I should like to find a nice little wife for the Bishop, for he has Crawleigh in his gift – the present incumbent is at the point of death, and the living is worth £1,800 a year. The duty is extremely light, and the county society unexceptional. I think I could be truly useful in such a sphere of action.'

V

The action of the 'Patent Oxy-Hydrogen Love-at-First-Sight Philtre' was rapid and powerful, and before evening there was scarcely a disengaged person (over thirteen years of age) in Ploverleigh. The Dowager Lady Fitz-Saracen, a fierce old lady of sixty, had betrothed herself to Alfred Creeper, of the Three Fiddlers, a very worthy man, who had been engaged in the public trade all his life, and had never yet had a mark on his licence. Colonel Pemberton, of The Grove, had fixed his affections on dear little Bessie Lane, the pupil teacher, and his son Willie (who had returned from Eton only the day before) had given out his engagement to kind old Mrs Partlet, the widow of the late sexton. In point of fact there was only one disengaged person in the village – the good and grave old Bishop. He was in the position of the odd player who can't find a seat in the 'Family Coach'. But, on the whole, Stanley Gay was rather glad of this, as he venerated the good old prelate, and in his opinion there was no one in the village at that time who was really good enough to be a Bishop's wife, except, indeed, the dear little brown-haired, soft-eyed maiden to whom Stanley himself was betrothed.

So far everything had worked admirably, and the unions effected through the agency of the philtre, if they were occasionally ill-assorted as regards the stations in life of the contracting parties, were all that could be desired in every other respect. Good, virtuous, straightforward, and temperate men were engaged to blameless women who were calculated to make admirable wives and mothers, and there was every prospect that Ploverleigh would become celebrated as the only Home of Perfect Happiness. There was but one sad soul in the village. The good old Bishop had drunk freely of the philtre, but there was no one left to love him. It was pitiable to see the poor love-lorn prelate as he wandered disconsolately through the smiling meadows of

Ploverleigh, pouring out the accents of his love to an incorporeal abstraction.

'Something must be done for the Bishop,' said Stanley, as he watched him sitting on a stile in the distance. 'The poor old gentleman is wasting to a shadow.'

The next morning, as Stanley was carefully reading through the manuscript sermon which had been sent to him by a firm in Paternoster Row for delivery on the ensuing Sabbath, little Jessie entered his library (with Zorah) and threw herself on a sofa, sobbing as if her heart would break.

'Why, Jessie – my own little love,' exclaimed Stanley. 'What in the world is the matter?'

And he put his arms fondly round her waist, and endeavoured to raise her face to his.

'Oh, no – no – Stanley – don't – you musn't – indeed, indeed, you musn't.'

'Why, my pet, what can you mean?'

'Oh, Stanley, Stanley – you will never, never forgive me.'

'Nonsense, child,' said he. 'My dear little Jessie is incapable of an act which is beyond the pale of forgiveness.' And he gently kissed her forehead.

'Stanley, you musn't do it – indeed you musn't.'

'No, you musn't do it, Muster Gay,' said Zorah.

'Why, confound you, what do you mean by interfering?' said Stanley in a rage.

'Ah, it's all very fine, I dare say, but I don't know what you're a-talking about.'

And Stanley, recollecting her infirmity, explained in panto-mime the process of confounding a person, and intimated that it would be put into operation upon her if she presumed to cut in with impertinent remarks.

'Stanley – Mr Gay –' said Jessie.

'*Mr* Gay!' ejaculated Stanley.

'I musn't call you Stanley any more.'

'Great Heaven, why not?'

'I'll tell you all about it if you promise not to be violent.'

And Gay, prepared for some terrible news, hid his head in his hands, and sobbed audibly.

'I loved you – oh so, so much – you were my life – my heart,' said the poor little woman. 'By day and by night my thoughts were with you, and the love came from my heart as the water from a well!'

Stanley groaned.

'When I rose in the morning it was to work for your happiness, and when I lay down in my bed at night it was to dream of the love that was to weave itself through my life.'

He kept his head between his hands and moved not.

'My life was for your life – my soul for yours! I drew breath but for one end – to love, to honour, to reverence you.'

He lifted his head at last. His face was ashy pale.

'Come to the point,' he gasped.

'Last night,' said Jessie, 'I was tempted to taste a bottle of the Elixir. It was but a drop I took on the tip of my finger. I went to bed thinking but of you. I rose today, still with you in my mind. Immediately after breakfast, I left home to call upon you, and as I crossed Bullthorn's meadow I saw the Bishop of Chelsea seated on a stile. At once I became conscious that I had placed myself unwittingly under the influence of the fatal potion. Horrified at my involuntary faithlessness – loathing my miserable weakness – hating myself for the misery I was about to weave around the life of a saint I had so long adored – I could not but own to myself that the love of my heart was given over, for ever, to that solitary and love-lorn prelate. Mr Gay (for by that name I must call you to the end), I have told you nearly all that you need care to know. It is enough to add that my love is, as a matter of course, reciprocated, and, but for the misery I have caused you, I am happy. But, full as my cup of joy may be, it will never be without a bitter aftertaste, for I cannot forget that my folly – my

47

wicked folly – has blighted the life of a man who, an hour ago, was dearer to me than the whole world!'

And Jessie fell sobbing on Zorah's bosom.

Stanley Gay, pale and haggard, rose from his chair, and staggered to a side-table. He tried to pour out a glass of water, but as he was in the act of doing so the venerable Bishop entered the room.

'Mr Gay, I cannot but feel that I owe you some apology for having gained the affections of a young lady to whom you were attached – Jessie, my love, compose yourself.'

And the Bishop gently removed Jessie's arms from Zorah's neck, and placed them about his own.

'My Lord,' said Mr Gay, 'I am lost in amazement. When I have more fully realized the unparalleled misfortune that has overtaken me I shall perhaps be able to speak and act with calmness. At the present moment I am unable to trust myself to do either. I am stunned – quite, quite stunned.'

'Do not suppose, my dear Mr Gay,' said the Bishop, 'that I came here this morning to add to your reasonable misery by presenting myself before you in the capacity of a successful rival. No. I came to tell you that poor old Mr Chudd, the vicar of Crawleigh has been mercifully removed. He is no more, and as the living is in my gift, I have come to tell you that, if it can compensate in any way for the terrible loss I have been the unintentional means of inflicting upon you, it is entirely at your disposal. It is worth £1,800 per annum – the duty is extremely light, and the local society is unexceptional.'

Stanley Gay pressed the kind old Bishop's hand.

'Eighteen hundred a year will not entirely compensate me for Jessie.'

'For Miss Lightly,' murmured the Bishop, gently.

'For Miss Lightly – but it will go some way towards doing so. I accept your lordship's offer with gratitude.'

'We shall always take an interest in you,' said the Bishop.

'Always – always,' said Jessie. 'And we shall be so glad to see you at the Palace – shall we not Frederick?'

'Well – ha – hum – yes – oh, yes, of course. Always,' said the Bishop. 'That is – oh, yes – always.'

The 14th of February was a great day for Ploverleigh, for on that date all the couples that had been brought together through the agency of the philtre were united in matrimony by the only bachelor in the place, the Rev. Stanley Gay. A week afterwards he took leave of his parishioners in an affecting sermon, and 'read himself in' at Crawleigh. He is still unmarried, and likely to remain so. He has quite got over his early disappointment, and he and the Bishop and Jessie have many a hearty laugh together over the circumstances under which the good old prelate wooed and won the bright-eyed little lady. Sir Caractacus died within a year of his marriage, and Zorah lives with her daughter-in-law at the Palace. The Bishop works hard at the art of pantomimic expression, but as yet with qualified success. He has lately taken to conversing with her through the medium of diagrams, many of which are very spirited in effect, though crude in design. It is not unlikely that they may be published before long. The series of twelve consecutive sketches, by which the Bishop informed his mother-in-law that, if she didn't mind her own business, and refrain from interfering between his wife and himself, he should be under the necessity of requiring her to pack up and be off, is likely to have a very large sale.

The Secret Panel

M. P. Shiel

The one thing that Walter Gilbert could not do was to preach –
and he was a preacher. He had been at St Jerome for months, and
the people were still wondering at the things which the parson
offered them for sermons. It was a Devonshire parish, paying
the incumbent £75 – a sum for which not much was to be
expected of the lungs beyond breathing. But the little congregation persisted in hoping for better things, since, in other respects,
the new man had so crept into their hearts. Rumour breathed of
charities eked out of those £75 stipends, of sick-bed tendernesses,
long tramps over-country to see a paralytic. It was noticed that
as he went with his long swing along lanes, smiting his thick
stick smartly upon the ground, he was fond of glancing at the
sky, always with a sort of simple half-laugh. If he met anyone,
the same half-laugh, as he flung out on his hand his 'How-d'ye-
do?' He seemed very attached to children, and would carry a
small boy on his shoulder quite a long way. He was very big,
with a light-coloured moustache, and wore a short morning-
coat, instead of the parson's frock. It was impossible not to be
caught and won by him. But he certainly could not preach. And
Farmer Brian's daughters, who had attended boarding-school at
Bath, said that he was not a 'gentleman'; which, in a sense, was
true.

One Saturday night he sat writing the morrow's sermon. The
parsonage was an old house in a mass of trees. The week had

50

been so full that he had found excuse to put off that dreaded task till now – those two harangues, that labour of Hercules. If he had only been content to utter simply the limpid good that was in him! – but, no, he must be ornate, he must do better than his poor best. '*Anything* will not do,' he said constantly, spurring himself. It was his sense of duty, really, which was to blame. But either his wits were not over-bright, or preaching was the one thing above all for which he was not made. When all was said and done, he was conscious that the simple congregation regarded his outpouring with a half-smile of mere tolerance. Sometimes he was near to despair; would thump his forehead, and say: 'Dunce! Thick-head!'

This night he wrote till one, and then the Sunday morning task was over. He read the sermon, and seemed not dissatisfied. For the present, he rose and went to bed.

At breakfast he once more read the sheets, and this time with loathing. How little of the human heart with its yearnings and out-goings was here! He did not know that even sublime works of art seem to their creators, after repeated readings, like stalest dulness. Yet at ten he was at the fatal scrawl again, reading from beginning to end. The thing would not do – this stiff, leaden thing. It seemed to him monstrous, so high and fine was his inner sense, that the word spoken to living and hungry creatures should be other than inspired – and he fell to his knees, agonized. He was alone in his chamber; his forehead struck against the wall. He began to pray . . . for some miracle to help him . . . if not, then for some work in the world which he could better do. Suddenly something moved, gave – at his forehead, where it rested heavily upon the wall. Astonished, he put up his hand. At his pressure a panel flew sharply back, and there was revealed to him an oblong opening in the thickness of the wall. He sprang to his feet, realizing that his head had touched a secret spring. In a corner of the opening, tied with a ribbon, he saw a packet of old papers.

Flushed, he hurried to a table, and untied the ribbon. The first wrapping was a blank sheet of foolscap; then came another, of parchment, covered with writing: 'This is the last will and testament of me, James Anthony Pritchard . . . £170,000 . . . to the sole power and disposition of the said Alice Jane Woodhouse . . .'

A duly-signed will, thirty years old? So it seemed. And now, tied by themselves, a good-sized packet . . . of letters? Hardly! He sat reading the uppermost; sat, till at eleven, the bell ceased tolling for service; then rose, tingling, flurried, frightened, in his hand the sere old sheets. They were scribbled in a woman's running writing.

He stammered no leaden things that day. When he sat down, pale, at the sermon-end, St Jerome was a little electric ganglion of thrills.

He remained there a year, continuing without fail the series of glowing sermons, full of humour, brilliant wisdom. But it was noticed that something of his simple-hearted jollity had passed from him. As to James Anthony Pritchard, as to Alice Jane Woodhouse, he made furtive enquiries, but heard nothing.

At the end of this time he was called to a living in Wales, where he remained two years; and here again occurred the same poor beginning, bursting suddenly into the same fine surprise. He received then an invitation to a substantial curacy in Derbyshire, which he felt an inner call to accept; and thither he accordingly went.

The church was in a valley, somewhat remote from Lyston, the straggling town; and near the church the parsonage, an old-time, low structure, half wooden, where Gilbert lived alone. By a lane at the back you ascended a hill, wound down into a wooded dell, and so reached the manor-house, the dwelling of the Doctor – a shaded place, a stately home. Gilbert, strolling here in the park one day, came upon a Miss Rosey swinging in a hammock, bowered all in brown shades. She lay asleep, half-sideways, the delicate undulations of her girlhood revealed to him. As he looked, her flush deepened, and she sprang up, laughing. He, too, laughed.

'I am only a bungler,' he said, 'not a thief. I was strolling, quite innocently, waiting for the Doctor.'

His laugh was too loud, and his hands hopelessly large. She noticed them with a little mental pout, as he stood.

'It is of no consequence,' she said; 'I fell asleep over the book you set me reading. On these hot days Morpheus becomes a god to be obeyed, instead of a servant to be summoned.'

'*Sesame and Lilies*? Do you like it?'

'It seems goodish. And *you* approve it. I rather pin my faith to your literary tastes, do you know?'

Her head perked saucily. Sometimes he had a terrible dread in his heart that she was laughing at him.

They walked among the trees, she swinging her stringed hat. Its straw and pink roses reproduced the colours of her hair and cheeks.

'What I wanted to know,' he said, 'was whether the Doctor will be able to preach tomorrow.'

Dr Grandford, a fine orator, always took the morning sermon, Gilbert preaching at night. But the Doctor had lately been showing signs of break-up.

'I'm *afraid* he won't be able,' she said. 'Do you know, he took yesterday to a *stick*? – making him look *so* quaint, my poor papa!'

'That, then, is *two* sermons for someone between now and tomorrow. Can't you write one for me, Miss Rosey?'

'I can at least give you all the sympathy I have to spare.'

'Is that much?'

'All I have to spare, sir.' Then, after a short silence: 'But, tell me – do you find it, in truth, a very great – bore?'

'It is far from easy, you know.'

'And I wanted to ask you – do you, as one somehow suspects, imagine that you do not preach – nicely?'

'My heart knows that, Miss Rosey.'

Her manner became perfectly earnest.

'But you *do*! Will you believe me? And more and more you do. Your sermons are becoming 'freer' – that is papa's word, and approbation from him is something, you know! If crude people think differently, why should you trouble? I, at least, like –'

She stopped. He was looking down upon the path, deeply sensitive to the gentle, womanly purpose of her words.

'You are kind to me,' he murmured, 'kinder than anyone I ever knew.'

A footman just then came announcing the arrival of the Doctor.

An hour after, Gilbert was still alone with Dr Grandford in the library. The Doctor stood, one forefinger smoothing down the strip of silver whisker on his pale, shaven face. He was large, white-haired, conveying a suggestion of immaculate cleanness and dignity. His suave and cultured voice uttered deliberate, nicely poised phrases. Gilbert sat before him.

'You surprise me,' the Doctor said. 'You cannot mean that you have been so – incautious, as to let yourself, ah, fall in love with Rosey?'

Dr Grandford was a younger son of noble old blood, an aristocrat of aristocrats. Gilbert looked upon the ground, fingering his shovel hat.

'I am afraid, sir, that something like that has happened, and I thought it right to mention it to you in the first place. Of course, I know –'

He stopped. The Doctor smoothed his strip of whisker.

'But have you grounds for imagining that such a notion would be received by my daughter with, ah, acquiescence?'

'No, sir; no grounds. That is, I have thought it not impossible.

I may be presumptuous. Miss Rosey is very good and gracious to me, sir.'

'There is no question of presumption,' said the Doctor; 'but you must see that there are – reasons. You are not, ah, firmly established: and my daughter has been richly nurtured. I may mention, too, that a calamity just befallen me would prevent any inequality between you from being remedied on *her* side –'

'A calamity, sir? I am sorry to hear of that.'

'It has made me quite ill, you see,' the Doctor said, with a pale smile. 'I tell you in confidence. My child is aware of nothing. The extent of the disaster, one does not yet know. But the concern in which my whole personalty has been involved has, ah, failed. You guess the consequences – debt, mortgages on my realty here, general impecuniosity. If the worst be true, I may have to depend upon the moneys accruing from tithes, and the income of the little church – and you see me daily grow feebler. In fact, I now largely depend upon your efforts, Mr Gilbert, and have been comforted by the knowledge that my trust is well placed. I have observed you, and, ah, like you. But as to this matter of my daughter –'

'Do not let that be an added trouble to you, sir!' cried Gilbert, brimming with sudden pity. 'I, for my part, will – at any rate, it can wait.'

'Well – but that is not what I wanted to say. I do not feel the impulse to thwart your inclination to that extent. Having gone so far, I should, if I were you, ah, speak to her. You will find your mind freer in consequence. But I do not conceal from you my anticipation that you will find your suit – unsuccessful.'

Gilbert grasped his hand, and walked home to the parsonage.

In the grey old church, with its effigies of centuries and melancholy half-lights, the congregation the next morning was thin. Dr Grandford, sitting in hood and surplice at the choir-end behind the pulpit, listened to Gilbert with sideward head, smoothing his whisker. Anyone looking would have noticed a slight twitching of his brows, a look of surprise on his placid face. And the surprise was general. The people leant forward, intent upon this new utterance. Rosey, in her curtained pew, contemplated her lap, slightly flushed, frowning. There were, then, unsuspected powers in him? Yet something troubled her – a little jarring on the nerves. Dr Johnson, the winey old practitioner of Lyston, swore in his pew a full-blooded, mental oath, muttering: 'That's not his own sermon, by Heaven!' The thought occurred to others. Yet, if not his, then whose? He would hardly dare to preach a published discourse, which any of his hearers might have read. Nor was he, as they all in their hearts knew, the kind of man to shirk his burthens by the cheapness of plagiarism. As for Gilbert, the words which were filling his whole mind were these: 'I now depend largely upon your efforts, Mr Gilbert.' They had been a nightmare upon his consciousness, and a goad at his will.

Lady Wixley, who, with her brood of young girls, had accompanied Rosey home after church, said, in the drawing-room:

'Did anyone notice anything extwaudnerwy in our sermon today?'

The Doctor was silent. There was still on his face that look of puzzlement – those twitching brows.

'Did *you*, Miss Grandford?'

Rosey was somewhat restless, peevish.

'It was a little – unusual, I think,' she said shortly, half turning her neck.

In the evening Dr Grandford, contrary to his wont of late, again drove to the church. It was full, and the sermon was even more brilliant than the morning's. In the midst of it a slight 'Oh!' broke involuntarily from Dr Grandford. Three choirboys distinctly heard it, and reported it far. Gilbert, in a flight of eloquence, had uttered the words:

'You cannot bind a zephyr in an embrace: it will escape you: it will away to the mountain-top and elude you: it will dance with wings to the uttermost sea to mock you!'

And the same night, the Doctor summoned Miss Rosey into his presence in the library. His brow was adamant in its stern calm. His hand rested upon the dry and rumply head, she sitting on a footstool by his chair, rather pale.

'Rosey, I have to tell you – something. I shall not detain you from your music. But it is as well that you hear this without delay. I know it to be possible that words may shortly be spoken to you by Mr, ah, Gilbert, which may set up a new relation between you. And in order that there may be no kind of doubt as to your course in such an event, I have to tell you my impression that Mr Gilbert is not a man of, ah, honour.'

She turned sharply, with face all inflamed, upon him.

'Oh, *papa* –'

'You are moved, Rosey.'

'Because – this is so strangely *unlike* you – dear papa! – and I am so positively *certain* that you must be wrong –'

The Doctor frowned.

'You make me conjecture, Rosey,' he said, 'that I did well in ordering this interview. Am I to understand that you are – *attached* – to Mr Gilbert?'

'I am pleased with his society, papa,' she answered, with extravagantly innocent round eyes of surprise.

'I see. Then you are, no doubt, a close listener to his discourses. You may, therefore, chance to remember a sentence of tonight's harangue beginning, "You cannot bind a zephyr in an embrace." Now, I say to you that that sentence has for years, by some extraordinary chance, been running in my own head. I know it perfectly well. So well that, having heard it, I was able to know also that today's sermons were quite certainly not Mr Gilbert's own. And you cannot, I think, hold a man honest who takes to himself credit, aye, and possible emolument and advancement in his future career, on the strength of another's thoughts. You must see that, I think.'

'Not his *own*, do you say, papa?'

'No.'

The roses had whitened in Rosey's cheeks.

'And *you* know whose they are?'

'No. I *should*, however. I have certainly heard or seen them. They are not unfamiliar to me.'

'He must be a very foolish man to act in that way,' she broke out. 'It seems so sudden and incredible – unless there be some mistake – some other point of view. But, of course, darling papa – it can be nothing to me –'

She was on his breast in a moment, her throat dry and aching; the old man patted her hair, kissing her face; and she ran from him to hide her moistening eyes.

The crash of the bankruptcy fell ruinously upon Dr Grandford: there was a month's confinement to his bed; then came a sad migration from the manor-house to the parsonage – the carriage and footmen were gone – and strange men walked with an air of ownership in the halls of an ancient race. Rosey, of course, now knew the truth, and her lips compressed haughtily. There are natures which require poverty to bring out all their latent pride, of birth, or culture, or loveliness. A week after taking up his lodgings in Lyston town, Gilbert at last found the chance of speaking, of which she had been clever to baulk him. 'There is little hope in life for me, Miss Rosey, if you do not care for me,' he said.

It was a proud-necked patrician who answered him. The Doctor, hearing her, would have pronounced her manner and voice-inflexions the perfection of tone and taste.

'You surprise me. May you not have allowed your fancies to over-reach your instincts, Mr Gilbert?'

'Ah, Miss Rosey –'

'I am sorry if you suffer. You will let the question drop now. You have business with papa?'

The Doctor had waited with almost peevish impatience to see if the series of sermons would cease. But they had revoltingly continued. At every fresh sight of the packed church he had had an impulse to interfere. At last he summoned Gilbert.

With a multiplicity of 'ah's', he lying a-bed, Gilbert sitting near, he said that circumstances over which he had no, ah, control had, to his great – annoyance, and, he might say, sorrow, compelled him to think about engaging another curate. He recognized the value of Gilbert's zeal, and had actually reported of him in that sense to the Bishop, who, he had reason to think, might, on his approaching visit to Lyston, have something to say to Gilbert.

The double blow fell upon the simple, tough fibre of Gilbert like a sledge upon a block of oak. He was stunned, but never winced. He started forth upon a headlong walk, away from men, over the lonely country. All life seemed slipped from him. 'I now depend largely upon your efforts, Mr Gilbert' – how the words had puffed him with a glad, boyish pride, pricking his uttermost energy! And it had ended in this: unconcerned dismissal – from all he cared for in life – from the old man, from her. To live without tie, all unrelated to the world – this, surely, is the supreme bitterness. To a man of affectionate soul it is a taste of purgatory. The night came down upon him far from home.

'Oh, Rosey, Rosey!' he cried, to the waving wood, 'if you had only pity, child!'

Had he done anything – neglected to do anything? The sermons! Those sermons of another mind! They were a rather sore place in his consciousness. Ought he ever to have preached them? God knew his motive, that it was pure. At their first discovery, he had promised himself never to utter them on any occasion when there was a chance that personal benefit might accrue to himself from them, hence, on going to a new place, while he could at all consider himself as being more or less on his trial, he spoke his own words only. And the finding of the sermons had seemed to him so directly an answer to his cry for help; and *now* it was Dr Grandford's expression of dependence upon him that had led him to keep the church, by these means, a centre of interest. He could not manage to blame himself; he looked deeply within, and found all clear and selfless. For a sensitively upright nature to commit a deception for the good of others may be a greater exhibition of self-sacrifice than to tell a truth at the cost of life itself. He tossed his head backward in cloudless appeal to God. But the sermons had nothing to do with it! It was all the crookedness of his own bitter fate. No one knew of the sermons, or could know. Some spears of rain dashed upon his face; he turned back, walking still in the same wild haste. The night was very black. Again and again from the shuddering breast came the half-cry: 'Oh, Rosey, Rosey, my child!'

Rosey was at his lodgings, waiting for him! The Bishop's visit to Lyston to confirm a flock of young people was only a few days off, and Rosey was to return to the cathedral town with him as governess to his little girls; this last bitterness of her poverty she had bravely brought herself to swallow. She had been paying farewell visits among the parish poor, and had undertaken now to tell Gilbert, in passing, that Mrs Grimes, the quarryman's mother, was near to death, and eager to see him. He was out. Should she wait a few minutes? The landlady showed her into his sitting-room. She stood in her cape, hatted and gloved, at a window, twirling her parasol. Two heavy oak sticks of his stood near; she took one and looked at it, then, as if it were hot, put it quickly from her. She walked listlessly, upon her parasol, to and fro. On the drawer of an escritoire there lay a manuscript in faded ink, which, as she passed, caught her eye. She stood fixed, for the life of her unable to lift her gaze from the sheets. That hand – surely she knew it – that strong, running scrawl! Could *two* people ever have written so peculiarly, and so similarly? It was hard to believe. And the sentence she read told her that here was the last sermon preached by Gilbert. She was lost in bewilderment. Not now did she wait a moment, but hurried forth, flustered, into the rain of the already late night.

The way to the parsonage lay through lanes and a long, darksome avenue of sycamores. She had reached this, when, quite close, she heard a heaved breath bearing her name. She could see nothing, but the 'Rosey, Rosey!' fell like a burthen upon her heart. The next moment she collided with Gilbert. He would have known her presence in a sunless world, she his . . . She was in his arms, her lips found out . . . There was a little, hard scar on her short upper-lip, the mark of a cut in childhood; kissing her, he felt it, with a thrill . . . In an instant she was flying like a roe, pursued by the wild pain of his cry: 'Rosey, Rosey, Rosey . . .'

She stopped suddenly and stood away from the path, fearing, hoping, that he might follow her. They were so soon to part! But he had no notion where she was. Panting, pressed against the tree-trunk, she could faintly hear him pass away from her. She stretched out an arm after him, and a low wail came from her.

'Oh, I did so love him!'

In the parsonage, wet, with haggard face, she walked straight to the Doctor's bedside.

'Papa,' she said, calmly, 'I have been to Mr Gilbert's rooms. I chanced to see his last sermon. It is unaccountable – and I do not know what bearing it may have upon your opinion of him – but, judging from the packet of old letters I have of my mamma's, this sermon was certainly written by her.'

The Doctor's hand went sharply up to his brow.

'My – my *good* child –'

'I thought I would tell you, dear papa.'

She turned and walked away, longing for solitude. The Doctor sat up, smoothing his whisker, deep in thought.

For two days he did not refer to Gilbert; but once, when he was unexpectedly announced, Rosey was surprised to notice a twinkle in the Doctor's grey eyes.

On the Saturday my lord Bishop arrived – a little, quick man, with a brisk, bird-like perk of the head. He had heard of Gilbert's pastoral qualities from the Doctor, and had it in mind to place him well. At dinner he said:

'Is he – tell me, now – a man of liberal utterance, this Mr Gilbert?'

'I can at least promise you a very, ah, tolerable discourse from him tomorrow evening,' replied the Doctor, with a twinkle, ending in a frown.

'Mr Gilbert cannot preach!' blurted out Rosey, with a flush like anger.

'Rosey! you are candid,' cried the Doctor.

The Bishop's head perked from one to the other.

'There is – come, now – clearly a difference of standpoint between the new age and the old,' he said, puzzled. 'Well – I shall keep an open mind, and judge for myself.'

There was confirmation at both services, the Bishop preaching in the morning. Dr Grandford constrained himself to attend both times, and read the lessons. Gilbert's coming departure from Lyston had got abroad, and he was generally understood to be in some measure on his trial before the Bishop. Expectation of special effort from him was on tip-toe, as his white robes slowly ascended the pulpit. Rosey bent a perfectly pallid face over the still open hymn-book in her lap. Gilbert's massive, slanting brow, slightly bald on the top, was beaded with moisture.

There was a strong mournfulness in him this night. He had a way of shaking his bent forefinger as he preached; but tonight, he buried both fists in the cushion, leaning forward on his arms, with a slow, solemn enunciation. He did not read; and the drop from the clever flow and utterance of the last few months to this stolid speech was tremendous. But the sermon differed as much from Gilbert's own laboured and artificial discourses of other days as from the borrowed sermons. For the first time, he spoke the words of life. As perfect love 'casteth out fear', so profound sorrow will not admit of embarrassment. In Gethsemane there was no flurry. He did not stammer – he was strongly clear and calm. The voice of this melancholy human heart held the mind of the people in a sterner grip that night than though he had had the tongue of angels.

Something or other deeply moved Dr Grandford. His face showed it. His hands trembled. In a flash the whole secret of motive and character had illumined him! – the reason why those borrowed sermons had not been preached on Gilbert's first coming to Lyston – something of the reason why they had been preached afterwards – the reason why one of them was not preached *now*! He divined the whole. This man he had supposed capable of appearing before the Bishop in borrowed plumes for his own advancement – and, lo, he was a man to whom his own advancement was as nothing.

He said, as Gilbert was leaving the vestry: 'Will you, ah, Mr Gilbert, lend me an arm to the parsonage?'

The Bishop, walking in front with Rosey along the lane, said: 'You told me – come, now – that Mr Gilbert could not preach?'

'I was mistaken, my lord.' She was trembling.

'He is not brilliant, certainly.'

'Neither is the bread by which men live,' she answered.

The Doctor, behind, was leaning heavily upon Gilbert. He said:

'I must speak to you – now. I have misjudged you. I must humble myself before you. The matter is this: for some months you have been preaching to me a series of my own sermons –'

'Sir, sir –' cried Gilbert.

'I did not know *that* fact – till a few days since, or should have told you. It was a circumstance discovered by Rosey at your rooms which opened my eyes. They must have been written by my wife at my dictation at least thirty years ago, and I had forgotten them wholly, except a single sentence. I knew, however, that they were not yours, and thought – but let that pass. I say to you now that I divine your motives, and honour them, and extol them.'

'But, sir, sir –' Gilbert was all in trance and amaze.

'What you have to do in the first place is to appease my curiosity. By what miracle did you obtain these writings?'

'I found them, sir, in a secret panel at St Jerome's parsonage, at Hurley, in –'

'You have been there, then? Well, but that partially explains it. For before inheriting the manor here, I, too, was incumbent at that very St Jerome's.'

They had reached the parsonage. The Doctor led Gilbert into the study. They sat facing each other.

'The fact of the secret panel,' said the Doctor, 'I can explain: In the parsonage lived with us my wife's sister and their grandfather, a Mr Pritchard. The house was, indeed, his property. He was an eccentric person, of great age, and very wealthy. A man of irreligious and essentially worldly mind, he yet conceived it necessary to his salvation to hear a sermon once a week; and as he was almost bedridden and unable to attend church, upon me was imposed the task of reading to him a weekly sermon, which he insisted should be specially written for him. I had to humour his whim: for a clever young man with energy and a command of florid language such as he loved, the labour was not great. He invariably took possession of the sermons after hearing them, and, I suppose, treasured them in this panel, which was known to himself alone.'

'But, sir – the will!' cried Gilbert, starting to his feet with sudden recollection.

'What will? Mr Pritchard died intestate.'

'James Anthony Pritchard's will! – bequeathing £170,000 to

Alice Jane Woodhouse! – signed, sir! – wrapping up the sermons!'

The Doctor's face on the red chair-back went white as death. His hands fluttered.

'She was – my wife's – ah, sister,' he panted. 'Rosey is her – heir. Mr Pritchard's wealth went to a cousin – this, this is salvation – and the providence – of God.'

'The will is in the hands of a lawyer in London, sir,' said Gilbert. 'I committed it to him for enquiries, which have proved unsuccessful. It is duly executed.'

The Doctor's eyes closed.

An hour later, when Gilbert rose, he, too, rose, scribbled some words, and handed them in an envelope to Gilbert.

'As you pass by the drawing-room, you might hand this to Rosey,' he said.

The Bishop, tired, had retired early. Rosey sat, with dejected eyes, alone. He came, handed her the note – a low cry from her! She read:

'Have no longer any fear, my child, that Mr Gilbert is not at all points worthy of us.'

'Miss Rosey!' – he had sat down rather awkwardly by her.

Instantly her sadness changed to lightest frolic.

'Is anything wrong, Mr Walter? You tend to sighs.'

'Ah – Rosey . . .' He was one big sigh.

'It is the Sabbath evening. Am I to understand that you are again making love to me?'

'Rosey! my breath of life – my zephyr from Heaven –'

He tried to take her. She was up, and gone from him.

'You cannot bind a zephyr in an embrace, sir,' she cried, with a curtsy; 'it will escape you: it will away to the mountain-top and elude you: it will dance with wings to the uttermost sea to mock you!'

Then with a little run, a little trouble and murmur of love, she was crouching before him, her upturned lips beseeching his kiss.

Christmas Day at Kirkby Cottage

Anthony Trollope

Chapter I

What Maurice Archer said about Christmas

'After all, Christmas is a bore!'

'Even though you should think so, Mr Archer, pray do not say so here.'

'But it is.'

'I am very sorry that you should feel like that; but pray do not say anything so very horrible.'

'Why not? and why is it horrible? You know very well what I mean.'

'I do not want to know what you mean; and it would make Papa very unhappy if he were to hear you.'

'A great deal of beef is roasted, and a great deal of pudding is boiled, and then people try to be jolly by eating more than usual. The consequence is, they get very sleepy, and want to go to bed an hour before the proper time. That's Christmas.'

He who made this speech was a young man about twenty-three years old, and the other personage in the dialogue was a young lady, who might be, perhaps, three years his junior. The 'Papa' to whom the lady had alluded was the Rev. John Lownd, parson of Kirkby Cliffe, in Craven, and the scene was the parsonage library, as pleasant a little room as you would wish to see, in which the young man who thought Christmas to be a bore was at present sitting over the fire, in the parson's armchair, with a novel in his hand, which he had been reading till he was interrupted by the parson's daughter. It was nearly time for him to dress for dinner, and the young lady was already dressed. She had entered the room on the pretext of looking for some book or paper, but perhaps her main object may have been to ask for some assistance from Maurice Archer in the work of decorating the parish church. The necessary ivy and holly branches had been collected, and the work was to be performed on the morrow. The day following would be Christmas Day. It must be acknowledged, that Mr Archer had not accepted the proposition made to him very graciously.

Maurice Archer was a young man as to whose future career in life many of his elder friends shook their heads and expressed much fear. It was not that his conduct was dangerously bad, or that he spent his money too fast, but that he was abominably conceited, so said these elder friends; and then there was the unfortunate fact of his being altogether beyond control. He had neither father, nor mother, nor uncle, nor guardian. He was the owner of a small property not far from Kirkby Cliffe, which gave him an income of some six or seven hundred a year, and he had altogether declined any of the professions which had been suggested to him. He had, in the course of the year now coming to a close, taken his degree at Oxford, with some academical honours, which were not high enough to confer distinction, and had already positively refused to be ordained, although, would he do so, a small living would be at his disposal on the death of a septuagenarian cousin. He intended, he said, to farm a portion of his own land, and had already begun to make amicable arrangements for buying up the interest of one of his two tenants. The rector of Kirkby Cliffe, the Rev. John Lownd, had been among his father's dearest friends, and he was now the parson's guest for the Christmas.

There had been many doubts in the parsonage before the young man had been invited. Mrs Lownd had considered that the visit would be dangerous. Their family consisted of two daughters, the youngest of whom was still a child; but Isabel was turned twenty, and if a young man were brought into the house, would it not follow, as a matter of course, that she should fall in love with him? That was the mother's first argument. 'Young people don't always fall in love,' said the father. 'But people will say that he is brought here on purpose,' said the mother, using her second argument. The parson, who in family matters generally had his own way, expressed an opinion that if they were to be governed by what other people might choose to say, their course of action would be very limited indeed. As for his girl, he did not think she would ever give her heart to any man before it had been asked; and as for the young man – whose father had been for over thirty years his dearest friend – if he chose to fall in love, he must run his chance, like other young men. Mr Lownd declared he knew nothing against him, except that he was, perhaps, a little self-willed; and so Maurice Archer came to Kirkby Cliffe, intending to spend two months in the same house with Isabel Lownd.

Hitherto, as far as the parents or the neighbours saw – and in their endeavours to see, the neighbours were very diligent – there had been no love-making. Between Mabel, the young daughter, and Maurice, there had grown up a violent friendship – so much so, that Mabel, who was fourteen, declared that Maurice Archer was 'the jolliest person' in the world. She called him Maurice, as did Mr and Mrs Lownd; and to Maurice, of course, she was Mabel. But between Isabel and Maurice it was always Miss Lownd and Mr Archer, as was proper. It was so, at least, with this difference, that each of them had got into a way of dropping, when possible, the other's name.

It was acknowledged throughout Craven – which my readers of course know to be a district in the northern portion of the West Riding of Yorkshire, of which Skipton is the capital – that Isabel Lownd was a very pretty girl. There were those who thought that Mary Manniwick, of Barden, excelled her; and others, again, expressed a preference for Fanny Grange, the pink-cheeked daughter of the surgeon at Giggleswick. No attempt shall here be made to award the palm of superior merit; but it shall be asserted boldly, that no man need desire a prettier girl with whom to fall in love than was Isabel Lownd. She was tall, active, fair, the very picture of feminine health, with bright grey eyes, a perfectly beautiful nose – as is common to almost all girls belonging to Craven – a mouth by no means delicately small, but eager, eloquent, and full of spirit, a well-formed short chin, with a dimple, and light brown hair, which was worn plainly smoothed over her brows, and fell in short curls behind her head. Of Maurice Archer it cannot be said that he was handsome. He had a snub nose; and a man so visaged can hardly be good-looking, though a girl with a snub nose may be very pretty. But he was a well-made young fellow, having a look of power about him, with dark-brown hair, cut very short, close shorn, with clear but rather small blue eyes, and an expression of countenance which allowed no one for a moment to think that he was weak in character, or a fool. His own place, called Hundlewick Hall, was about five miles from the parsonage. He had been there four or five times a week since his arrival at Kirkby Cliffe, and had already made arrangements for his own entrance upon the land in the following September. If a marriage were to come of it, the arrangement would be one very comfortable for the father and mother at Kirkby Cliffe. Mrs Lownd had already admitted as much as that to herself, though she still trembled for her girl. Girls are so prone to lose their hearts, whereas the young men of these days are so very cautious and hard! That, at least, was Mrs Lownd's idea of girls and young men; and even at this present moment she was hardly happy about her child. Maurice, she was sure, had spoken never a word that might not have been proclaimed from the church tower; but her girl, she thought, was not quite the same as she had been before the young man had come among them. She was somewhat less easy in her manner, more preoccupied, and seemed to labour under a conviction that the presence in the house of Maurice Archer must alter the nature of her life. Of course it had altered the nature of her life, and of course she thought a great deal of Maurice Archer.

It had been chiefly at Mabel's instigation that Isabel had invited the co-operation of her father's visitor in the adornment of the church for Christmas Day. Isabel had expressed her opinion that Mr Archer didn't care a bit about such things, but Mabel declared that she had already extracted a promise from him. 'He'll do anything I ask him,' said Mabel proudly. Isabel, however, had not cared to undertake the work in such company, simply under her sister's management, and had proffered the request herself. Maurice had not declined the task – had indeed promised his assistance in some indifferent fashion – but had accompanied his promise by a suggestion that Christmas was a bore! Isabel had rebuked him, and then he had explained. But his explanation, in Isabel's view of the case, only made the matter worse. Christmas to her was a very great affair indeed – a festival to which the roast beef and the plum pudding were, no doubt, very necessary; but not by any means the essence, as he had chosen to consider them. Christmas a bore! No; a man who thought Christmas to be a bore should never be more to her than a mere acquaintance. She listened to his explanation, and then left the room, almost indignantly. Maurice, when she had gone, looked after her, and then read a page of his novel; but he was thinking of Isabel, and not of the book. It was quite true that he had never said a word to her that might not have been declared from the church tower; but, nevertheless, he had thought about her a good deal. Those were days on which he was sure that he was in love with her, and would make her his wife. Then there came days on which he ridiculed himself for the idea. And now and then there was a day on which he asked himself whether he was sure that she would take him were he to ask her. There was sometimes an air with her, some little trick of the body, a manner of carrying her head when in his presence, which he was not physiognomist enough to investigate, but which in some way suggested doubts to him. It was on such occasions as this that he was most in love with her; and now she had left the room with that particular motion of her head which seemed almost to betoken contempt.

'If you mean to do anything before dinner you'd better do it at once,' said the parson, opening the door. Maurice jumped up, and in ten minutes was dressed and down in the dining-room. Isabel was there, but did not greet him.

'You'll come and help us tomorrow,' said Mabel, taking him by the arm and whispering to him.

'Of course I will,' said Maurice.

'And you won't go to Hundlewick again till after Christmas?'

'It won't take up the whole day to put up the holly.'

'Yes, it will – to do it nicely – and nobody ever does any work the day before Christmas.'

'Except the cook,' suggested Maurice. Isabel, who heard the words, assumed that look of which he was already afraid, but said not a word. Then dinner was announced, and he gave his arm to the parson's wife.

Not a word was said about Christmas that evening. Isabel had threatened the young man with her father's displeasure on account of his expressed opinion as to the festival being a bore, but Mr Lownd was not himself one who talked a great deal about any Church festival. Indeed, it may be doubted whether

71

his more enthusiastic daughter did not in her heart think him almost too indifferent on the subject. In the decorations of the church he, being an elderly man, and one with other duties to perform, would of course take no part. When the day came he would preach, no doubt, an appropriate sermon, would then eat his own roast beef and pudding with his ordinary appetite, would afterwards, if allowed to do so, sink into his armchair behind his book – and then, for him, Christmas would be over. In all this there was no disrespect for the day, but it was hardly an enthusiastic observance. Isabel desired to greet the morning of her Saviour's birth with some special demonstration of joy. Perhaps from year to year she was somewhat disappointed – but never before had it been hinted to her that Christmas was a bore.

On the following morning the work was to be commenced immediately after breakfast. The same thing had been done so often at Kirkby Cliffe, that the rector was quite used to it. David Drum, the clerk, who was also schoolmaster, and Barty Cross-grain, the parsonage gardener, would devote their services to the work in hand throughout the whole day, under the direction of Isabel. Mabel would of course be there assisting, as would also two daughters of a neighbouring farmer. Mrs Lownd would go down to the church about eleven, and stay till one, when the whole party would come up to the parsonage for refreshment. Mrs Lownd would not return to the work, but the others would remain there till it was finished, which finishing was never accomplished till candles had been burned in the church for a couple of hours. Then there would be more refreshments; but on this special day the parsonage dinner was never comfortable and orderly. The rector bore it all with good humour, but no one could say that he was enthusiastic in the matter. Mabel, who delighted in going up ladders, and leaning over the pulpit, and finding herself in all those odd parts of the church to which her imagination would stray during her father's sermons, but which were ordinarily inaccessible to her, took great delight in the work. And perhaps Isabel's delight had commenced with similar feelings. Immediately after breakfast, which was much hurried on the occasion, she put on her hat and hurried down to the church, without a word to Maurice on the subject. There was another whisper from Mabel, which was answered also with a whisper, and then Mabel also went. Maurice took up his novel, and seated himself comfortably by the parlour fire.

But again he did not read a word. Why had Isabel made herself so disagreeable, and why had she perked up her head as she left the room in that self-sufficient way, as though she was determined to show him that she did not want his assistance? Of course, she had understood well enough that he had not intended to say that the ceremonial observance of the day was a bore. He had spoken of the beef and the pudding, and she had chosen to pretend to misunderstand him. He would not go near the church. And as for his love, and his half-formed resolution to make her his wife, he would get over it altogether. If there were one thing more fixed with him than another, it was that on no consideration would he marry a girl who should give herself airs. Among them they might decorate the church as they pleased, and when he should see their handywork – as he would do, of course, during the service of Christmas Day – he would pass it by without a remark. So resolving, he again turned over a page or two of his novel, and then remembered that he was bound, at any rate, to keep his promise to his friend Mabel. Assuring himself that it was on that plea that he went, and on no other, he sauntered down to the church.

Chapter II

Kirkby Cliffe Church

Kirkby Cliffe Church stands close upon the River Wharfe, about a quarter of a mile from the parsonage, which is on a steep hillside running down from the moors to the stream. A prettier little church or graveyard you shall hardly find in England. Here, no large influx of population has necessitated the removal of the last home of the parishioners from beneath the shelter of the parish church. Every inhabitant of Kirkby Cliffe has, when dead, the privilege of rest among those green hillocks. Within the building is still room for tablets commemorative of the rectors and their wives and families, for there are none others in the parish to whom such honour is accorded. Without the walls, here and there, stand the tombstones of the farmers; while the undistinguished graves of the peasants lie about in clusters which, solemn though they be, are still picturesque. The church itself is old, and may probably be doomed before long to that kind of destruction which is called restoration; but hitherto, it has been allowed to stand beneath all its weight of ivy, and has known but little change during the last two hundred years. Its old oak pews, and ancient exalted reading-desk and pulpit are offensive to many who come to see the spot; but Isabel Lownd is of opinion that neither the one nor the other could be touched, in the way of change, without profanation.

In the very porch Maurice Archer met Mabel, with her arms full of ivy branches, attended by David Drum. 'So you have come at last, Master Maurice?' she said.

'Come at last! Is that all the thanks I get? Now let me see what it is you're going to do. Is your sister here?'

'Of course she is. Barty is up in the pulpit, sticking holly branches round the sounding-board, and she is with him.'

'T' boorde's that rotten an' maaky, it'll be doon on Miss

Is'bel's heede, an' Barty Crossgrain ain't more than or'nary saft-handed,' said the clerk.

They entered the church, and there it was, just as Mabel had said. The old gardener was standing on the rail of the pulpit, and Isabel was beneath, handing up to him nails and boughs, and giving him directions as to their disposal.

'Naa, miss, naa; it wonot do that a-way,' said Barty. 'Thou'll ha' me on to t' stanes – thou wilt, that a-gait. Lard-a-mussy, miss, thou munnot clim' up, or thou'lt be doon, and brek thee banes, thee ull!'

So saying, Barty Crossgrain, who had contented himself with remonstrating when called upon by his young mistress to imperil his own neck, jumped on to the floor of the pulpit and took hold of the young lady by both her ankles. As he did so, he looked up at her with anxious eyes, and steadied himself on his own feet, as though it might become necessary for him to perform some great feat of activity. All this Maurice Archer saw, and Isabel saw that he saw it. She was not well pleased at knowing that he should see her in that position, held by the legs by the old gardener, and from which she could only extricate herself by putting her hand on the old man's neck as she jumped down from her perch. But she did jump down, and then began to scold Crossgrain, as though the awkwardness had come from fault of his.

'I've come to help, in spite of the hard words you said to me yesterday, Miss Lownd,' said Maurice, standing on the lower steps of the pulpit. 'Couldn't I get up and do the things at the top?' But Isabel thought that Mr Archer could not get up and 'do the things at the top'. The wood was so far decayed that they must abandon the idea of ornamenting the sounding-board, and so both Crossgrain and Isabel descended into the body of the church.

Things did not go comfortably with them for the next hour. Isabel had certainly invited his co-operation, and therefore could not tell him to go away; and yet, such was her present feeling towards him, she could not employ him profitably, and with ease to herself. She was somewhat angry with him, and more angry with herself. It was not only that she had spoken hard words to him, as he had accused her of doing, but that, after the speaking of the last words, she had been distant and cold in her manner to him. And yet he was so much to her! She liked him so well! – and though she had never dreamed of admitting to herself that she was in love with him, yet – yet it would be pleasant to have the opportunity of asking herself whether she could not love him, should he ever give her a fair and open opportunity of searching her own heart on the matter. There had now sprung up some half-quarrel between them, and it was impossible that it could be set aside by any action on her part. She could not be otherwise than cold and haughty in her demeanour to him. Any attempt at reconciliation must come from him, and the longer she continued to be cold and haughty, the less chance there was that it would come. And yet she knew that she had been right to rebuke him for what he had said. 'Christmas a bore!' She would rather lose his friendship for ever than hear such words from his mouth, without letting him know what she thought of them. Now he was there with her, and his coming could not but be taken as a sign of repentance. Yet she could not soften her manners to him, and become intimate with him, and playful, as had been her wont. He was allowed to pull about the masses of ivy, and to stick up branches of holly here and there at discretion; but what he did was done under Mabel's direction, and not under hers – with the aid of one of the farmer's daughters, and not with her aid. In silence she continued to work round the chancel and communion-table, with Crossgrain, while Archer, Mabel and David Drum used their taste and diligence in the nave and aisles of the little church. Then Mrs Lownd came among them, and things went more easily; but hardly a word had been spoken between Isabel and Maurice when, after sundry hints from David

Drum as to the lateness of the hour, they left the church and went up to the parsonage for their luncheon.

Isabel stoutly walked on first, as though determined to show that she had no other idea in her head but that of reaching the parsonage as quickly as possible. Perhaps Maurice Archer had the same idea, for he followed her. Then he soon found that he was so far in advance of Mrs Lownd and the old gardener as to be sure of three minutes' uninterrupted conversation; for Mabel remained with her mother, making earnest supplication as to the expenditure of certain yards of green silk tape, which she declared to be necessary for the due performance of the work which they had in hand.

'Miss Lownd,' said Maurice, 'I think you are a little hard upon me.'

'In what way, Mr Archer?'

'You asked me to come down to the church, and you haven't spoken to me all the time I was there.'

'I asked you to come and work, not to talk,' she said.

'You asked me to come and work with you.'

'I don't think that I said any such thing; and you came at Mabel's request, and not at mine. When I asked you, you told me it was all – a bore. Indeed you said much worse than that. I certainly did not mean to ask you again. Mabel asked you, and you came to oblige her. She talked to you, for I heard her; and I was half disposed to tell her not to laugh so much, and to remember that she was in church.'

'I did not laugh, Miss Lownd.'

'I was not listening especially to you.'

'Confess, now,' he said, after a pause; 'don't you know that you misinterpreted me yesterday, and that you took what I said in a different spirit from my own.'

'No; I do not know it.'

'But you did. I was speaking of the holiday part of Christmas, which consists of pudding and beef, and is surely subject to ridicule, if one chooses to ridicule pudding and beef. You answered me as though I had spoken slightingly of the religious feeling which belongs to the day.'

'You said that the whole thing was . . . I won't repeat the word. Why should pudding and beef be a bore to you, when it is prepared as a sign that there shall be plenty on that day for people who perhaps don't have plenty on any other day of the year? The meaning of it is, that you don't like it all, because that which gives unusual enjoyment to poor people, who very seldom have any pleasure, is tedious to you. I don't like you for feeling it to be tedious. There! that's the truth. I don't mean to be uncivil, but –'

'You are very uncivil.'

'What am I to say, when you come and ask me?'

'I do not well know how you could be more uncivil, Miss Lownd. Of course it is the commonest thing in the world, that one person should dislike another. It occurs every day, and people know it of each other. I can perceive very well that you dislike me, and I have no reason to be angry with you for disliking me. You have a right to dislike me, if your mind runs that way. But it is very unusual for one person to tell another so to his face – and more unusual to say so to a guest.'

Maurice Archer, as he said this, spoke with a degree of solemnity to which she was not at all accustomed, so that she became frightened at what she had said. And not only was she frightened, but very unhappy also. She did not quite know whether she had or had not told him plainly that she disliked him, but she was quite sure that she had not intended to do so. She had been determined to scold him – to let him see that, however much of real friendship there might be between them, she would speak her mind plainly, if he offended her; but she certainly had no desire to give him cause for lasting wrath against her.

'However,' continued Maurice, 'perhaps the truth is best after all, though it is so very unusual to hear such truths spoken.'

'I didn't mean to be uncivil,' stammered Isabel.

'But you meant to be true?'

'I meant to say what I felt about Christmas Day.' Then she paused a moment. 'If I have offended you, I beg your pardon.'

He looked at her and saw that her eyes were full of tears, and his heart was at once softened towards her. Should he say a word to her, to let her know that there was – or, at any rate, that henceforth there should be no offence? But it occurred to him that if he did so, that word would mean so much, and would lead perhaps to the saying of other words, which ought not to be shown without forethought. And now, too, they were within the parsonage gate, and there was no time for speaking.

'You will go down again after lunch?' he asked.

'I don't know – not if I can help it. Here's papa.' She had begged his pardon – had humbled herself before him. And he had not said a word in acknowledgement of the grace she had done him. She almost thought that she did dislike him – really dislike him. Of course he had known what she meant, and he had chosen to misunderstand her and to take her, as it were, at an advantage. In her difficulty she had abjectly apologized to him, and he had not even deigned to express himself as satisfied with what she had done. She had known him to be conceited and masterful; but that, she had thought, she could forgive, believing it to be the common way with men – imagining, perhaps, that a man was only the more worthy of love on account of such fault; but now she found that he was ungenerous also, and deficient in that chivalry without which a man can hardly appear at advantage in a woman's eyes. She went on into the house, merely touching her father's arm, as she passed him, and hurried up to her own room.

'Is there anything wrong with Isabel?' asked Mr Lownd.

'She has worked too hard, I think, and is tired,' said Maurice. Within ten minutes they were all assembled in the dining-room, and Mabel was loud in her narrative of the doings of the morning. Barty Crossgrain and David Drum had both declared the sounding-board to be so old that it mustn't even be touched, and she was greatly afraid that it would tumble down some day and 'squash papa' in the pulpit. The rector ridiculed the idea of any such disaster; and then there came a full description of the morning's scene, and of Barty's fears lest Isabel should 'brek her banes'.

'His own wig was almost off,' said Mabel, 'and he gave Isabel such a lug by the leg that she very nearly had to jump into his arms.'

'I didn't do anything of the kind,' said Isabel.

'You had better leave the sounding-board alone,' said the parson.

'We have left it alone, papa,' said Isabel, with great dignity. 'There are some other things that can't be done this year.' For Isabel was becoming tired of her task, and would not have returned to the church at all could she have avoided it.

'What other things?' demanded Mabel, who was as enthusiastic as ever. 'We can finish all the rest. Why shouldn't we finish it? We are ever so much more forward than we were last year, when David and Barty went to dinner. We've finished the Granby-Moor pew, and we never used to get to that till after luncheon.' But Mabel on this occasion had all the enthusiasm to herself. The two farmer's daughters, who had been brought up to the parsonage as usual, never on such occasions uttered a word. Mrs Lownd had completed her part of the work; Maurice could not trust himself to speak on the subject; and Isabel was dumb. Luncheon, however, was soon over, and something must be done. The four girls of course returned to their labours, but Maurice did not go with them, nor did he make any excuse for not doing so.

'I shall walk over to Hundlewick before dinner,' he said, as soon as they were all moving. The rector suggested that he would hardly be back in time. 'Oh, yes; ten miles – two hours and a half; and I shall have two hours there besides. I must see what they are doing with our own church, and how they mean to keep Christmas there. I'm not quite sure that I shan't go over there again tomorrow.' Even Mabel felt that there was something wrong, and said not a word in opposition to this wicked desertion.

He did walk to Hundlewick and back again, and when at Hundlewick he visited the church, though the church was a mile beyond his own farm. And he added something to the store provided for the beef and pudding of those who lived upon his own land; but of this he said nothing on his return to Kirkby Cliffe. He walked his dozen miles, and saw what was being done about the place, and visited the cottages of some who knew him, and yet was back at the parsonage in time for dinner. And during his walk he turned many things over in his thoughts, and endeavoured to make up his mind on one or two points. Isabel had never looked so pretty as when she jumped down into the pulpit, unless it was when she was begging his pardon for her want of courtesy to him. And though she had been, as he described it to himself, 'rather down upon him', in regard to what he had said of Christmas, did he not like her the better for having an opinion of her own? And then, as he had stood for a few minutes leaning on his own gate, and looking at his own house at Hundlewick, it had occurred to him that he could hardly live there without a companion. After that he had walked back again, and was dressed for dinner, and in the drawing-room before any one of the family.

With poor Isabel the afternoon had gone much less satisfactorily. She found that she almost hated her work, that she really had a headache, and that she could put no heart into what she was doing. She was cross to Mabel, and almost surely to David Drum and Barty Crossgrain. The two farmer's daughters were allowed to do almost what they pleased with the holly

branches – a state of things which was most unusual – and then
Isabel, on her return to the parsonage, declared her intention of
going to bed! Mrs Lownd, who had never before known her to
do such a thing, was perfectly shocked. Go to bed, and not come
down the whole of Christmas Eve! But Isabel was resolute. With
a bad headache she would be better in bed than up. Were she to
attempt to shake it off, she would be ill the next day. She did not
want anything to eat, and would not take anything. No; she
would not have any tea, but would go to bed at once. And to bed
she went.

She was thoroughly discontented with herself, and felt that
Maurice had, as it were, made up his mind against her for ever.
She hardly knew whether to be angry with herself or with him;
but she did know very well that she had not intended really to
quarrel with him. Of course she had been in earnest in what she
had said; but he had taken her words as signifying so much more
than she had intended! If he chose to quarrel with her, of course
he must; but a friend could not, she was sure, care for her a great
deal who would really be angry with her for such a trifle. Of
course this friend did not care for her at all – not the least, or he
would not treat her so savagely. He had been quite savage to her,
and she hated him for it. And yet she hated herself almost more.
What right could she have had first to scold him, and then to tell
him to his face that she disliked him? Of course he had gone
away to Hundlewick. She would not have been a bit surprised if
he had stayed there and never come back again. But he did come
back, and she hated herself as she heard their voices as they all
went in to dinner without her. It seemed to her that his voice was
more cheery than ever. Last night and all the morning he had
been silent and almost sullen, but now, the moment that she was
away, he could talk and be full of spirits. She heard Mabel's
ringing laughter downstairs, and she almost hated Mabel. It
seemed to her that everybody was gay and happy because she
was upstairs in her bed, and ill. Then there came a peal of

laughter. She was glad that she was upstairs in bed, and ill. Nobody would have laughed, nobody would have been gay, had she been there. Maurice Archer liked them all, except her – she was sure of that. And what could be more natural after her conduct to him? She had taken upon herself to lecture him, and of course he had not chosen to endure it. But of one thing she was quite sure, as she lay there, wretched in her solitude – that now she would never alter her demeanour to him. He had chosen to be cold to her, and she would be like frozen ice to him. Again and again she heard their voices, and then, sobbing on her pillow, she fell asleep.

Chapter III

Showing how Isabel Lownd told a Lie

On the following morning – Christmas morning – when she woke, her headache was gone and she was able, as she dressed, to make some stern resolutions. The ecstasy of her sorrow was over, and she could see how foolish she had been to grieve as she had grieved. After all, what had she lost, or what harm had she done? She had never fancied that the young man was her lover, and she had never wished – so she now told herself – that he should become her lover. If one thing was plainer to her than another, it was this – that they two were not fitted for each other. She had sometimes whispered to herself, that if she were to marry at all, she would fain marry a clergyman. Now, no man could be more unlike a clergyman than Maurice Archer. He was, she thought, irreverent, and at no pains to keep his want of reverence out of sight, even in that house. He had said that Christmas was a bore, which, to her thinking, was abominable. Was she so poor a creature as to go to bed and cry for a man who had given her no sign that he even liked her, and of whose ways she disapproved so greatly, that even were he to offer her his hand she would certainly refuse it? She consoled herself for the folly of the preceding evening by assuring herself that she had really worked in the church till she was ill, and that she would have gone to bed, and must have gone to bed, had Maurice Archer never been seen or heard of at the parsonage. Other people went to bed when they had headaches, and why should not she? Then she resolved, as she dressed, that there should be no sign of illness, no bit of ill-humour on her, on this sacred day. She would appear among them all full of mirth and happiness, and would laugh at the attack brought upon her by Barty Crossgrain's sudden fear in the pulpit; and she would greet Maurice Archer with all possible cordiality, wishing him a merry Christmas as she gave him her hand, and would make him understand in a moment that she had altogether forgotten their mutual bickerings. He should understand that, or should, at least, understand that she willed that it should all be regarded as forgotten. What was he to her, that any thought of him should be allowed to perplex her mind on such a day as this?

She went downstairs, knowing that she was the first up in the house – the first, excepting the servants. She went into Mabel's room, and kissing her sister, who was only half awake, wished her many, many, many happy Christmases.

'Oh, Bell,' said Mabel, 'I do so hope you are better!'

'Of course I am better. Of course I am well. There is nothing for a headache like having twelve hours round of sleep. I don't know what made me so tired and so bad.'

'I thought it was something Maurice said,' suggested Mabel.

'Oh, dear, no. I think Barty had more to do with it than Mr Archer. The old fellow frightened me so when he made me think I was falling down. But get up, dear. Papa is in his room, and he'll be ready for prayers before you.'

Then she descended to the kitchen, and offered her good wishes to all the servants. To Barty, who always breakfasted there on Christmas mornings, she was especially kind, and said something civil about his work in the church.

'She'll 'bout brek her little heart for t'young mon there, an' he's naa true t' her,' said Barty, as soon as Miss Lownd had closed the kitchen door; showing, perhaps, that he knew more of the matter concerning herself than she did.

She then went into the parlour to prepare the breakfast, and to put a little present, which she had made for her father, on his plate – when, whom should she see but Maurice Archer!

It was a fact known to all the household, and a fact that had not recommended him at all to Isabel, that Maurice never did come downstairs in time for morning prayers. He was always the last; and, though in most respects a very active man, seemed to be almost a sluggard in regard to lying in bed late. As far as she could remember at the moment, he had never been present at prayers a single morning since the first after his arrival at the parsonage, when shame, and a natural feeling of strangeness in the house, had brought him out of his bed. Now he was there half an hour before the appointed time, and during that half-hour she was doomed to be alone with him. But her courage did not for a moment desert her.

'This is a wonder!' she said, as she took his hand. 'You will have a long Christmas Day, but I sincerely hope that it may be a happy one.'

'That depends on you,' said he.

'I'll do everything I can,' she answered. 'You shall only have a very little bit of roast beef, and the unfortunate pudding shan't be brought near you.' Then she looked in his face, and saw that his manner was very serious – almost solemn – and quite unlike his usual ways. 'Is anything wrong?' she asked.

'I don't know; I hope not. There are things which one has to say which seem to be so very difficult when the time comes. Miss Lownd, I want you to love me.'

'What!' She started back as she made the exclamation, as

though some terrible proposition had wounded her ears. She had ever dreamed of his asking for her love, she had dreamed of it as a thing that future days might possibly produce – when he should be altogether settled at Hundlewick, and when they should have got to know each other intimately by the association of years.

'Yes, I want you to love me, and to be my wife. I don't know how to tell you; but I love you better than anything and everything in the world – better than all the world put together. I have done so from the first moment that I saw you; I have. I knew how it would be the very first instant I saw your dear face, and every word you have spoken, and every look out of your eyes, has made me love you more and more. If I offended you yesterday, I will beg your pardon.'

'Oh, no,' she said.

'I wish I had bitten my tongue out before I had said what I did about Christmas Day. I do, indeed. I only meant, in a half-joking way, to – to – to –. But I ought to have known you wouldn't like it, and I beg your pardon. Tell me, Isabel, do you think that you can love me?'

Not half an hour since she had made up her mind that, even were he to propose to her – which she then knew to be absolutely impossible – she would certainly refuse him. He was not the sort of man for whom she would be a fitting wife; and she had made up her mind also, at the same time, that she did not at all care for him, and that he certainly did not in the least care for her. And now the offer had absolutely been made to her! Then came across her mind an idea that he ought in the first place to have gone to her father; but as to that she was not quite sure. Be that as it might, there he was, and she must give him some answer. As for thinking about it, that was altogether beyond her. The shock to her was too great to allow of her thinking. After some fashion, which afterwards was quite unintelligible to herself, it seemed to her, at that moment, that duty, and maidenly reserve, and filial obedience, all required her to reject him instantly. Indeed, to have accepted him would have been quite beyond her power.

'Dear Isabel,' said he, 'may I hope that some day you will love me?'

'Oh! Mr Archer, don't,' she said. 'Do not ask me.'

'Why should I not ask you?'

'It can never be.' This she said quite plainly, and in a voice that seemed to him to settle his fate for ever; and yet at the moment her heart was full of love towards him. Though she could not think, she could feel. Of course she loved him. At the very moment in which she was telling him that it could never be, she was elated by an almost ecstatic triumph, as she remembered all her fears, and now knew that the man was at her feet.

When a girl first receives the homage of a man's love, and receives it from one whom, whether she loves him or not, she thoroughly respects, her earliest feeling is one of victory – such a feeling as warmed the heart of a conqueror in the Olympian games. He is the spoil of her spear, the fruit of her prowess, the quarry brought down by her own bow and arrow. She, too, by some power of her own which she is hitherto quite unable to analyse, has stricken a man to the very heart, so as to compel him for the moment to follow wherever she may lead him. So it was with Isabel Lownd as she stood there, conscious of the eager gaze which was fixed upon her face, and fully alive to the anxious tones of her lover's voice. And yet she could only deny him. Afterwards, when she thought of it, she could not imagine why it had been so with her; but, in spite of her great love, she continued to tell herself that there was some obstacle which could never be overcome – or was it that a certain maidenly reserve sat so strong within her bosom that she could not bring herself to own to him that he was dear to her?

'Never!' exclaimed Maurice, despondently.

'Oh, no!'

'But why not? I will be very frank with you, dear. I did think you liked me a little before that affair in the study.' Like him a little! Oh, how she had loved him! She knew it now, and yet not for worlds could she tell him so. 'You are not still angry with me, Isabel?'

'No; not angry.'

'Why should you say never? Dear Isabel, cannot you try to love me?' Then he attempted to take her hand, but she recoiled at once from his touch, and did feel something of anger against him in that he should thus refuse to take her word. She knew not what it was that she desired of him, but certainly he should not attempt to take her hand, when she told him plainly that she could not love him. A red spot rose to each of her cheeks as again he pressed her.

'Do you really mean that you can never, never love me?' She muttered some answer, she knew not what, and then he turned from her, and stood looking out upon the snow which had fallen during the night. She kept her ground for a few seconds, and then escaped through the door, and up to her own bedroom. When once there, she burst out into tears. Could it be possible that she had thrown away for ever her own happiness, because she had been too silly to give a true answer to an honest question? And was this the enjoyment and content which she had promised herself for Christmas Day? But surely, surely he would come to her again. If he really loved her as he had declared, if it was true that ever since his arrival at Kirkby Cliffe he had thought of her as his wife, he would not abandon her because in the first tumult of her surprise she had lacked courage to own to him the truth; and then in the midst of her tears there came upon her that delicious recognition of a triumph which, whatever be the victory won, causes such elation to the heart! Nothing, at any rate, could rob her of this – that he had loved her. Then, as a thought suddenly struck her, she ran quickly across the passage, and in a moment was upstairs, telling her tale with her mother's arm close folded round her waist.

In the meantime Mr Lownd had gone down to the parlour, and had found Maurice still looking out upon the snow. He, too, with some gentle sarcasm, had congratulated the young man on his early rising, as he expressed the ordinary wish of the day.

'Yes,' said Maurice, 'I had something special to do. Many happy Christmases, sir! I don't know much about its being happy to me.'

'Why, what ails you?'

'It's a nasty sort of day, isn't it?' said Maurice.

'Does that trouble you? I rather like a little snow on Christmas Day. It has a pleasant, old-fashioned look. And there isn't enough to keep even an old woman at home.'

'I dare say not,' said Maurice, who was still beating about the bush, having something to tell, but not knowing how to tell it. 'Mr Lownd, I should have come to you first, if it hadn't been for an accident.'

'Come to me first! What accident?'

'Yes; only I found Miss Lownd down here this morning, and I asked her to be my wife. You needn't be unhappy about it, sir. She refused me point blank.'

'You must have startled her, Maurice. You have startled me, at any rate.'

'There was nothing of that sort, Mr Lownd. She took it all very easily. I think she does take things easily.' Poor Isabel! 'She just told me plainly that it never could be so, and then she walked out of the room.'

'I don't think she expected it, Maurice.'

'Oh, dear no! I'm quite sure she didn't. She hadn't thought about me any more than if I were an old dog. I suppose men do make fools of themselves sometimes. I shall get over it, sir.'

'Oh, I hope so.'

'I shall give up the idea of living here. I couldn't do that. I shall probably sell out the property, and go to Africa.'

'Go to Africa!'

'Well, yes. It's as good a place as any other, I suppose. It's wild, and a long way off, and all that kind of thing. As this is Christmas, I had better stay here today, I suppose.'

'Of course you will.'

'If you don't mind, I'll be off early tomorrow, sir. It's a kind of thing, you know, that does flurry a man. And then my being here may be disagreeable to her – not that I suppose she thinks about me any more than if I were an old cow.'

It need hardly be remarked that the rector was a much older man than Maurice Archer, and that he therefore knew the world much better. Nor was he in love. And he had, moreover, the advantage of a much closer knowledge of the young lady's character than could be possessed by the lover. And, as it happened, during the last week, he had been fretted by fears expressed by his wife – fears which were altogether opposed to Archer's present despondency and African resolutions. Mrs Lownd had been uneasy – almost more than uneasy – lest poor dear Isabel should be stricken at her heart; whereas, in regard to that young man, she didn't believe that he cared a bit for her girl. He ought not to have been brought into the house. But he was there, and what could they do? The rector was of opinion that things would come straight – that they would be straightened not by any lover's propensities on the part of his guest, as to which he protested himself to be altogether indifferent, but by his girl's good sense. His Isabel would never allow herself to be seriously affected by a regard for a young man who had made no overtures to her. That was the rector's argument; and perhaps, within his own mind, it was backed by a feeling that, were she so weak, she must stand the consequence. To him it seemed to be an absurd degree of caution that two young people should not be brought together in the same house lest one should fall in love with the other. And he had seen no symptoms of such love. Nevertheless his wife had fretted him, and he had been uneasy. Now the shoe was altogether on the other foot. The young man was the despondent lover, and was asserting that he must go instantly to Africa, because the young lady treated him like an old dog, and thought no more about him than of an old cow.

A father in such a position can hardly venture to hold out hopes to a lover, even though he may approve of the man as a suitor for his daughter's hand. He cannot answer for his girl, nor can he very well urge upon a lover the expediency of renewing his suit. In this case Mr Lownd did think, that in spite of the cruel, determined obduracy which his daughter was said to have displayed, she might probably be softened by constancy and perseverance. But he knew nothing of the circumstances, and could only suggest that Maurice should not take his place for the first stage on his way to Africa quite at once.

'I do not think you need hurry away because of Isabel,' he said, with a gentle smile.

'I couldn't stand it – I couldn't indeed,' said Maurice, impetuously. 'I hope I didn't do wrong in speaking to her when I found her here this morning. If you had come first I should have told you.'

'I could only have referred you to her, my dear boy. Come – here they are; and now we will have prayers.'

As he spoke, Mrs Lownd entered the room, followed closely by Mabel, and then at a little distance by Isabel. The three maid-servants were standing behind in a line, ready to come in for prayers. Maurice could not but feel that Mrs Lownd's manner to him was especially affectionate; for, in truth, hitherto she had kept somewhat aloof from him, as though he had been a ravening wolf. Now she held him by the hand, and had a spark of motherly affection in her eyes, as she, too, repeated her Christmas greeting. It might well be so, thought Maurice. Of course she would be more kind to him than ordinary, if she knew that he was a poor blighted individual. It was a thing of course that Isabel should have told her mother; equally a thing of course that he should be pitied and treated tenderly. But on the next day he would be off. Such tenderness as that would kill him.

As they sat at breakfast, they all tried to be very gracious to each other. Mabel was sharp enough to know that something special had happened, but could not quite be sure what it was. Isabel struggled very hard to make little speeches about the day, but cannot be said to have succeeded well. Her mother, who had known at once how it was with her child, and had required no positive answers to direct questions to enable her to assume that Isabel was now devoted to her lover, had told her girl that if the man's love were worth having, he would surely ask her again. 'I don't think he will, Mamma,' Isabel had whispered, with her face half-hidden on her mother's arm. 'He must be very unlike other men if he does not,' Mrs Lownd had said, resolving that the opportunity should not be wanting. Now she was very gracious to Maurice, speaking before him as though he were quite one of the family. Her trembling maternal heart had feared him, while she thought that he might be a ravening wolf, who would steal away her daughter's heart, leaving nothing in return; but now that he had proved himself willing to enter the fold as a useful domestic sheep, nothing could be too good for him. The parson himself, seeing all this, understanding every turn in his wife's mind, and painfully anxious that no word might be spoken which should seem to entrap his guest, strove diligently to talk as though nothing was amiss. He spoke of his sermon, and of David Drum, and of the allowance of pudding that was to be given to the inmates of the neighbouring poorhouse. There had been a subscription, so as to relieve the rates from the burden of the plum-pudding, and Mr Lownd thought that the farmers had not been sufficiently liberal.

'There's Furness, at Loversloup, gave us half a crown. I told him he ought to be ashamed of himself. He declared to me to my face that if he could find puddings for his own bairns, that was enough for him.'

'The richest farmer in these parts, Maurice,' said Mrs Lownd.

'He holds above three hundred acres of land, and could stock double as many, if he had them,' said the would-be indignant rector, who was thinking a great deal more of his daughter than of the poor-house festival. Maurice answered him with a word or two, but found it very hard to assume any interest in the question of the pudding. Isabel was more hard-hearted, he thought, than even Farmer Furness, of Loversloup. And why should he trouble himself about these people – he, who intended to sell his acres, and go away to Africa? But he smiled and made some reply, and buttered his toast, and struggled hard to seem as though nothing ailed him.

The parson went down to church before his wife, and Mabel went with him. 'Is anything wrong with Maurice Archer?' she asked her father.

'Nothing, I hope,' said he.

'Because he doesn't seem to be able to talk this morning.'

'Everybody isn't a chatter-box like you, Mab.'

'I don't think I chatter more than Mamma, or Bell. Do you know, Papa, I think Bell has quarrelled with Maurice Archer.'

'I hope not. I should be very sorry that there should be any quarrelling at all – particularly on this day. Well, I think you've done it very nicely; and it is none the worse because you've left the sounding-board alone.' Then Mabel went over to David Drum's cottage, and asked after the condition of Mrs Drum's plum-pudding.

No one had ventured to ask Maurice Archer whether he would stay in church for the sacrament, but he did. Let us hope that no undue motive of pleasing Isabel Lownd had any effect upon him at such a time. But it did please her. Let us hope also that, as she knelt beside her lover at the low railing, her young heart was not too full of her love. That she had been thinking of him throughout her father's sermon – thinking of him, then resolving that she would think of him no more, and then thinking of him more

than ever – must be admitted. When her mother had told her that
he would come again to her, she had not attempted to assert that,
were he to do so, she would again reject him. Her mother knew
all her secret, and, should he not come again, her mother would
know that she was heart-broken. She had told him positively
that she would never love him. She had so told him, knowing
well that at the very moment he was dearer to her than all the
world beside. Why had she been so wicked as to lie to him? And
if now she were punished for her lie by his silence, would she
not be served properly? Her mind ran much more on the subject
of this great sin which she had committed on that very morning
– that sin against one who loved her so well, and who desired to
do good to her – than on those general arguments in favour of
Christian kindness and forbearance which the preacher drew
from the texts applicable to Christmas Day. All her father's
eloquence was nothing to her. On ordinary occasions he had no
more devoted listener; but, on this morning, she could only
exercise her spirit by repenting her own unchristian conduct.
And then he came and knelt beside her at that sacred moment! It
was impossible that he should forgive her, because he could not
know that she had sinned against him.

There were certain visits to her poorer friends in the immediate
village which, according to custom, she would make after church.
When Maurice and Mrs Lownd went up to the parsonage, she
and Mabel made their usual round. They all welcomed her, but
they felt that she was not quite herself with them, and even
Mabel asked her what ailed her.

'Why should anything ail me? – only I don't like walking in
the snow.'

Then Mabel took courage. 'If there is a secret, Bell, pray tell
me. I would tell you any secret.'

'I don't know what you mean,' said Isabel, almost crossly.

'Is there a secret, Bell? I'm sure there is a secret about
Maurice.'

'Don't – don't,' said Isabel.

'I do like Maurice so much. Don't you like him?'

'Pray do not talk about him, Mabel.'

'I believe he is in love with you, Bell; and, if he is, I think you ought to be in love with him. I don't know how you could have anybody nicer. And he is going to live at Hundlewick, which would be such great fun. Would not Papa like it?'

'I don't know. Oh, dear! – oh, dear!' Then she burst out into tears, and, walking out of the village, told Mabel the whole truth. Mabel heard it with consternation, and expressed her opinion that, in these circumstances, Maurice would never ask again to make her his wife.

'Then I shall die,' said Isabel frankly.

Chapter IV

Showing how Isabel Lownd repented her Fault

In spite of her piteous condition and near prospect of death, Isabel Lownd completed her round of visits among her old friends. That Christmas should be kept in some way by every inhabitant of Kirkby Cliffe, was a thing of course. The district is not poor, and plenty on that day was rarely wanting. But Parson Lownd was not what we call a rich man; and there was no resident squire in the parish. The farmers, comprehending well their own privileges, and aware that the obligation of gentle living did not lie on them, were inclined to be close-fisted; and thus there was sometimes a difficulty in providing for the old and the infirm. There was a certain ancient widow in the village, of the name of Mucklewort, who was troubled with three orphan grandchildren and a lame daughter; and Isabel had, some days since, expressed a fear up at the parsonage that the good things of this world might be scarce in the old widow's cottage.

Something had, of course, been done for the old woman, but not enough, as Isabel had thought. 'My dear,' her mother had said, 'it is no use trying to make very poor people think that they are not poor.'

'It is only one day in the year,' Isabel had pleaded.

'What you give in excess to one, you take from another,' replied Mrs Lownd, with the stern wisdom which experience teaches. Poor Isabel could say nothing further, but had feared greatly that the rations in Mrs Mucklewort's abode would be deficient. She now entered the cottage, and found the whole family at that moment preparing themselves for the consumption of a great Christmas banquet. Mrs Mucklewort, whose temper was not always the best in the world, was radiant. The children were silent, open-eyed, expectant, and solemn. The lame aunt was in the act of transferring a large lump of beef, which seemed to be commingled in a most inartistic way with potatoes and cabbage, out of a pot on to the family dish. At any rate there was plenty; for no five appetites – had the five all been masculine, adult, and yet youthful – could, by any feats of strength, have emptied that dish at a sitting. And Isabel knew well that there had been pudding. She herself had sent the pudding; but that, as she was well aware, had not been allowed to abide its fate till this late hour of the day.

'I'm glad you're all so well employed,' said Isabel. 'I thought you had done dinner long ago. I won't stop a minute now.'

The old woman got up from her chair, and nodded her head, and held out her withered old hand to be shaken. The children opened their mouths wider than ever, and hoped there might be no great delay. The lame aunt curtsyed and explained the circumstances.

'Beef, Miss Isabel, do take a mortal time t' boil; and it ain't no wise good for t' bairns to have it any ways raw.' To this opinion Isabel gave her full assent, and expressed her gratification that the amount of beef should be sufficient to require so much cooking. Then the truth came out.

'Muster Archer just sent us over from Rowdy's a meal's meat with a vengeance; God bless him!' crooned out the old woman, and the children muttered some unintelligible sound, as though aware that duty required them to express some Amen to the prayer of their elders. Now Rowdy was the butcher living at Grassington, some six miles away – for at Kirkby Cliffe there was no butcher. Isabel smiled all round upon them sweetly, with her eyes full of tears, and then left the cottage without a word.

He had done this because she had expressed a wish that these people should be kindly treated – had done it without a syllable spoken to her or to anyone – had taken trouble, sending all the way to Grassington for Mrs Mucklewort's beef! No doubt he had given other people beef, and had whispered no word of his kindness to anyone at the rectory. And yet she had taken upon herself to rebuke him, because he had not cared for Christmas Day. As she walked along, silent, holding Mabel's hand, it seemed to her that of all men he was the most perfect. She had rebuked him, and had then told him – with incredible falseness – that she did not like him; and after that, when he had proposed to her in the kindest, noblest manner, she had rejected him – almost as though he had not been good enough for her! She felt now as though she would like to bite the tongue out of her head for such misbehaviour.

'Was not that nice of him?' said Mabel. But Isabel could not answer the question. 'I always thought he was like that,' continued the younger sister. 'If he were my lover, I'd do anything he asked me, because he is so good-natured.'

'Don't talk to me,' said Isabel. And, Mabel, who comprehended something of the condition of her sister's mind, did not say another word on their way back to the parsonage.

It was the rule of the house that on Christmas Day they should dine at four o'clock – a rule which almost justified the very strong expression with which Maurice first offended the young lady whom he loved. To dine at one or two o'clock is a practice which has its recommendations. It suits the appetite, is healthy, and divides the day into two equal halves, so that no man so dining fancies that his dinner should bring to him an end of his usual occupations. And to dine at six, seven, or eight is well adapted to serve several purposes of life. It is convenient, as inducing that gentle lethargy which will sometimes follow the pleasant act of eating at a time when the work of the day is done; and it is both fashionable and comfortable. But to dine at four is almost worse than not to dine at all. The rule, however, existed at Kirkby Cliffe parsonage in regard to this one special day in the year, and was always obeyed.

On this occasion Isabel did not see her lover from the moment in which he left her at the church door till they met at table. She had been with her mother, but her mother had not said a word to her about Maurice. Isabel knew very well that they two had walked home together from the church, and she had thought that her best chance lay in the possibility that he would have spoken of what had occurred during the walk. Had this been so, surely her mother would have told her; but not a word had been said; and even with her mother Isabel had been too shame-faced to ask a question. In truth, Isabel's name had not been mentioned between them, nor had any allusion been made to what had taken place during the morning. Mrs Lownd had been too wise and too wary – too well aware of what was really due to her daughter – to bring up the subject herself; and he had been silent, subdued, and almost sullen. If he could not get an acknowledgement of affection from the girl herself, he certainly would not endeavour to extract a cold compliance by the mother's aid. Africa, and a disruption of all the plans of his life, would be better to him than that. But Mrs Lownd knew very well how it was with him; knew how it was with them both; and was aware that in such a condition things should be allowed to arrange themselves. At dinner, both she and the rector were full of mirth and good humour, and Mabel, with great glee, told the story of Mrs Mucklewort's dinner.

'I don't want to destroy your pleasure,' she said, bobbing her head at Maurice; 'but it did look so nasty! Beef should always be roast beef on Christmas Day.'

'I told the butcher it was to be roast beef,' said Maurice, sadly.

'I dare say the little Muckleworts would just as soon have it boiled,' said Mrs Lownd. 'Beef is beef to them, and a pot for boiling is an easy apparatus.'

'If you had beef, Miss Mab, only once or twice a year,' said her father, 'you would not care whether it were roast or boiled.' But Isabel spoke not a word. She was most anxious to join the conversation about Mrs Mucklewort, and would have liked much to give testimony to the generosity displayed in regard to quantity; but she found that she could not do it. She was absolutely dumb. Maurice Archer did speak, making, every now and then, a terrible effort to be jocose; but Isabel from first to last was silent. Only by silence could she refrain from a renewed deluge of tears.

In the evening two or three girls came in with their younger brothers, the children of farmers of the better class in the neighbourhood, and the usual attempts were made at jollity. Games were set on foot, in which even the rector joined, instead of going to sleep behind his book, and Mabel, still conscious of her sister's wounds, did her very best to promote the sports. There was blindman's-buff, and hide and seek, and snapdragon, and forfeits, and a certain game with music and chairs – very prejudicial to the chairs – in which it was everybody's object to sit down as quickly as possible when the music stopped. In the game Isabel insisted on playing, because she could do that alone. But even to do this was too much for her. The sudden pause could hardly be made without a certain hilarity of spirit, and her spirits were unequal to any exertion. Maurice went through his work like a man, was blinded, did his forfeits, and jostled for the chairs with the greatest diligence; but in the midst of it all he, too, was as solemn as a judge, and never once spoke a single word to Isabel. Mrs Lownd, who usually was not herself much given to the playing of games, did on this occasion make an effort, and absolutely consented to cry the forfeits; but Mabel was wonderfully quiet, so that the farmers' daughters hardly perceived that there was anything amiss.

It came to pass, after a while, that Isabel had retreated to her room – not for the night, as it was as yet hardly eight o'clock – and she certainly would not disappear till the visitors had taken their departure – a ceremony which was sure to take place with the greatest punctuality at ten, after an early supper. But she had escaped for a while, and in the meantime some frolic was going on which demanded the absence of one of the party from the room, in order that mysteries might be arranged of which the absent one should remain in ignorance. Maurice was thus banished, and desired to remain in desolation for the space of five minutes; but, just as he had taken up his position, Isabel descended with slow, solemn steps, and found him standing at her father's study door. She was passing on, and had almost entered the drawing-room, when he called her.

'Miss Lownd,' he said. Isabel stopped, but did not speak; she was absolutely beyond speaking. The excitement of the day had been so great, that she was almost overcome by it, and doubted, herself, whether she would be able to keep up appearances till the supper should be over, and she should be relieved for the night. 'Would you let me say one word to you?' said Maurice. She bowed her head and went with him into the study.

Five minutes had been allowed for the arrangement of the mysteries, and at the end of the five minutes Maurice was authorized, by the rules of the game, to return to the room. But he did not come, and upon Mabel's suggesting that possibly he might not be able to see his watch in the dark, she was sent to fetch him. She burst into the study, and there she found the truant and her sister, very close, standing together on the hearthrug. 'I didn't know you were here, Bell,' she exclaimed. Whereupon Maurice, as she declared afterwards, jumped round the table after her, and took her in his arms and kissed her. 'But you must come,' said Mabel, who accepted the embrace with perfect goodwill.

'Of course you must. Do go, pray, and I'll follow – almost immediately.' Mabel perceived at once that her sister had altogether recovered her voice.

'I'll tell 'em you're coming,' said Mabel, vanishing.

'You must go now,' said Isabel. 'They'll all be away soon, and then you can talk about it.' As she spoke, he was standing with his arm round her waist, and Isabel Lownd was the happiest girl in all Craven.

Mrs Lownd knew all about it from the moment in which Maurice Archer's prolonged absence had become cause of complaint among the players. Her mind had been intent upon the matter, and she had become well aware that it was only necessary that the two young people should be alone together for a few moments. Mabel had entertained great hopes, thinking, however, that perhaps three or four years must be passed in melancholy gloomy doubts before the path of true love could be made to run smooth; but the light had shone upon her as soon as she saw them standing together. The parson knew nothing about it till the supper was over. Then, when the front door was open, and the farmers' daughters had been cautioned not to get themselves more wet than they could help in the falling snow, Maurice said a word to his future father-in-law.

'She has consented at last, sir. I hope you have nothing to say against it.'

'Not a word,' said the parson, grasping the young man's hand, and remembering, as he did so, the extension of the time over which that phrase 'at last' was supposed to spread itself.

Maurice had been promised some further opportunity of

'talking about it', and of course claimed a fulfilment of the promise. There was a difficulty about it, as Isabel, having now been assured of her happiness, was anxious to talk about it all to her mother rather than to him; but he was imperative, and there came at last for him a quarter of an hour of delicious triumph in that very spot on which he had been so scolded for saying that Christmas was a bore.

'You were so very sudden,' said Isabel, excusing herself for her conduct in the morning.

'But you did love me?'

'If I do now, that ought to be enough for you. But I did, and I've been so unhappy since; and I thought that, perhaps, you would never speak to me again. But it was all your fault; you were so sudden. And then you ought to have asked Papa first – you know you ought. But, Maurice, you will promise me one thing. You won't ever again say that Christmas Day is a bore!'

The Perfect Crime

Ormond Greville

Farmer Greenwood, a big, stout, red-faced man, was in a disputatious mood, and the other men in the billiard room of the Parish Hall, though they never allowed themselves to smile, were thoroughly enjoying the fun. He had had a glass, as the saying is, and had finished a very erratic game of billiards, and now he was expressing his opinions more freely than usual.

'You chaps all think Parson's a saint. Jumping Jehoshaphat! I'll lay he's much like the rest of us, and we aren't saints that I know of – not even you, Dick Burge, not by a long chalk!'

Dick Burge, who was, amongst other things, parish clerk, undertaker and a contractor in a small way, winked at the others and said, 'Don't know as I ever set up to be, Mr Greenwood. But Parson's nigher to being a saint than anyone *I* ever see.' He puffed at his pipe and added, 'And I've seen a lot of men who ought to have been – three bishops, two deans, and a score of archdeacons, canons and suchlike. Lor' bless me, when it becomes a matter of a talk with Saint Peter, they'll have more to explain away than Parson, and you may lay your shirt on that!'

'You're just like a lot of females,' said the farmer contemptuously, 'taken in by a good-looking face. You're like my missus, who talks to me about his health and says he don't eat enough. Why, I've heard her chatter to my Jane about his lovely voice and eyes and his beautiful smile! She says he's like St Paul! Pah!

Why, he's as strong as a young horse, and no more like St Paul than I am.'

Joe Harris, the blacksmith and motor-agent, remarked here:

'I never heard that St Paul was as strong as Samson. But what have you got against Parson, anyway, Mr Greenwood?'

Greenwood finished his glass before replying.

'Well,' he said, 'I've not got nothin' agin him, except that ever since he came to Oldthorpe, nine years ago come midsummer, everyone in the parish talks as if he was perfect, and as for the women, they're clean daft about him!'

Dick Burge put in, 'But he never gives any of them a look, for all the eyes they make at him – you'll allow that, although he hasn't a wife to look after him, like you have, Mr Greenwood!'

'Confound the man!' said the farmer, 'I know that. He can't be caught out in anything, drat him, that's what makes me mad. It's not human nature for a man not to smoke, *nor* drink, *nor* swear, *nor* have his bit of fun with the girls, nor do nothin' at all. I've always found that the men who set up to be plaster saints have a secret somewhere! Jumping Jehoshaphat! I'll lay this one's the same . . .'

But Bill Hackett, who was a retired builder and said to be the warmest man in the village, broke in here, and told Greenwood that he ought to be ashamed of himself.

'That's as may be,' said Greenwood. 'I'm no plaster saint!' and as some reminiscence in proof of that assertion smote him, he began to roll about with laughter.

He then ordered drinks for all of them, still highly amused with his thoughts, the nature of which the others seemed to understand, for one of them observed: 'We all know what you were, Jim Greenwood, in the time of Parson Gregory.'

'Why,' said Joe Harris, 'look at the words you used to rap out.' He proceeded to point out that since Parson Quaile got at him, his favourite oath had taken the place of a much more blasphemous one. This accusation was met by Greenwood with gusts of laughter and the assertion that he didn't mind obliging anyone who was civil, even a parson.

'But he gets you to church,' said Dick Burge.

'When it's too wet to get about the farm,' said Greenwood, and added, 'but I don't deny he can preach. What a gift for talking! It's as good as a play to listen to him.'

And then Bill Hackett interposed by asking Burge whether there would be anything said by the parson at the funeral of Joshua Pook the next day.

They all had known Joshua Pook, who had recently died at his comfortable house in the parish. He was an auctioneer and estate agent, with offices in the Cathedral town, only three or four miles from Oldthorpe.

'I don't know,' replied Burge. 'What could he say about him, anyway, though he was once a sidesman, to be sure?'

And then they proceeded to make comments on Mr Pook, from which it became apparent that they none of them had either liked or respected him, for all the many years he had lived among them. Mr Hackett observed that his reputation for honesty in the town was such that no man trusted him a yard.

'He's no loss to anyone so far as I can see.'

'And I don't think Parson cared for him much,' said Dick Burge. 'I saw them talking a short time ago after Church, and I thought to myself that Parson couldn't abide him.'

And this brought them to the old topic, and they were still discussing it when closing time came, and they all went out into the windy night.

The subject of this discussion, the Reverend George Theophilus Quaile, was peacefully writing in his study at the Oldthorpe Rectory. He had long been engaged on a life of Julian the Apostate, but it was advancing slowly owing to the many demands of his parish on his time. For there was never a more conscientious rector, and it was quite unusual for him to find that he could give two consecutive hours to his history.

The work had been started originally as a kind of sedative. It kept away distressing thoughts: it occupied any spare time before he felt the need of sleep: it helped him to secure peaceful slumber. The interest of the subject had taken possession of his mind, and he sometimes blamed himself for thinking of the complex character and perplexing motives of the Roman Emperor when he ought to have been thinking of his next sermon.

It was a simply furnished room; with a low ceiling, which Quaile could touch with his hand, when he stood upright, for he was over six feet in height. The only remaining work of the builders was a beautiful Queen Anne fireplace. The windows had been converted into Gothic by a clerical disciple of Horace Walpole. The walls were completely covered with books in every sort of binding and every kind of condition. There were a couple of old oars fastened against the cornice, evidence of successes on the Cam twenty years before. Almost the only furniture was a very long, narrow table of oak, littered with books, papers, two heavy inkstands, an ebony ruler, a couple of candlesticks, a lamp and a Bible-box.

A log fire was burning in the grate and there was a pile of logs beside it. The Rector's reputation for strength in the neighbourhood was largely due to the fact that he was accustomed to fell and trim his own trees in a wood which formed part of the glebe, and it was a subject of talk in the parish, not unmixed with pride, that he could wield a woodman's axe as well or better than any professional.

It was nearly midnight when he gave a sigh and rose to his feet. He had finished the important chapter dealing with the massacre of Alexandria, and the behaviour of Julian to Athanasius. He threw a few more logs on the fire, for he still had an hour's work before him on the parish accounts, and, lighting an old pipe, gave himself up to reflection.

Unexpectedly, he found he was happier than he had been since his university days. He had got the parish into something like reasonable order. There were no crying scandals and the poor were decently housed. He had as many offers of assistance and of money as he could do with. The Bishop, a man chary of praise, had been more than complimentary of late. The parish church was crowded on Sundays, and he was accustomed to preach, either there or elsewhere, including the Cathedral, to a rapt congregation. His reputation in the diocese was spotless. Indeed, he could not help knowing that he was talked of by enthusiasts as if he were a saint.

His lips, at this thought, formed a sardonic smile. For the Reverend Theophilus Quaile had not always been a pattern among men. At Cambridge, and for a few years afterwards, he had been more than gay, if not worse. The hedonist had become an ascetic suddenly, as the result of a tragic occurrence which had nearly driven him to suicide; and he was only just able, now, after fifteen years, to think calmly of the terrible incident of the death of Margaret Powell in his rooms after a Covent Garden Ball. He saw her again in the eyes of the mind with all her remarkable loveliness and charm; and he was still filled with love, pity and remorse.

No one could condemn him as severely as he condemned himself. A lifetime of devotion to others could hardly, he thought to himself, atone. The coroner's inquest was still a nightmare in the retrospect, and the bribing of three Press reporters to suppress their copy was a distasteful close to a horrible morning . . . And then, after some long weeks of misery, when death would have been welcome, he found peace in religion and social service. If this is to be called a conversion, he had experienced it . . .

And then, some years later, after taking Orders, and after he had become Rector of Oldthorpe, and when he had thought confidently that the past was buried except in his own heart, Joshua Pook came on the scene. He had become an inhabitant of the parish and was accustomed to drive daily into the town to conduct a doubtful, if not a disreputable business as an auctioneer. The Rector, who had heard of his reputation, had tried to avoid him as far as possible: but one day Joshua Pook had sought a private interview, and then a blow had fallen on poor Quaile.

By what seemed a most untoward chance, Pook was a half-brother of Margaret, and he had made it his business to know the whole terrible story. His arrival and settlement in Oldthorpe was not an accident. He was in great straits for money, and partly by appeals to the Rector's feelings, and partly by putting his claim as one for compensation, he had induced him to pay him money. In some strange and illogical way the Rector felt that he was making atonement and expiation.

Once this fatal step was taken the rest was easy. More pressure was brought to bear, and more money was paid. Finally the Rector, who wanted every penny of his income for his parish, struck, and said he would pay no more. Pook then resorted to the open method of blackmail. The story he was in a position to tell was a scandalous one: with his own embellishments it would sound terrible.

The Rector cared little for himself; but his influence in the parish was as necessary to him as life itself. After a struggle, he gave in on the terms of paying an annual sum to Pook. And now Pook was dead, and he was to be buried next day.

The Rector felt that a cloud had been lifted from his brain. The secret was to be buried with the auctioneer. The book was getting on. He loved his work. He felt younger and stronger than he had felt for years.

He sat down at his table, and, taking the ebony ruler, he had just drawn a line along a sheet of foolscap paper when he heard a tap at the window.

He looked up, fancying that it might be caused by the wind; but it was repeated. He went to the window and, drawing back the curtain, opened it. He saw a man dimly made visible by the light of the room.

The man said, 'It's Longhurst, James Longhurst,' and added, 'Mr Pook's clerk.'

'What do you want here at this time of night? Is it something to do with the funeral?'

'Nothing to do with that, at least, not exactly, governor; but it's something private, deadly private, and I've come at this hour to make sure of a private interview.'

The Rector paused. He could not imagine what the man wanted. But late as it was, it might be of importance. He was not a man to feel any fear, or to be swayed by considerations of prudence, so he said: 'Well, I'll let you in, though you might have come earlier.'

And in a few moments he was back in his room, looking at an undersized, rat-like man, with ferrety eyes and ginger hair.

'Sit down,' said the Rector, 'and tell me what I can do for you.'

Longhurst looked round the room, twisting a cloth cap in his hands, as if uncertain how to begin.

'It's perishing cold outside,' he said, looking at the fire.

'Well,' said the Rector, 'warm yourself at the fire and tell me your private business.'

Longhurst went to the fire, which was blazing, and after cramming his cap into a pocket, held his hands to it, looking back over his shoulder towards the Rector.

'Pretty snug here,' he said; 'there isn't such a thing as a drink handy, I suppose?'

'You can have a glass of water,' was the reply. 'I don't drink either beer or spirits myself, and there are, I believe, none in the house.'

'Gosh!' said the man. 'Water? I don't call that a drink.'

'Well,' said the Rector with a smile, 'the sooner you tell me your business, the sooner you will be back home where I suppose there is what you would call a drink. So speak on!'

'It's deadly private, governor! That's why I've walked out at this time of night, unbeknownst to a living soul.'

'The servants have been in bed and asleep for about three hours, and there's no one to listen. Come! What is it about?'

'It's about Josh Pook, whom you're burying tomorrow.'

'Well, what about him?' said the Rector.

'You used to pay him a hundred and fifty a year,' said the man, looking quickly over his left shoulder to see how the Rector would take this statement.

There was a long pause.

'And what has that to do with you?' said the Rector at last.

'I know what you paid it for.'

The blow had fallen, and a number of wholly unpleasant thoughts raced through the Rector's mind.

'Well?' he said.

Longhurst did not at first reply. He seemed to be in doubt as to how to continue the interview. At last he turned round from the fire and said, 'There's nothing extra to be gained by beating about the bush! You've got to continue the annuity to me.'

'Why should I?'

'For the same reason.'

'And what is that?'

'Silence, I guess,' said Longhurst.

The Rector rose to his feet quickly and advanced towards the man who, shrinking back and putting a hand in his pocket, cried out, 'Don't touch me! I've a revolver in my pocket.'

The Rector stopped.

'You worm!' he said. 'Did you think I was going to dirty my hands on you?'

'Now, now,' said the man, 'there's nothing to be gained by that kind of talk. You're up against it and you'd better take it quietly.'

The Rector sat down again.

'Go on,' he said, 'I'm listening.' And taking up the ruler, he began ruling some fresh lines for his accounts.

Longhurst produced from his inside pocket some flimsy paper.

'I found these while turning out a private drawer of Mr Pook's yesterday. They seemed interesting and I read them. Golly! Oh, what a surprise! Scandal about the Reverend Theophilus Quaile! Spicy stuff, too! And all ready for the newspapers. And all about the Reverend Quaile who preaches religion and moral sob-stuff in the Cathedral, and who hobnobs with the Bishop. I've seen him myself. Why, the copy's worth a guinea a line to the *P——Gazette* or to the *True Briton*! But more to you, governor, a precious sight more!'

The Rector made no reply.

'Come,' said the man, 'I'll read you a bit,' and he proceeded to read a sensational account of the tragedy, full of imaginary conversations and inaccurate detail.

The Rector paused for a moment in his work, holding the ruler tightly in his right hand.

Longhurst went on reading extracts here and there. He came to a description of Margaret, and smacked his lips over it.

'Be quiet!' said the Rector, in a low, emphatic voice.

Longhurst went on with a coarse laugh. The Rector rose to his feet.

'She seems to have been hot stuff,' said Longhurst, 'and I'll bet a monkey you and she . . .'

The sentence was never finished.

The Rector never knew exactly how it happened. The act was instinctive. With the ruler he had struck, as if to fell the man to the earth. He moved his head and received the blow on his temple. He sank down, a heap of dirty clothes.

The Rector stood looking at the body for a long time without touching it.

He then stooped and found with his hand that the heart had ceased to beat. He got a small mirror and placed it before the man's open mouth. There was no sign of moisture on the glass.

It was true, then; he had killed the blackmailer.

He felt no regret, but an enormous disquietude. What was to be done?

The Rector was a man with great powers of imagination. As he sat down again at his table, he visualized in a series of scenes – as if he were looking at a film, all that would follow if he straightway informed the police of everything that had happened. He saw the embarrassed village policeman arriving, the sergeant coming later, the questions put to him and his answers, his arrest, his interview with the inspector of police in the town, the inside of the jail! Would they allow him bail? He thought not. And then he saw himself as the principal figure at the inquest, with hundreds of curious people of both sexes staring at him, and he heard his own answers to the pitiless questions put to him by a hatchet-faced counsel, who seemed not to understand his terrible anxiety not to say anything which might tarnish the reputation of Margaret.

His mind made a jump to his trial in the assize court by a small, red-faced judge, before a jury of men (and two women), who looked like half-wits. He heard his conviction for manslaughter; for his mind refused to think of another possibility, and then the sentence of the judge, in solemn tones. The warder touched him on the shoulder and he walked down some stairs to a prison van.

And then he was in prison for an interminable time, with degraded fellow-prisoners, callous warders, and – a curious freak of his mind – a low-church prison chaplain who cordially disliked him, the exact counterpart of the only clergyman with whom the Rector had ever had a quarrel. The chaplain's visits and conversation were almost more than the Rector could bear . . .

And then he saw himself having a final interview with the governor of the prison, and walking out of the gates . . .

One or two sympathetic friends came to meet him, but their honest sympathy showed him the depth to which he had fallen

. . . He was given to understand that he had no future as one of the working clergy in England. His only chance was to begin life over again; preferably in the colonies.

The Rector at this point struck the table with the fatal ruler and exclaimed aloud, 'By Heaven, I will not give up my work here. I would sooner die!'

He turned his gaze to the untidy object between him and the fireplace. The body, the body! The only obstacle! How could it be made to disappear – and disappear for ever?

He drew nearer to it and, turning it over, looked steadily at the weak, futile, vicious face. His imagination pictured for him the man's life. He thought, as he had often thought of others, 'Poor foolish wretch! Perhaps he never in all his life had a single decent friend.' His anger left him and was replaced by his accustomed sympathy for erring mankind.

He paused, and then said in a low, determined tone, 'He must have Christian burial!'

And upon this thought, all things became clear to the priest, and his further acts seemed to follow an inevitable course, as if, indeed, they were those of an automaton guided by an exterior will.

Taking the body in his arms as easily as if it were a child, he walked with it to the front door and let himself out.

The wind had got up, and the many elms in the garden were moaning in the gale; but it was not raining. He walked to the garage and placed the body in the back of the old car. He covered it with the rug.

He drove out of the door, and then stopped. He shut the door and got from the neighbouring tool-house and potting-shed a spade, a pick, a piece of rope and two sacks.

The churchyard was little more than a hundred yards away. He drove slowly without lights. The lane was completely desolate. He parked the car in a dark lane under some over-hanging trees and entered the churchyard.

The wind was still rising and seemed to threaten the stability of the trees, and the clouds, fitfully visible by the light of a setting moon, were scudding across the sky. The Rector took his tools and walked quickly to the side of the newly dug grave destined to receive, in a few hours, the mortal remains of Joshua Pook. It was close to a row of elms, and the place was so dark that, except at moments when the moon gave a faint light, the Rector could scarcely see the ancient and lofty church spire thirty or forty yards away. The sexton had covered the opening with planks, which the Rector removed. He took one, however, and placed it across the middle of the opening, and with its assistance lowered himself into the grave and began to dig.

Fortunately, digging was an occupation to which he was accustomed, or strong as he was, he would soon have been exhausted. As it was, the thought occurred to him, after half an hour's work, that the sexton was not overpaid. For the first time since the fatal interview he smiled.

At one end of the opening he was much troubled with the roots of a tree, and he was glad he had brought the pick. He worked hard, and it did not seem to him very long before he had excavated about two feet of soil. With the aid of the plank he swung himself up. The keen air seemed to go through him, and he wiped his forehead and put on the coat which he had removed.

When he reached the car, he found that the body was beginning to get stiff; but he managed, without much difficulty, to place it at full length beside the grave. He went back for the rope and the stable lantern. He tied the rope under the arms of the body and, standing at one end of the grave, he carefully lowered it down. Taking the stable lantern he went down himself, untied the rope and arranged the corpse in its final resting place.

It did not take more than a few minutes to shovel the soil down, so that the body was covered to the extent of over a foot. He trod the soil firmly down over it and smoothed it over with the spade. After a careful examination, by the light of the lantern, he hoisted himself out, filled the two sacks with excavated soil, and rearranged the planks and the earth, leaving everything round the grave just as he had found it. He carried his two sacks to the car.

There was a running stream close to the road side, and there he emptied his sacks of soil. He drove home very slowly, for he thought there might be trees down across the road, but he only encountered some moderate sized branches.

The gale was dropping when he reached the Rectory garage. He cleaned out the car, replaced the sacks and the rope, and returned to the house. By the old clock in the hall he noted that it was quarter-past four. Except for its loud ticking the house was silent, as silent as the grave. When the trite phrase crossed his mind, he shuddered.

He entered the sitting-room, where the lamp was still burning; everything was as he left it, except that there were only a few bright embers in the hearth. Its familiar appearance gave him a sense of tightening at the heart; it seemed to him that he had been away a year and was returning a different man. He tidied up his desk and carefully wiped the ebony ruler. The hearth-rug showed no signs of any unusual happening. He removed some dirt from his shoes and brushed his clothes before going to bed.

He slept a dreamless sleep.

The funeral of Joshua Pook, which took place at midday, attracted a large congregation. Nearly every adult in the parish came, for the dead man, though not a favourite, had been a resident among them for a long time and, moreover, there was curiosity to hear what the Rector could find to say about him.

He said nothing beyond the words of the service for the burial of the dead, which he uttered in his magnificent voice and in his usual impressive manner. The female members of the assembly noticed, however, that he looked paler and more ascetic than ever; and Mrs Greenwood and several others wished that they were allowed to look after him. When he came to the words, 'Thou knowest, O Lord, the secrets of our hearts,' he made an unusual pause. The men present thought that he was reflecting on the guilty secrets of the deceased sinner; but in this they were mistaken. When the coffin was brought to the grave the Rector, standing at the head of it, was noticed to look down into the opening – as if there was something to be seen at the bottom. But, of course, there was nothing! The coffin was lowered down in the customary way. 'Earth to earth, dust to dust, ashes to ashes . . .'

That night, a little after eleven, Farmer Greenwood, Bill Hackett, Joe Harris and Dick Burge were walking homewards together from the parish room. Their way led past the churchyard, and not very far from the spot where they had attended the burial of Joshua Pook and where there was now an oblong mound of soil. Not unnaturally they looked towards the spot, and to their surprise they saw beside it a kneeling figure. They stopped and gazed, open-mouthed.

'It's the Parson,' said Joe Harris.

'Praying, begad!' said Greenwood.

'Beside the grave of Pook,' said Hackett.

They were silent while they took in the fact; and then they made their respective comments, which were terse.

'Holy Moses!' said Hackett.

'That scalliwag!' said Joe Harris.

'That's why!' said Dick Burge.

'Jumping Jehoshaphat!' said the farmer.

And they walked on, ruminating on the incident.

How were they to know that the Reverend Theophilus Quaile had committed the perfect crime, never to be discovered by man, and was now praying to God for forgiveness?

The Vicarage Clock

Christopher Park

As I looked out through the lead-panes of the vicarage window my eyes blinked in the golden light of the setting sun and I knew in that moment that, for generations, this room must always have been the priest's study. Immediately opposite and slightly to my right about a hundred yards away lay the old, stone church with its square clock-tower. All the faces of the clock showed the correct time except the one facing the vicarage which seemed to be stuck at five to twelve. But presumably this would not have caused much concern among the village folk as the twenty or so little dwellings that made up the tiny Wiltshire hamlet of Nether Brookfield all lay to the left and across the river on the other side of the church. So the only inconvenience would have been to the inhabitants of the vicarage itself and, presumably, they had other means of telling the time.

As if on cue, there was a tremendous whirring and I turned round to watch as a beautiful old grandfather clock set behind a chaise-longue and between the bookcases of the back study wall began to strike 7 p.m. As it did so I became aware of perhaps yet another reason why this room had been chosen as my late friend's study, as much as it had been by his father and his father before him. And though this was a time of mourning for the whole household, it somehow seemed doubly appropriate on this Easter Saturday that a shadow of a crucifix should be shed over the tall body and face of the clock. I turned my gaze back into the setting sun and, now that the light was less intense as the ruddy disc had begun to sink behind the hill beyond the river, I could make out what had given rise to this rather macabre image. For there, silhouetted on the skyline, stood an old windmill, its sails set in such a fashion that, with the sun behind them, they formed the arms of a Roman cross.

As the seventh chime of the clock died away, the church bells themselves began to strike the hours. Then the whole house was still and all that could be heard was the twittering of birds from the small hedged garden outside and the occasional sound of voices from the village beyond. A tranquil scene indeed, but one which I would have given anything to have witnessed under pleasanter circumstances. For yesterday my old schoolfriend had died in this very room.

I sat down at his desk again and picked up where I'd left off. According to his housekeeper he had been working right up to the hour of his death, which had, by curious coincidence, been at five to twelve yesterday evening, Good Friday. I only wish I had got there a day earlier, but I'd been held up in London with some legal business involving my ex-wife.

Ours had been a short-lived marriage – barely a year – and I had decided to do some travelling to try and broaden my mind and at the same time perhaps to find some answers. I was still young enough, in my mid-forties, not to mind a few hardships en route and so decided I could just about afford a year away. So, to give my plans some sort of structure, I decided that I would visit a group of my old schoolfriends who were now scattered around the globe. We had gone under the name of the Apostles in our teenage years, as there were twelve of us in all. However, there the similarity had ended, for instead of worshipping God we had all – convinced Fido-fanciers to a man since we were knee-high to a dachshund – sworn allegiance to the cult of the Dog.

In my present peripatetic state I was naturally deficient in the pooch department, but I was intrigued to see what developments my friends had made since we'd last been together. We had all kept vaguely in touch over the past thirty years and I was particularly interested to follow up the career of my friend Bryan. This was not only to inspect his current canine companion at first hand but also to see what conclusions he had reached on life, the universe and everything, after changing direction in his late thirties. After his mother's death he had given up a successful business career in the City and become a missionary priest and then, when his father passed away some five years ago, he had taken over the family's hereditary incumbency of the picturesque, rural parish of Nether Brookfield.

This, my instincts told me, had some particular and personal import for me as, having been intrigued by the offbeat theology of a relative of my ex-wife's, I had myself begun to wonder if there might not be something in this God business after all, Christian or otherwise. And then when my world fell apart with the destruction of my home and marriage, the details of which are too painful to relate, I became even more receptive to ideas of teleology and the possibility that there might be some kind of meaning to existence. Thus my travel plans began to take on the nature of a pilgrimage.

So when I had written off to Bryan and asked him if I could drop by sometime I was delighted when he had invited me over for Easter. Indeed, I had been looking forward to seeing him preach in the lovely old country church he'd described, and in my mind's eye could imagine the daffodils waving in the churchyard outside, the thatched cottages in the village and the wheat beginning to sprout in the wide, undulating fields that stretched off into the faraway distance where, he'd said, on a clear day you could just make out the spire of Salisbury Cathedral. It had seemed a picture of calm and tranquillity where all was right in the world, God was in his heaven, and Nature was never red in tooth or claw.

My first disappointment had been the delay which had kept me in London. I had phoned through my apologies to his housekeeper (Bryan was at church) and later booked into a dingy hotel in Earls Court where I had spent an uncomfortable night. I had then caught a train to Salisbury and eventually arrived, after waiting an age for a bus in the direction of Blandford Forum, at the vicarage sometime after two. My second disappointment had been the fact that instead of the joys of spring and the song of the lark I was met by pouring rain and floods, where the brook – after which the village is named – had burst its banks. But the final sadness as I walked past the high box-hedges and up the muddy pathway to the ancient, ivy-covered vicarage and rapped the cast-iron knocker was to be greeted not by the cheery Rev. B. Clowes but by a tearful housekeeper.

The news of Bryan's heart attack had been a great shock to everyone, and naturally my first instinct had been to find a hotel and leave the housekeeper and her pretty red-haired daughter to their grief. But then they'd insisted that I should stay as I had been his friend and he had no other relatives except his brother – whom she called 'Mr B.' to differentiate him from 'Rev. B.' – who was very ill but who would be coming over the next day to sign various papers.

Somehow I'd forgotten Bryan's twin brother Bernard. He hadn't been at school with us because he had always been very sick as a child and had been brought up, as a result, in the vicarage. Thus it didn't surprise me that he was still prone to bouts of illness. However, I was a little taken aback, but very flattered, when the housekeeper, whose name was Dorothy and who was, as I later discovered, the daughter of the village baker, asked me to try and sort out some of Bryan's papers. For her part, she couldn't face going into his study for the moment and anyway, she said, she was no 'scollard' and might throw away something important.

So here I now sat, leafing through the pile of papers on Bryan's desk. After putting various bank and credit-card statements and other business affairs into a pile on the floor, I started sifting through a pile of printed texts. From what I could make out, these seemed to be a set of publishers' proofs that Bryan had been correcting when he died. Indeed it may have been these that hastened his demise, as Dorothy told me that he had been working all evening on them to try and finish them for the publishers by Tuesday morning as he would be so tied up with church affairs over Easter.

From what I could gather he had got about halfway into the book, which was a translation into verse of the collected Latin enigmas of St Aldhelm, the seventh-century Bishop of Sherborne and Abbot of Malmesbury. I was very impressed as I had no idea that Bryan had become such a scholar. True, at school he had always been pretty good at maths – and hence his later success as a financial whizz-kid – but from what I recall his main leisure reading had been 'sword and sorcery' books, science fiction and fantasy curios such as *Lord of the Rings*. Latin and Greek had never come into it. He had certainly changed over the years.

As I continued to delve, I came across a handwritten note, hastily scribbled 'From B. to B.' and containing another riddle, which ran as follows:

> This thing all things devours:
> Birds, beasts, trees, flowers;
> Gnaws iron, bites steel;
> Grinds hard stones to meal;
> Slays king, ruins town,
> And beats high mountain down.

An inspired guess made me think that it must have been from Bernard to Bryan, as this would confirm Dorothy's own appellation of the two brothers. However, the answer to the enigma was lacking, as well as the source, so there was no way of telling whether it was ancient or modern. My first thought was 'water' but somehow it didn't seem to fit properly, and just as my mind wandered off into other possibilities – further distracting me from the important task in hand of sorting out Bryan's paperwork – there was a knock at the door and the housekeeper's daughter came in with a cup of tea.

'Mama says that dinner will be in about half an hour, sir,' she said as she held out the rattling cup with its saucer in her right hand and clutched an ancient Jack Russell under her left arm.

I thanked her and put the cup on the floor as there was no space on the table. When I then asked her what her name was she replied, 'Sophia'.

'That's a pretty name,' I said. 'Do you know what it means?'

'Yes, sir . . . um . . . it means "knowledge" in . . . um . . . Ancient Greek.' Then, struggling now with both hands to keep hold of the squirming dog, which seemed to have its two front legs in plaster, she continued: 'Um, yes, and Mr B. says – do keep still, Sissy – Mr B. says that he must become a philosopher because he says I am his favourite little girl in all the world and . . . and he loves me a lot and . . . um . . . because he would then be philo-Sophia which means "I love Sophia" or something, which is also Ancient Greek. But Mr B. is so unwell that I don't know and, anyway, and Mama says that now that I am eight I can have a guinea-pig which will be very nice because . . . um . . . my friend Jenny . . .'

She was interrupted by her mother calling from the stairs, and was turning to go when I asked what was wrong with the dog's legs.

'Oh, he got . . . um . . . caught up in something on the farm and the doctor's had to put them in splints and the Rev. B. made a wonderful thing which you must see and . . . um, Sissy's very happy until she's better, but you must come and see . . .'

Again the housekeeper called from the stairs, this time more insistently and saying to bring Sissy down this instant.

'But why's he called Sissy?' I asked. 'That's a girl's name, isn't it?'

'Oh yes . . . um . . . but he was originally called Tom because all the dogs have been called Tom but . . . um . . . once he broke his legs the Rev. B. said we should call him . . . um . . . Sisyphus and he explained why and how it was Greek too and um . . . that we could change his name back again later if we wanted to but not if we didn't want to and that it was like getting married and changing your name, and Sissy is easier to say and Tom doesn't seem to notice anyway and . . .'

At this point Dorothy's head appeared around the door and, with apologies for the interruptions, led the child away to leave me in peace.

Pleased to see that Bryan had indeed owned a dog in true schoolboy Apostle tradition, I picked up the cup of tea and leaned against the bookcase to drink it, fearful of spilling any on the papers on the desk.

Then, looking around the room in the fast fading light, I started piecing together aspects of Bryan's all-too-brief life. As I recalled, according to my theologically trained former in-law, whose topsy-turvy views on religion had set me off on this pilgrimage among my old chums in the first place, the psychologist William James (brother of the writer Henry) had said somewhere that a room tells you an awful lot about a person. And looking around Bryan's study, I could see things that not only revealed aspects of his own life but also of all the previous incumbents going back for generations.

For a start there was the majestic vicarage clock itself – that must have been over a hundred years old at the very least, and something told me that it hadn't been bought second-hand at a local antiques shop. The beautifully polished cabinet was made, I guessed, out of mahogany and walnut, and if you turned the little key and opened the door in the front you could see inside the two massive solid cylinders of cast iron which worked the mechanism. And in front of them swung, with a metronome-like movement, the giant, flat saucer of brass that was the pendulum. The face itself was a delight of scrolled, antique metalwork hands and polished wood and at the top was painted a pictur-esque, rural scene, not unlike the one from the study window, with a little village and a church clock and amazingly – though I had to pinch myself to believe it was true – the church clock was stopped at five to twelve! I looked again and there was, yes, also a tiny windmill on the hill, so it looked as though this must have been a special commission from some long-dead relative of the Clowes family. Or at least the painting evidently was. Which led me to wonder exactly how long the mechanism in the church tower had been broken . . .

As I mulled this over, my gaze took in the rest of the room by degrees and, turning on the light and pulling the curtains, I noticed that as well as books there were a large number of idols of varying kinds – no doubt trophies brought back from far and wide after missionary expeditions by members of successive generations of this family, including Bryan. Here were a Mexican corn god, a miniature totem pole, a wooden Ganesh elephant from India, a green Maori tiki and, filled with pot-pourri, a large seated Buddha, among many others. I also spotted a long piece of wood leaning against the grandfather clock. When I picked it up, it made a strange rushing sound. Having seen one in a shop in London I recognized this as a South American 'rain-stick', though what its purpose was, beyond aural delight, I had no idea. Replacing it carefully, my eye then caught sight of a framed colour photograph, taken when Bryan's parents were still alive, and featuring both sons. It also showed a Jack Russell puppy which was probably Sissy in his youth, when he had still been known as Tom and had the use of both front limbs.

Looking from one twin to the other it was almost impossible to tell them apart, such was the extraordinary similarity of the two faces, and indeed if this had been a monochrome picture I would have been hard put to identify Bryan. But as it was colour it was easy because Bryan, of course, had red hair like his mother and at the time of the picture was wearing ordinary, though extremely well-cut, man-about-town business clothes, whereas his brother was in clerical garb. I'd had no idea that his brother had also taken holy orders but it would have been natural enough in such a family. No doubt all would be revealed on Sunday when I met Bernard.

The bizarre thing, of course, was that Bryan should ever have turned out so very different from the rest of them. When they had visited the school, his parents had always seemed very reserved and quiet people and no doubt Bernard, though I had never met him, was much the same. But my recollection of Bryan, even at school – let alone in the tales I have since heard of his flamboyant lifestyle from other members of our group – was that until he saw the light he was a real tearaway. He had earned pots of money in the City in the early 80s and was by all accounts living the life of Reilly – flash sports cars, sex, drink, drugs, and rock and roll. And then came, for whatever reason, this sudden change. I thus felt doubly sorry that he had died before I had met up with him again and perhaps learnt what had brought this on. Indeed, we might have had a lot in common . . .

But it was all too late now. I put my cup down beside the Buddha and looked through the notes again. As I was tidying away the riddle proofs I remarked inwardly on how similar Bernard's handwriting in his letter, 'From B. to B.' was to Bryan's but then thought nothing more of it. After all, my own brother's script is much the same as mine; there's always a natural family resemblance among siblings. And of course in their case they were twins, so it was hardly surprising.

However, what I hadn't expected to find – but which I suppose I had always rather hoped would be somewhere tucked away in some secret corner – was a large hardcover book, about as thick as my thumb. I opened the cover and found myself reading a private journal. There was nothing on the first page to indicate that it was by him, but I recognized the flourishes and the idiosyncratic cursive script from the letters we had exchanged in the past few weeks: it was Bryan's private memoir of the years since his father's death.

I'd only had a chance to flip through a few pages before the gong sounded for dinner, so I closed up the book – using the riddle letter to mark my place – and went downstairs.

I had intended returning to the study that evening, but a combination of fatigue and Dorothy's good red wine thwarted my plans. I was also interested in hearing more about Bryan's final days from the person who'd seen him last. Out of a rather old-fashioned deference, the housekeeper wouldn't join me to eat at the same table, but as she brought in each course I was able to have brief conversations with her and piece together recent events.

Thus it appeared that Bryan had been very troubled in the last few weeks before his death and the thing that had borne in on his mind the most had been the fact that he would have to move out of the vicarage. With ever-dwindling congregations and cuts in church administration costs it appeared that he had been asked to cover services at some other parishes in the neighbourhood as well as his own – he would in effect have to become a sort of time-share priest. Of itself, of course, this was not an insurmountable problem and it would not have necessitated his having to move. But it had been pointed out to him that there would obviously be considerable advantages to be had if he were more centrally based among his new parishes. And in addition, though his family had owned the vicarage building outright for generations, the upkeep and expenses of it had always been borne by the Church. And now that the place was really beginning to show its age, these maintenance costs were starting to become quite significant. The employment of a full-time, live-in house-keeper and her daughter had also been seen as an unnecessary drain on the Church's meagre resources by the powers-that-be.

As a result, Bryan had been contemplating selling up the family home and moving to a small cottage a few miles away. But, as I could imagine, he'd been in an agony of indecison. Added to which, it appeared that his brother's illness was now terminal and he was dying of the cancer which had taken away his mother. This in itself would have been bad enough but, being a twin, he found himself suffering almost as much pain as Mr B. himself. All this Dorothy related between the soup, meat and dessert courses with such a sad and caring look that I felt quite touched by her loyalty.

The Rev. B.'s body, it appeared, had been removed to the undertakers, and as there were no independent witnesses to the death, an autopsy would be made in the next few days. However, there was little doubt that a heart attack or stroke would be revealed to have been the cause of death, brought on most probably by overwork and stress induced by severe anxiety over the future of the vicarage.

Another commendable concern of my old schoolfriend was for the welfare of Dorothy and her dear little daughter, the house-keeper went on. Pouring me a glass of port as I stretched out in front of the open fire in the drawing-room after dinner, she made light of her situation, saying that the Rev. B. needn't have worried himself on their account and that she could always go back to work in her father's bakery if need be. But privately I made a mental note to have a word with Bernard in this regard when he came tomorrow to sort out Bryan's business affairs, assuming that he was well enough himself to be able to put a word in with the solicitors.

The wind outside began to pick up at about 10.30 p.m. and when Dorothy poked her head around the door to show me to my room half an hour later I could hear the vicarage clock upstairs striking the hour in ominous tones. The wooden steps creaked as we ascended to the spare room and I experienced a kind of shudder as we passed the open door to Bryan's bedroom, which was curious in the circumstances as he had died in the study. Perhaps another relative had passed away there in previous times, I thought, and mentioned this to Dorothy.

'Oh yes, sir,' she replied. 'The Rev. B.'s grandfather died peacefully in his bed in that room but we've got no ghosts here, if that's what you mean. None that I've heard of, at least.'

This last comment, meant no doubt to be reassuring, had rather the opposite effect on me. As we entered the guest room, which faced Bryan's bedroom a few feet further down the corridor, my sense of unease increased. It was a pleasant enough room, decorated with some Hogarth prints and with a floral wallpaper of some kind, but unfortunately the door would not lock as it was so old and gnarled that it hung at an angle on its hinges. As a result, my view from the single bed against one wall was of the open door to Bryan's bedroom.

I wished Dorothy goodnight and waited until I could hear her settled in her room at the other end of the corridor. Then, for my own peace of mind, I placed the bedside lamp on the floor and put the small table it had been on against the door to close it, though the wind, now blowing up a storm and hurling rain against the window-panes, produced an icy draught which constantly threatened to push the lightweight table away across the ancient floorboards.

Somehow, though – despite the howling gale outside and my strange sense of insecurity – I got to sleep and dreamed of myself in the role of the biblical Joseph in Egypt – very appropriate, I thought later, for someone spending the night in a vicarage. However, in my version of the story, I was not solving Pharaoh's vision of the seven thin and seven fat cattle but rather the anonymous riddle that I had seen on Bryan's desk:

This thing all things devours:
Birds, beasts, trees, flowers;
Gnaws iron, bites steel . . .

In my dream I was just about to whisper in Pharaoh Bryan's ear the solution to the riddle, which would also, I felt, somehow release me from all my own troubles and have something to do with the meaning of life, when I was awoken by a sound in the room. Rolling over – I had been facing the wall – I suddenly noticed to my horror that the little table was being slowly pushed open by the door and watched, rigid with fear, as its legs scraped along the floor. Terrified at first, I then progressively relaxed as I listened to the wind outside and noticed how its gusts coincided with the erratic movements of the door and the table.

Somewhat comforted by this realization, I was just about to get out of bed to close the door again when I froze. Something was not right. There was now another noise – this time coming from the opposite direction to the stairs up which I had ascended. A steady clomping sound. Thump, thump, thump the noise went, at least twenty times. Nervously, I tried to convince myself that it was again just the wind. Who was I kidding? I looked at my watch. It was three in the morning on Easter Sunday. Perhaps Bryan had been resurrected from the dead, I thought frivolously. He had, after all, like Jesus, died on Good Friday and this was the third day. But then I thought again. Don't be ridiculous, it's just an old house, you're tired, it's been a stressful day . . . My thoughts stopped dead in their tracks as, gazing through the door on to the corridor I saw a small, dark shape glide rapidly and silently along the carpet and into Bryan's room!

I am sure the hair stood to attention on my head and time certainly seemed to stand still as I tried to evaluate what I had just seen. Then a few moments later, and with equal rapidity, the shape re-emerged, slid past my door again, and disappeared down the corridor followed by another twenty or so bumping sounds. Now wide awake, I turned on the bedside light, jammed the door shut with one of my shoes and took the other back to bed with me as a defensive weapon in case whatever I had seen decided to come a-visiting.

I was awoken in the grey drizzle of Sunday morning by a loud banging and instantly grabbed for my shoe before realizing that it was only Dorothy waking me for breakfast. Half an hour later, and extremely weary from a sleepless night, I descended the staircase to the dining-room and, over coffee and scrambled eggs on toast, quizzed Dorothy about the incident I had witnessed in the early hours of the morning.

She laughed when she heard my description of the bumping sounds and the shape that had slid so eerily into Bryan's room.

'Oh, I'm sorry, sir, I should have mentioned about little Sissy. You see, he always used to sleep in the Rev. B.'s bedroom and he must have come in, found him not there and gone out again.'

'But surely that was no dog I saw, not moving the way it did,' I replied, only partially comforted by this explanation. 'And what about the strange bumping sounds?'

At this point Sophia came in, together with the ancient little Jack Russell terrier himself. But this time, instead of being carried with difficulty by the little girl, he motored in under his own steam. And motoring is a pretty accurate description of his movements as, to my amazement, he propelled himself along on wheels! Now I understood why Bryan had called him Sisyphus, after the character in Greek myth who was condemned to push a huge rock up a mountain for eternity. Bryan, ever ingenious, had fashioned a sort of wheelchair apparatus for the poor disabled creature. A leather harness went over the dog's shoulders and around his back, thereby protecting his outstretched stiff plaster forelegs and giving him mobility – like pushing a pram.

The bumping sound was explained shortly afterwards when Dorothy showed me another staircase which led from the kitchen up to the corridor off which I had been sleeping. Here, up against the right-hand banister, could be seen a long plank which was crossed at intervals of roughly six inches or so by thin wooden struts. To demonstrate how Bryan had helped the poor dog to get up the stairs on his own, Sophia placed him at the bottom and we watched as he positioned the wheels of the contraption on the plank. He then raced up the incline, bumping over each strut as he did so, these in turn helping to give him a footing like the rungs on a ladder. Much relieved, I laughed with the rest of them as Sissy barked and wagged his tail at the top, and then I returned to finish my coffee.

As it was Easter Sunday, and in deference to Bryan's memory, I suggested to Dorothy that perhaps we ought to go over to the church, but I soon realized my mistake. Though Bryan would naturally have preached in his own church rather than the neighbouring parishes under his aegis on Easter Sunday, his death had obviously prevented that and there wasn't any ecclesiastical locum available. As a result, any of the congregation who wished to had been advised to travel the five miles or so to Salisbury Cathedral and worship there. However, as buses were a rarity in these parts at the best of times – and trains non-existent – those who had cars had been asked to give lifts to friends and neighbours. The problem was that there were very few in the village who drove and spaces were at a premium. In consequence, I opted to stay behind with the dog while Dorothy and Sophia went in the family bread van, promising to prepare a late lunch on their return for myself and Mr B., when he arrived.

Back up in Bryan's study after the van had pulled off down the main road out of the village, I could hear the rain beginning to patter down again and, looking out of the window at the bridleway on the far side of the church, felt sorry for the lone horseman splashing along in the shower in the direction of Salisbury, followed by two children on bicycles.

The vicarage clock struck eleven, swiftly followed by the chimes from the church tower opposite. By the time I had cleared away some more letters, estate agents' brochures and old parish magazines from the desk, the windmill on the hill was barely visible through the drizzle. Sissy came bonking up his stair-ladder again and stretched out under the chaise-longue as I then settled down to read Bryan's journal.

I don't know what I had expected, really. I hadn't seen my friend for the best part of twenty years. Though he had been a live-wire at school and, as I recalled, wrote with great imagination and panache – we'd called him Algy, after Algernon Swinburne, as he'd been very flamboyant and had similar long flowing auburn hair – he had obviously changed with the passage of time. Not only had I been surprised by his facility with classical languages, but I was now also confronted by the writings of a deeply introspective character. And of course his sudden and dramatic change of career from womanizing, hard-drinking, City playboy to a quiet, country parson was a complete *volte-face*. I looked forward to learning more about what had happened to him. Perhaps, I hoped, the answer would be revealed to me in these pages. I read on.

The reason for his beginning his journal, it transpired, was to try and come to grips with the fact of his father's death. Apparently it had been neither noble nor, like his grandfather's, peaceful, but the result of an unhappy accident. One February the inhabitants of Nether Brookfield had decided to hold a fancy-dress carnival, culminating in a dance at the village hall. Bryan's father, for some bizarre reason, had opted to go disguised as the devil and had cycled over to join in the fun. Unfortunately, once inside the hall the heavens had opened and the brook, already full to overflowing by earlier downpours, had burst its banks – as it is so often wont to do – and flooded the surrounding fields. As a result, when the vicar eventually left the village, somewhat the worse for drink, he found the bridge inaccessible and thus tried to find an alternative route over one of the narrower but deeper parts of the river.

Leaving his bicycle on one bank he then must have tried to leap the gap, slipped in the mud and plunged into the foaming brook and quickly drowned. Unfortunately, such was the power of the flood that his body was washed downstream and he wasn't found for some days. Identification of his body was also difficult as, not only was he not wearing his clerical garb but his features had also been disfigured by the action of the stones in the river and the appetite of flocks of crows. 'God's creatures obviously hadn't heard that "carnival" comes for the Latin for "meat farewell" ', as Bryan's phrase in the journal put it.

This experience had obviously had a considerable effect on Bryan, who had not only to identify the body – a grisly enough task in any death but worse so in this case – but also to officiate during the burial as no one else was available. Added to which, it was at much the same time that news had reached him of his brother's terminal cancer. As a result, it seems that it was at this point, at least according to the testimony of his journal, that his faith seriously began to waiver. Indeed, not only did he feel that Christianity had somehow let him down but that also the whole contemporary practice of the religion was bogus. An entry for the day he died gives the general flavour of his argument:

16 April, Good Friday

Merciful Father, I've got to go into St Luke's now and preach the wonder of Christ's word, preach that this was the Son of God who died for us sinners that we might enjoy eternal life. It's the oldest of the Christian festivals and the most important in the Christian year yet its very name is pagan – from Eostre, the goddess of the dawn – and more people are interested in chocolate eggs and bunny-rabbits – ancient fertility symbols one and all – than a man's sacrifice.

And what about the images themselves? Look at this study in which I sit writing this journal – filled with totems and idols from religions despised by Christians – 'Thou shalt not make any graven image of the Lord thy God'. We, my relatives and I for generations, and many like us, have travelled the world trying to show poor benighted souls the error of their ways. And yet what do we do? Paint pictures of God, Jesus, the Virgin Mary and the saints – all curiously golden-haired and white-skinned when in reality they would have been dark-haired, swarthy Mediterranean Semitic types – and make statues and stained-glass replicas of them. What's the difference between a silver crucifix and a golden calf? Why is the Christian fish symbol and a string of rosary beads different from a drawing of the river-gods or a load of magic seashells? Jesus wasn't even born at Christmas, for goodness' sake. The church establishment just annexed the Roman sun-festival and the Nordic Yule. And even the Christian festival wasn't recognized as such until the fourth century, and then only in Rome . . .

The soul-searching continued in similar vein for some ten pages or so, interspersed with much agonizing about his twin brother's illness and the potential sale of the vicarage.

I warrant that none of this material, of course, would have been seen as in any way problematic or difficult to counter by a priest who was strong in his faith. After all, that is presumably what faith is all about. But to find this kind of doubt in a practising servant of God was, to say the least, a little unnerving. And I for one was somewhat thrown by the apparent contradictions of history and religion that were raised, here and elsewhere in the journal. Indeed, these were some of the very areas of conflict that I had aired with my ex-wife's relative before I set out on this pilgrimage and I was beginning to wonder where it would end in my own mind. I was also beginning to realize that, with this kind of torture going through his mind on a daily basis – not to mention the additional worries about having to leave the ancestral home and so forth – perhaps, in a sense, Bryan's heart attack may have been a blessing in disguise.

My inclination was to skip on as fast as possible to the end of the book to see whether he had come to terms with all this before he died and thus, perhaps rather selfishly, to see what I could learn from his experience for my own edification. However, just as I'd reached a point where he'd seemed to be agreeing with an excommunicated heretic called Spinoza that God and Nature were one, I heard the door-knocker bang and, preceded by a yapping Sissy, went down to investigate.

Before I could reach the bottom of the stairs, the door was pushed open from outside by a rotund, ruddy-faced woman carrying a tray of hot cross-buns – I'd forgotten that some country people still don't lock their houses. She was greeted with much barking and tail-wagging from Sissy.

'Oh, excuse me, sir,' the woman said as she deposited the tray on a table in the hallway next to the hatstand and beneath an old wall-mounted barometer. 'I thought I'd take the opportunity of nipping across between the showers to let you have these for your afternoon tea. I'm Dorothy's mother, from the bakery . . .'

I thanked her for her gift and invited her to stay a while as the others were due back soon, but she insisted on going, tapping the barometer as she looked out the open door at the brief patch of blue sky that had appeared above.

'No, thank you all the same, sir, but I'd best be on my way in case it comes down again. Terrible news about the reverend, of course, but he'll be with the Lord now, I'm sure. A good man he was, unlike some I could mention . . .'

I didn't quite get the drift of this general indictment of humanity but made the appropriate noises as she continued. 'Dorothy tells me that you knew the boys at school. I expect a lot has changed since then, mind you. I gather young Mr B. is turning up this afternoon from Salisbury, poor soul. Do give him my best regards and tell him we're all looking forward to seeing him at the wedding, God willing . . .'

'Oh, OK, I'll pass on the message,' I replied, not entirely sure what to make of it and unable to detain her any longer as she splashed out towards the village.

With the sudden change in the weather, it quickly became very stuffy indoors – the central heating had been turned on full most of the morning – and as I re-entered Bryan's study I was tempted to open a window. However, as soon as I did so a breeze blew all the riddle proofs on to the floor. So I gave up the attempt and, still drowsy from lack of sleep the previous night, picked the sheets up again and walked over to the desk.

As the bright sunlight now illuminated the study quite well I decided to take the journal over to the chaise-longue in front of the grandfather clock and continue my reading there. As it happened, the wind had also blown over a few pages in the book and I found myself reading some more outpourings from Bryan's anguished pen, this time – by coincidence – about the clock itself.

It turned out that it had in fact been originally purchased in Salisbury by Bryan's great-grandfather when he had first taken over the living. However, as transport had been thin on the ground in those days, he had been unable to find a way of bringing it home. Not put out, and being a strongly built man, he then – so family tradition had it – strapped it to his back and, trusting to God, carried it the full five miles back from the city on foot.

One of the reasons for buying the clock, Bryan's narrative revealed, had nothing to do with its quality – though it was manifestly a fine piece of craftmanship. Rather it was the fact that his great-grandfather, never well paid as a priest, had despaired of ever being able to afford to get the church clock opposite mended and he had no other means of telling the time. This fact thus proved that the hands had indeed been stuck at five to twelve for at least a hundred years. Bryan also mentioned that it had been his ancient relative who had commissioned the landscape view of the church and village which had been painted on the top of the vicarage clock to commemorate this.

But what followed in the journal was interesting:

> . . . and now I am having to move out of the vicarage and family tradition will be broken. Indeed it is far more than that, as a whole sequence of inheritance will change. Not only has the vicarage itself been handed down from father to son as ministers of God's Holy Church but also this beautiful clock, which my great-grandfather carried home on his back, has always stood here and whoever has lived in this house has always been born under its watchful gaze. And I have to face up to the fact that it is, sadly, unlikely now that I will marry and have children. I have never been confident of my own health and, indeed, with my brother's illness now coming to a head I have an awful feeling of foreboding about my own mortality. The doctors say he is unlikely to last out the year and if I have to move, even if I do survive, the vicarage will be gone from the family's hands for ever. And so will the tradition of handing down the vicarage clock to someone born in the house where it stood . . .

There then followed seemingly endless pages of self-mortification about his imagined inadequacies as a priest, and I must confess that after a while the tone of it began to pall – guilty though this made me feel – especially as I soon became aware that all I really wanted to read were more of his views of Spinoza. Added to which, the stuffiness of the room and the comforting curves of the chaise-longue were beginning to start a chain-reaction in my sleep-deprived and rather weary body.

In short, I must have dozed off, because the next thing I became aware of was the vicarage clock beside my head striking one. I lazily blinked my eyes open and, looking towards the window opposite, could see nothing but a giant cross. Thinking that I was just seeing the shadow of the windmill from the hill again, I at first thought nothing of it but then, by degrees, my befuddled thoughts came into order as I realized that I was facing the wrong way for this to be possible, and blinked again.

It was then that the ghastly truth of the manifestation became clear. Standing opposite me with his arms outstretched was the gruesome reincarnation of my friend Bryan!

'Toby,' he cried, slowly and with a croaking voice as he moved towards my reclining figure on the chaise-longue, arms still akimbo. And as he did so I could see that his eyes were yellow, his face like dry paper and covered in a thin red stubble the colour of his long, tangled hair, while on his wrists were the marks of the stigmata, bloody evidence of the nails that had pinned Jesus to the cross two thousand years ago.

I cringed back into the chair, my eyes wide with fright, and tried to put out my hands to hold the hideous thing off . . .

I must have blacked out because the next thing I knew was that I was lying on the floor with Dorothy's worried face bending over me and Sissy alternately barking and licking my right cheek.

Groggy at first but gaining strength all the time as the breeze from the now open window brought me round and, aided by some brandy that Dorothy was making me sip, I asked what had happened.

'It seems that you must have fainted when Mr B. came up to see you, sir. As he's not at all well I suggested that he should go down to the drawing-room and wait for you there. If you're feeling better now perhaps you could join him while I get on with lunch? But only if you feel well enough yourself, of course.'

I started to stand up. 'You sure you're all right now, sir?' I nodded my thanks. 'Well, that's all right then. But mind how you go. Oh and thank you for taking in the hot cross-buns from my mother.'

Now that I was on my feet again I began to recover quite quickly and soon found I was able to get down the stairs.

I steeled myself as I walked into the drawing-room. The sight of the spectral figure of my old schoolfriend slumped in an armchair facing the window appalled and confused me in equal measure. I was at a complete loss for words.

As I entered, he turned round slowly from his chair and looked at me with those horrible, glazed yellow eyes.

'Bryan, Bryan, but how can you be alive still? . . .' I eventually managed to stammer out, half in fear and half in reproach.

'Dear Toby, how nice to see you again after all these years,' the dry voice whispered, obviously labouring under great pain. 'I'm sorry about my appearance – it's the cancer, you see – got to the liver . . . jaundice . . . and they've doped me up to the eyeballs to kill the pain. Not much fun.'

He grinned that quick grin he used to have as a teenager.

'Truth is, it's not me that's dead – not yet at least – but Bernard. You remember? My twin brother. A little deception I fear, from a loving sibling. It was he who had written to you, trying to cover up for me. I'm sure if you had read further on in his journal you would have discovered the truth. You see, I never did change, always been a bit of a rat. But then I also got rather ill, in more ways than one. Three to be precise . . .'

I sat down slowly to try and take all this in, at the same time realizing that every breath he took was made with great difficulty and whatever drugs he was on to mask the pain were slowing down his speech to a slur.

'. . . Not physically so at first, though this, Illness No. 3' – he pointed at his face and wasted body – 'came later.'

'No,' he said, resting the journal on his knees, 'my main

trouble, Illness No. 1 – totally self-inflicted – was all in my head. Life was going too well for me and something went terribly wrong. I'm sure Bernard with the fine classical education he received at home would have called it *hubris*, the pride that comes before a fall.'

He grinned again.

'As you know, I was doing rather well in the City – loads of money, fast cars, beautiful women – in fact everything I ever wanted. Trouble is, as I learnt to my cost, money does tend to make you think that you are invincible, perhaps even god-like. I went too far, they tell me, too far . . .'

He paused for a moment as Dorothy briefly popped her head round the doorway to check that we were still OK.

'I went mad, Toby, crazy. I bullied people, smashed things up. I had so much money it wasn't a problem – buy another one, buy a hundred. I was a law unto myself. I could do anything, anything. Money is power, and I was drunk with it.

'One day, out of my head on something – alcohol, drugs, I forget which – a terrible temptation overtook me. I came round here to see Dad – he was still alive then, of course – and sound off about something that was bothering me about religion, I forget what. God and Mammon I expect, or the camel and the eye of a needle, whatever. I was always banging on about something and when you're brought up with religion it affects you one way or the other. I thought I knew it all.'

He paused again and looked at me with those yellow eyes.

'Anyway, he and my saintly twin brother were both out, probably at church – Bernard was just about to go off on his first mission then. And the door being open, as it always is, I started to wander about the house.

'Hearing a noise from the kitchen I then spotted the pretty, young girl you now know as Dorothy. This was about ten years ago and she hadn't met me then – why should she have? I was rarely in this part of the country – usually too busy having a good time in the Bahamas, the French Riviera or some other playboy resort. And, of course, she wasn't his housekeeper then but was just around running errands for her dad's bakery, probably dropping something off. Anyway, seeing me come in she assumed I was Bernard, as so many people have naturally done in bygone years. A wicked idea then entered my crazed brain. I played on our similarity – it was a game Bernard and I had often played in our childhood with him as the urbane Dr Jekyll and me as the awful Mr Hyde – and pretended that I'd just dyed my hair for a laugh and what did she think?'

His breathing was getting heavy now, but he managed to continue.

'In short, Toby, she somehow allowed herself to trust me more than she should have in the circumstances. OK – I seduced her. There, it's out. I seduced Dorothy under my own father's roof and did so with her believing I was my brother, a missionary priest. It was so easy, saying that I would be a long time away without seeing a white woman and all that nonsense and that if there was a baby then we would be married when I came back and not to mention anything to a soul . . . and . . . it worked. I put a bun in the oven of the baker's daughter.'

He laughed a brief cold laugh.

'And then, of course, Bernard did go off overseas, in reality, within a few days. And Dorothy did become pregnant. Like a good girl, she never told Dad and if the news got out in the village then it was all hushed up. When Dad took her on as his live-in housekeeper he knew she was pregnant, of course, but not by whom, and he did what he did out of Christian charity. He hadn't expected her to give birth under his own roof, but that couldn't be helped – the baby came on suddenly in the middle of the night and there was no time to get her over to Salisbury Hospital. And if my ears don't deceive me, the living proof is right outside this window.'

He pointed across at the front of the house and there, through the glass, I could see Sophia playing with Sissy outside in the sunshine.

'She doesn't understand yet, of course. She's too young. But she will do soon. You noticed the hair, I expect . . .'

Suddenly the scales fell from my eyes and I began to understand.

'But what about Dorothy, when did she find out about you . . . ?' I began, but Bryan interrupted.

'Yes, Dorothy found out about me at Dad's funeral. It only took one look at the pair of us together for the game to be up. But even then she never said anything, she was so confused. Bernard kept her on as his own housekeeper and he never knew till his dying day that Sophia was my child.'

'But that means . . .' I began.

'No, please, old friend, please let me finish. I've not got much more to say. Anyway, once my crazy power illness wore off and I realized what I had done, things started going even more wrong in my head. I started smashing things up for no reason at all. Not to show how much power I had but just because they were there. And this was Illness No. 2. I was institution-alized. Had delusions – all kinds of mixed-up things about religion and that, I banged holes in my hands with nails to make stigmata. Thought I was Jesus, Ezekiel and Moses all rolled into one – you name it, I was Mr Holiness himself, a crazy fallen angel. They put me in a strait-jacket and all I could talk about was "Strait is the gate . . ." It was bad, very bad. This is what Bernard tried to protect you from. Sure, I'd got religion again after Dad's death – just like he said – but it was a nightmare attack and it didn't go away. Not, that is, until I got my final illness, the one that's killing me now, and that . . .' he gasped for breath, 'is about me done, in more ways than one.'

I got a lift back to Salisbury Station in the baker's van fairly soon after lunch. It had been a difficult meal, not only because there had been so much for me to digest mentally but also because Bryan's confession had taken an awful lot out of him physically. In addition he had insisted on Dorothy joining us at the table, as an equal, which she had felt very awkward about at first, though Sophia enjoyed it immensely.

The wedding, which in my mistaken belief about the true identity of my friend I had assumed that Bryan/Bernard would be conducting in some ecclesiastical capacity, was actually to be, of course, his own to Dorothy, as I discovered from our conversation at lunch. It would take place the day after Bernard's funeral, assuming that Bryan was well enough.

Our farewells had been difficult, too. I had come to this beautiful part of rural Wiltshire expecting to meet an old school chum who might help me find some direction in my life. Instead, I had found something quite unexpected, quite different. Indeed, my old friend Bryan, whom it transpired was never the man I thought he was, was now, confusingly, a changed man. And as I made my departure he promised to use his still prodigious wealth to repair, at last, the church clock and to live with Dorothy and Sophia in the vicarage once he and Dorothy were married.

As I stood at the door, it began to rain again and I came back inside the porch. Then something that had been nagging at my mind suddenly occurred to me and I strode back into the house to retrieve the journal from the drawing-room where Bryan had left it. The place in the narrative concerning the vicarage clock was still marked by the letter containing the riddle, 'From B. to B.' and, handing it to Bryan, I suggested he might read that passage with particular interest. I also mentioned that I would be keen to learn the solution to the enigma in the letter sometime, if he happened to know it.

We had waved goodbye and as the van drove off I looked back at the family standing in the porch. The shower quickly passed and as we drew away from the house I could just make out the old windmill on the hill, still silhouetted like a crucifix but now, as the sun broke through the clouds, crowned with the glittering bars of not one but two rainbows, almost like a halo.

More business in London kept me from both Bernard's funeral and Bryan and Dorothy's wedding, but I got a postcard from Sophia in the Bahamas saying what a wonderful time they were all having on honeymoon together. Dorothy's Christmas card was less happy – Bryan had finally succumbed to the cancer that had held him in its grip for so many long and painful years. He had borne it bravely in the end and had, I'd thought, finally made his peace with his maker, who- or whatever that might be.

The final communication I had with his family before I disappeared on my travels again was a photograph of Dorothy (holding Bernard's now-published copy of St Aldhelm), Sophia and Sissy – with his legs fully mended – standing in front of the vicarage clock, the cruciform shadow of the windmill falling over the entire group. And in a little mirror behind I could make out the reflection of the church tower. Despite the reversal of the image it could clearly be seen that the church clock now told the same time as the one in the vicarage study: half-past three. Pinned to the back of the photograph was a note in Dorothy's hand and a crumpled sheet of paper:

I know Bryan would have wanted you to have a copy of this. In his will he left the house and everything in it to me with one exception: the vicarage clock. This, as you helped us realize, was very important to his brother and the family. And as Sophia was born in this house it is she who will inherit the clock, and when I die, the vicarage as well. Future generations, I hope, will thank you for this gift of knowledge, as we do.

Much love, Dorothy Clowes

P.S. Bryan also asked me to enclose this riddle which he told me you'd been interested in.

I folded back the letter and looked at the page with the handwritten riddle attached. It was the same letter 'From B. to B.' that I had used as a bookmark in Bernard's journal. However, Bryan had made a few additions to the original in the shaky handwriting that had marked his final days:

Dear Toby,
You wanted to know about the riddle which I sent to Bernard:

> This thing all things devours:
> Birds, beasts, trees, flowers;
> Gnaws iron, bites steel;
> Grinds hard stones to meal;
> Slays king, ruins town,
> And beats high mountain down.

Well, he never did get the chance to try and crack it. Did you? It comes from J.R.R. Tolkien's *The Hobbit*. The solution? 'Time.'

The Enemies

Dylan Thomas

It was morning in the green acres of the Jarvis valley, and Mr Owen was picking the weeds from the edges of his garden path. A great wind pulled at his beard, the vegetable world roared under his feet. A rook had lost itself in the sky, and was making a noise to its mate; but the mate never came, and the rook flew into the west with a woe in its beak. Mr Owen, who had stood up to ease his shoulders and look at the sky, observed how dark the wings beat against the red sun. In her draughty kitchen Mrs Owen grieved over the soup. Once, in past days, the valley had housed the cattle alone; the farm-boys came down from the hills to holla at the cattle and to drive them to be milked; but no stranger set foot in the valley. Mr Owen, walking lonely through the country, had come upon it at the end of a late summer evening when the cattle were lying down still, and the stream that divided it was speaking over the pebbles. Here, thought Mr Owen, I will build a small house with one storey, in the middle of the valley, set around by a garden. And, remembering clearly the way he had come along the winding hills, he returned to his village and the questions of Mrs Owen. So it came about that a house with one storey was built in the green fields; a garden was dug and planted, and a low fence put up around the garden to keep the cows from the vegetables.

That was early in the year. Now summer and autumn had gone over; the garden had blossomed and died; there was frost at the weeds. Mr Owen bent down again, tidying the path, while the wind blew back the heads of the nearby grasses and made an oracle of each green mouth. Patiently he strangled the weeds; up came the roots, making war in the soil around them; insects were busy in the holes where the weeds had sprouted, but, dying between his fingers, they left no stain. He grew tired of their death, and tireder of the fall of the weeds. Up came the roots, down went the cheap, green heads.

Mrs Owen, peering into the depths of her crystal, had left the soup to bubble on unaided. The ball grew dark, then lightened as a rainbow moved within it. Growing hot like a sun, and cooling again like an arctic star, it shone in the folds of her dress where she held it lovingly. The tea-leaves in her cup at breakfast had told of a dark stranger. What would the crystal tell her? Mrs Owen wondered.

Up came the roots, and a crooked worm, disturbed by the probing of the fingers, wriggled blind in the sun. Of a sudden the valley filled all its hollows with the wind, with the voice of the roots, with the breathing of the nether sky. Not only a mandrake screams; torn roots have their cries; each weed Mr Owen pulled out of the ground screamed like a baby. In the village behind the hill the wind would be raging, the clothes on the garden lines would be set to strange dances. And women with shapes in their wombs would feel a new knocking as they bent over the steamy tubs. Life would go on in the veins, in the bones, the binding flesh, that had their seasons and their weathers even as the valley binding the house about with the flesh of the green grass.

The ball, like an open grave, gave up its dead to Mrs Owen. She stared on the lips of women and the hairs of men that wound into a pattern on the face of the crystal world. But suddenly the patterns were swept away, and she could see nothing but the shapes of the Jarvis hills. A man with a black hat was walking down the paths into the invisible valley beneath. If he walked any nearer he would fall into her lap. 'There's a man with a black hat walking on the hills,' she called through the window. Mr Owen smiled and went on weeding.

It was at this time that the Reverend Mr Davies lost his way; he had been losing it most of the morning, but now he had lost it altogether, and stood perturbed under a tree on the rim of the Jarvis hills. A great wind blew through the branches, and a great grey-green earth moved unsteadily beneath him. Wherever he looked the hills stormed up to the sky, and wherever he sought to hide from the wind he was frightened by the darkness. The farther he walked, the stranger was the scenery around him; it rose to undreamed-of heights, and then fell down again into a valley no bigger than the palm of his hand. And the trees walked like men. By a divine coincidence he reached the rim of the hills just as the sun reached the centre of the sky. With the wide world rocking from horizon to horizon, he stood under a tree and looked down into the valley. In the fields was a little house with a garden. The valley roared around it, the wind leapt at it like a boxer, but the house stood still. To Mr Davies it seemed as though the house had been carried out of a village by a large bird and placed in the very middle of the tumultuous universe.

But as he climbed over the craggy edges and down the side of the hill, he lost his place in Mrs Owen's crystal. A cloud displaced his black hat, and under the cloud walked a very old phantom, a shape of air with stars all frozen in its beard, and a half-moon for a smile. Mr Davies knew nothing of this as the stones scratched his hands. He was old, he was drunk with the wine of the morning, but the stuff that came out of his cuts was a human blood.

Nor did Mr Owen, with his face near the soil and his hands on the necks of the screaming weeds, know of the transformation in the crystal. He had heard Mrs Owen prophesy the coming of the black hat, and had smiled as he always smiled at her faith in the powers of darkness. He had looked up when she called, and, smiling, had returned to the clearer call of the ground. 'Multiply, multiply,' he had said to the worms disturbed in their channelling, and had cut the brown worms in half so that the halves might breed and spread their life over the garden and go out, contaminating, into the fields and the bellies of the cattle.

Of this Mr Davies knew nothing. He saw a young man with a beard bent industriously over the garden soil; he saw that the house was a pretty picture, with the face of a pale young woman pressed up against the window. And, removing his black hat, he introduced himself as the rector of a village some ten miles away.

'You are bleeding,' said Mr Owen.

Mr Davies's hands, indeed, were covered in blood.

When Mrs Owen had seen to the rector's cuts, she sat him down in the armchair near the window, and made him a strong cup of tea.

'I saw you on the hill,' she said, and he asked her how she had seen him, for the hills are high and a long way off.

'I have good eyes,' she answered.

He did not doubt her. Her eyes were the strangest he had seen.

'It is quiet here,' said Mr Davies.

'We have no clock,' she said, and laid the table for three.

'You are very kind.'

'We are kind to those that come to us.'

He wondered how many came to the lonely house in the valley, but did not question her for fear of what she would reply. He guessed she was an uncanny woman loving the dark because it was dark. He was too old to question the secrets of darkness, and now, with the black suit torn and wet and his thin hands bound with the bandages of the stranger woman, he felt older than ever. The winds of the morning might blow him down, and the sudden dropping of the dark be blind in his eyes. Rain might pass through him as it passes through the body of a ghost. A tired, white-haired old man, he sat under the window, almost invisible against the panes and the white cloth of the chair.

Soon the meal was ready, and Mr Owen came in unwashed from the garden.

'Shall I say grace?' asked Mr Davies when all three were seated around the table.

Mrs Owen nodded.

'O Lord God Almighty, bless this our meal,' said Mr Davies. Looking up as he continued his prayer, he saw that Mr and Mrs Owen had closed their eyes. 'We thank Thee for the bounties that Thou hast given us.' And he saw that the lips of Mr and Mrs Owen were moving softly. He could not hear what they said, but he knew that the prayers they spoke were not his prayers.

'Amen,' said all three together.

Mr Owen, proud in his eating, bent over the plate as he had bent over the complaining weeds. Outside the window was the brown body of the earth, the green skin of the grass, and the breasts of the Jarvis hills; there was a wind that chilled the animal earth, and a sun that had drunk up the dews on the fields; there was creation sweating out of the pores of the trees; and the grains of sand on far-away seashores would be multiplying as the sea rolled over them. He felt the coarse foods on his tongue; there was a meaning in the rind of the meat, and a purpose in the lifting of food to mouth. He saw, with a sudden satisfaction, that Mrs Owen's throat was bare.

She, too, was bent over her plate, but was letting the teeth of her fork nibble at the corners of it. She did not eat, for the old powers were upon her, and she dared not lift up her head for the greenness of her eyes. She knew by the sound which way the wind blew in the valley; she knew the stage of the sun by the curve of the shadows on the cloth. Oh, that she could take her crystal, and see within it the stretches of darkness covering up this winter light. But there was a darkness gathering in her mind, drawing in the light around her. There was a ghost on her left; with all her strength she drew in the intangible light that moved around him, and mixed it in her dark brains.

Mr Davies, like a man sucked by a bird, felt desolation in his veins, and, in a sweet delirium, told of his adventures on the hills, of how it had been cold and blowing, and how the hills went up and down. He had been lost, he said, and had found a dark retreat to shelter from the bullies in the wind; but the darkness had frightened him, and he had walked again on the hills where the morning tossed him about like a ship on the sea. Wherever he went he was blown in the open or frightened in the narrow shades. There was nowhere, he said pityingly, for an old man to go. Loving his parish, he had loved the surrounding lands, but the hills had given under his feet or plunged him into the air. And, loving his God, he had loved the darkness where men of old had worshipped the dark invisible. But now the hill caves were full of shapes and voices that mocked him because he was old.

'He is frightened of the dark,' thought Mrs Owen, 'the lovely dark.' With a smile, Mr Owen thought: 'He is frightened of the worm in the earth, of the copulation in the tree, of the living grease in the soil.' They looked at the old man, and saw that he was more ghostly than ever. The window behind him cast a ragged circle of light round his head.

Suddenly Mr Davies knelt down to pray. He did not understand the cold in his heart nor the fear that bewildered him as he knelt, but, speaking his prayers for deliverance, he stared up at the shadowed eyes of Mrs Owen and at the smiling eyes of her husband. Kneeling on the carpet at the head of the table, he stared in bewilderment at the dark mind and the gross dark body. He stared and he prayed, like an old god beset by his enemies.

Mr Marmaduke and the Minister

Wilkie Collins

I

September 13th – Winter seems to be upon us, on the Highland Border, already.

I looked out of window, as the evening closed in, before I barred the shutters and drew the curtains for the night. The clouds hid the hilltops on either side of our valley. Fantastic mists parted and met again on the lower slopes, as the varying breeze blew them. The blackening waters of the lake before our window seemed to anticipate the coming darkness. On the more distant hills the torrents were just visible, in the breaks of the mist, stealing their way over the brown ground like threads of silver. It was a dreary scene. The stillness of all things was only interrupted by the splashing of our little waterfall at the back of the house. I was not sorry to close the shutters, and confine the view to the four walls of our sitting-room.

The day happened to be my birthday. I sat by the peat-fire, waiting for the lamp and the tea-tray, and contemplating my past life from the vantage-ground, so to speak, of my fifty-fifth year.

There was wonderfully little to look back on. Nearly thirty

years since, it pleased an all-wise Providence to cast my lot in this remote Scottish hamlet, and to make me Minister of Cauldkirk, on a stipend of seventy-four pounds sterling per annum. I and my surroundings have grown quietly older and older together. I have outlived my wife; I have buried one generation among my parishioners, and married another; I have borne the wear and tear of years better than the kirk in which I minister and the manse (or parsonage-house) in which I live – both sadly out of repair, and both still trusting for the means of reparation to the pious benefactions of persons richer than myself. Not that I complain, be it understood, of the humble position which I occupy. I possess many blessings; and I thank the Lord for them. I have my little bit of land and my cow. I have also my good daughter, Felicia; named after her deceased mother, but inheriting her comely looks, it is thought, rather from myself.

Neither let me forget my elder sister, Judith; a friendless single person, sheltered under my roof, whose temperament I could wish somewhat less prone to look at persons and things on the gloomy side, but whose compensating virtues Heaven forbid that I should deny. No; I am grateful for what has been given me (from on high), and resigned to what has been taken away. With what fair prospects did I start in life! Springing from a good old Scottish stock, blest with every advantage of education that the institutions of Scotland and England in turn could offer; with a career at the Bar and in Parliament before me – and all cast to the winds, as it were, by the measureless prodigality of my unhappy father, God forgive him! I doubt if I had five pounds left in my purse, when the compassion of my relatives on the mother's side opened a refuge to me at Cauldkirk, and hid me from the notice of the world for the rest of my life.

September 14*th* – Thus far I had posted up my Diary on the evening of the 13th, when an event occurred so completely unexpected by my household and myself, that the pen, I may say, dropped incontinently from my hand.

It was the time when we had finished our tea, or supper – I hardly know which to call it. In the silence, we could hear the rain pouring against the window, and the wind that had risen with the darkness howling round the house. My sister Judith, taking the gloomy view according to custom – copious draughts of good Bohea and two helpings of such a mutton ham as only Scotland can produce had no effect in raising her spirits – my sister, I say, remarked that there would be ships lost at sea and men drowned this night. My daughter Felicia, the brightest-tempered creature of the female sex that I have ever met with, tried to give a cheerful turn to her aunt's depressing prognostication. 'If the ships must be lost,' she said, 'we may surely hope that the men will be saved.' 'God willing,' I put in – thereby giving to my daughter's humane expression of feeling the fit religious tone that was all it wanted – and then went on with my written record of the events and reflections of the day. No more was said. Felicia took up a book. Judith took up her knitting.

On a sudden, the silence was broken by a blow on the house-door.

My two companions, as is the way of women, set up a scream. I was startled myself, wondering who could be out in the rain and the darkness, and striking at the door of the house. A stranger it must be. Light or dark, any person in or near Cauldkirk, wanting admission, would know where to find the bell-handle at the side of the door. I waited awhile to hear what might happen next. The stroke was repeated, but more softly. It became me as a man and a minister to set an example. I went out into the passage, and I called through the door, 'Who's there?'

A man's voice answered – so faintly that I could barely hear him – 'A lost traveller.'

Immediately upon this my cheerful sister expressed her view of the matter through the open parlour door. 'Brother Noah, it's a robber. Don't let him in!'

What would the Good Samaritan have done in my place? Assuredly he would have run the risk and opened the door. I imitated the Good Samaritan.

A man, dripping wet, with a knapsack on his back and a thick stick in his hand, staggered in, and would I think have fallen in the passage if I had not caught him by the arm. Judith peeped out at the parlour door, and said, 'He's drunk.' Felicia was behind her, holding up a lighted candle the better to see what was going on. 'Look at his face, aunt,' says she. 'Worn out with fatigue, poor man. Bring him in, father – bring him in.'

Good Felicia! I was proud of my girl. 'He'll spoil the carpet,' says sister Judith. I said, 'Silence, for shame!' and brought him in, and dropped him dripping into my own armchair. Would the Good Samaritan have thought of his carpet or his chair? I did think of them, but I overcame it. Ah, we are a decadent generation in these latter days!

'Be quick, father!' says Felicia; 'he'll faint if you don't give him something!'

I took out one of our little drinking cups (called among us a 'quaigh'), while Felicia, instructed by me, ran to the kitchen for the cream-jug. Filling the cup with whisky and cream in equal proportions, I offered it to him. He drank it off as if it had been so much water. 'Stimulant and nourishment, you'll observe, sir, in equal portions,' I remarked to him. 'How do you feel now?'

'Ready for another,' says he.

Felicia burst out laughing. I gave him another. As I turned to hand it to him, sister Judith came behind me, and snatched away the cream-jug. Never a generous person, sister Judith, at the best of times – more especially in the matter of cream.

He handed me back the empty cup. 'I believe, sir, you have saved my life,' he said. 'Under Providence,' I put in – adding, 'But I would remark, looking to the state of your clothes, that I have yet another service to offer you, before you tell us how you came into this pitiable state.' With that reply, I led him upstairs, and set before him the poor resources of my wardrobe, and left him to do the best he could with them. He was rather a small man, and I am in stature nigh on six feet. When he came down to us in my clothes, we had the merriest evening that I can remember for years past. I thought Felicia would have had an hysteric fit; and even sister Judith laughed – he did look such a comical figure in the minister's garments.

As for the misfortune that had befallen him, it offered one more example of the preternatural rashness of the English traveller in countries unknown to him. He was on a walking tour through Scotland; and he had set forth to go twenty miles a-foot, from a town on one side of the Highland Border to a town on the other, without a guide. The only wonder is that he found his way to Cauldkirk, instead of perishing of exposure among the lonesome hills.

'Will you offer thanks for your preservation to the Throne of Grace, in your prayers tonight?' I asked him. And he answered, 'Indeed I will!'

We have a spare room at the manse; but it had not been inhabited for more than a year past. Therefore we made his bed, for that night, on the sofa in the parlour; and so left him, with the fire on one side of his couch, and the whisky and the mutton ham on the other in case of need. He mentioned his name when we bade him good-night. Marmaduke Falmer of London, son of a minister of the English Church Establishment, now deceased. It was plain, I may add, before he spoke, that we had offered the hospitality of the manse to a man of gentle breeding.

September 15*th* – I have to record a singularly pleasant day; due partly to a return of the fine weather, partly to the good social gifts of our guest.

Attired again in his own clothing, he was, albeit wanting in height, a finely proportioned man, with remarkably small hands and feet; having also a bright mobile face, and large dark eyes of an extraordinary diversity of expression. Also, he was of a sweet and cheerful humour; easily pleased with little things, and amiably ready to make his gifts agreeable to all of us. At the same time, a person of my experience and penetration could not fail to perceive that he was most content when in company with Felicia. I have already mentioned my daughter's comely looks and good womanly qualities. It was in the order of nature that a young man (to use his own phrase) getting near to his thirty-first birthday should feel drawn by sympathy towards a well-favoured young woman in her four-and-twentieth year. In matters of this sort I have always cultivated a liberal turn of mind, not forgetting my own youth.

As the evening closed in, I was sorry to notice a certain change in our guest for the worse. He showed signs of fatigue – falling asleep at intervals in his chair, and waking up and shivering. The spare room was now well aired, having had a roaring fire in it all day.

I begged him not to stand on ceremony, and to betake himself at once to his bed. Felicia (having learned the accomplishment from her excellent mother) made him a warm sleeping-draught of eggs, sugar, nutmeg and spirits, delicious alike to the senses of smell and taste. Sister Judith waited until he had closed the door behind him, and then favoured me with one of her dismal predictions. 'You'll rue the day, brother, when you let him into the house. He is going to fall ill on our hands.'

II

November 28th – God be praised for all His mercies! This day, our guest, Marmaduke Falmer, joined us downstairs in the sitting-room for the first time since his illness.

He is sadly deteriorated, in a bodily sense, by the wasting rheumatic fever that brought him nigh to death; but he is still young, and the doctor (humanly speaking) has no doubt of his speedy and complete recovery. My sister takes the opposite view. She remarked, in his hearing, that nobody ever thoroughly got over a rheumatic fever. Oh, Judith! Judith! it's well for humanity that you're a single person! If, haply, there had been any man desperate enough to tackle such a woman in the bonds of marriage, what a pessimist progeny must have proceeded from you!

Looking back over my Diary for the last two months and more, I see one monotonous record of the poor fellow's sufferings; cheered and varied, I am pleased to add, by the devoted services of my daughter at the sick man's bedside. With some help from her aunt (most readily given when he was nearest to the point of death), and with needful services performed in turn by two of our aged women in Cauldkirk, Felicia could not have nursed him more assiduously if he had been her own brother. Half the credit of bringing him through it belonged (as the doctor himself confessed) to the discreet young nurse, always ready through the worst of the illness, and always cheerful through the long convalescence that followed. I must also record to the credit of Marmaduke that he was indeed duly grateful. When I led him into the parlour, and he saw Felicia waiting by the armchair, smiling and patting the pillows for him, he took her by the hand, and burst out crying. Weakness, in part, no doubt – but sincere gratitude at the bottom of it, I am equally sure.

November 29*th* – However, there are limits even to sincere gratitude. Of this truth Mr Marmaduke seems to be insufficiently aware. Entering the sitting-room soon after noon today, I found our convalescent guest and his nurse alone. His head was resting on her shoulder; his arm was round her waist – and (the truth before everything) Felicia was kissing him.

A man may be of a liberal turn of mind, and may yet consistently object to freedom when it takes the form of unlicensed embracing and kissing; the person being his own daughter, and the place his own house. I signed to my girl to leave us; and I advanced to Mr Marmaduke, with my opinion of his conduct just rising in words to my lips – when he staggered me with amazement by asking for Felicia's hand in marriage.

'You need feel no doubt of my being able to offer to your daughter a position of comfort and respectability,' he said. 'I have a settled income of eight hundred pounds a year.'

His raptures over Felicia; his protestations that she was the first woman he had ever really loved; his profane declaration that he preferred to die, if I refused to let him be her husband – all these flourishes, as I may call them, passed in at one of my ears and out at the other. But eight hundred pounds sterling per annum, descending as it were in a golden avalanche on the mind of a Scottish minister (accustomed to thirty years' annual contemplation of seventy-four pounds) – eight hundred a year, in one young man's pocket, I say, completely overpowered me. I just managed to answer, 'Wait till tomorrow' – and hurried out of doors to recover my self-respect, if the thing was to be anywise done. I took my way through the valley. The sun was shining, for a wonder. When I saw my shadow on the hillside, I saw the Golden Calf as an integral part of me, bearing this inscription in letters of flame – 'Here's another of them!'

November 30*th* – I have made amends for yesterday's back-sliding; I have acted as becomes my parental dignity and my sacred calling.

The temptation to do otherwise has not been wanting. Here is sister Judith's advice: 'Make sure that he has got the money first; and, for Heaven's sake, nail him!' Here is Mr Marmaduke's proposal: 'Make any conditions you please, so long as you give me your daughter.' And, lastly, here is Felicia's confession. 'Father, my heart is set on him. Oh, don't be unkind to me for the first time in your life!'

But I have stood firm. I have refused to hear any more words on the subject from any one of them, for the next six months to come.

'So serious a venture as the venture of marriage,' I said, 'is not to be undertaken on impulse. As soon as Mr Marmaduke can travel, I request him to leave us, and not to return again for six months. If, after that interval, he is still of the same mind, and my daughter is still of the same mind, let him return to Cauldkirk, and (premising that I am in all other respects satisfied) let him ask me for his wife.'

There were tears, there were protestations; I remained immovable. A week later, Mr Marmaduke left us, on his way by easy stages to the south. I am not a hard man. I rewarded the lovers for their obedience by keeping sister Judith out of the way, and letting them say their farewell words (accompaniments included) in private.

III

May 28*th* – A letter from Mr Marmaduke, informing me that I may expect him at Cauldkirk, exactly at the expiration of the six months' interval – viz., on June the seventh.

Writing to this effect, he added a timely word on the subject of his family. Both his parents were dead; his only brother held a civil appointment in India, the place being named. His uncle (his father's brother) was a merchant resident in London; and to this near relative he referred me, if I wished to make enquiries about him. The names of his bankers, authorized to give me every information in respect to his pecuniary affairs, followed. Nothing could be more plain and straightforward. I wrote to his uncle, and I wrote to his bankers. In both cases the replies were perfectly satisfactory – nothing in the slightest degree doubtful, no prevarications, no mysteries. In a word, Mr

Marmaduke himself was thoroughly well vouched for, and Mr Marmaduke's income was invested in securities beyond fear and beyond reproach. Even sister Judith, bent on picking a hole in the record somewhere, tried hard, and could make nothing of it.

The last sentence in Mr Marmaduke's letter was the only part of it which I failed to read with pleasure.

He left it to me to fix the day for the marriage, and he entreated that I would make it as early a day as possible. I had a touch of the heartache when I thought of parting with Felicia, and being left at home with nobody but Judith. However, I got over it for that time; and, after consulting my daughter, we decided on naming a fortnight after Mr Marmaduke's arrival – that is to say, the twenty-first of June. This gave Felicia time for her preparations, besides offering to me the opportunity of becoming better acquainted with my son-in-law's disposition. The happiest marriage does indubitably make its demands on human forbearance; and I was anxious, among other things, to assure myself of Mr Marmaduke's good temper.

IV

June 22nd – The happy change in my daughter's life (let me say nothing of the change in *my* life) has come: they were married yesterday. The manse is a desert; and sister Judith was never so uncongenial a companion to me as I feel her to be now. Her last words to the married pair, when they drove away, were: 'Lord help you both; you have all your troubles before you!'

I had no heart to write yesterday's record, yesterday evening, as usual. The absence of Felicia at the supper-table completely overcame me. I, who have so often comforted others in their afflictions, could find no comfort for myself. Even now that the day has passed, the tears come into my eyes, only with writing about it. Sad, sad weakness! Let me close my Diary, and open the Bible – and be myself again.

June 23*rd* – More resigned since yesterday; a more becoming and more pious frame of mind – obedient to God's holy will, and content in the belief that my dear daughter's married life will be a happy one.

They have gone abroad for their holiday – to Switzerland, by way of France. I was anything rather than pleased when I heard that my son-in-law proposed to take Felicia to that sink of iniquity, Paris. He knows already what I think of balls and playhouses, and similar devils' diversions, and how I have brought up my daughter to think of them – the subject having occurred in conversation among us more than a week since. That he could meditate taking a child of mine to the headquarters of indecent jiggings and abominable stage-plays, of spouting rogues and painted Jezebels, was indeed a heavy blow.

However, Felicia reconciled me to it in the end. She declared that her only desire in going to Paris was to see the picture-galleries, the public buildings, and the fair outward aspect of the city generally. 'Your opinions, father, are my opinions,' she said; 'and Marmaduke, I am sure, will so shape our arrangements as to prevent our passing a Sabbath in Paris.' Marmaduke not only consented to this (with the perfect good temper of which I have observed more than one gratifying example in him), but likewise assured me that, speaking for himself personally, it would be a relief to him when they got to the mountains and the lakes. So that matter was happily settled. Go where they may, God bless and prosper them!

Speaking of relief, I must record that Judith has gone away to Aberdeen on a visit to some friends. 'You'll be wretched enough here,' she said at parting, 'all by yourself.' Pure vanity and self-complacence! It may be resignation to her absence, or it may be natural force of mind, I began to be more easy and composed the moment I was alone, and this blessed state of feeling has continued uninterruptedly ever since.

V

September 5th – A sudden change in my life, which it absolutely startles me to record. I am going to London!

My purpose in taking this most serious step is of a twofold nature. I have a greater and a lesser object in view.

The greater object is to see my daughter, and to judge for myself whether certain doubts on the vital question of her happiness, which now torment me night and day, are unhappily founded on truth. She and her husband returned in August from their wedding-tour, and took up their abode in Marmaduke's new residence in London. Up to this time, Felicia's letters to me were, in very truth, the delight of my life – she was so entirely happy, so amazed and delighted with all the wonderful things she saw, so full of love and admiration for the best husband that ever lived. Since her return to London, I perceive a complete change.

She makes no positive complaint, but she writes in a tone of weariness and discontent; she says next to nothing of Marmaduke, and she dwells perpetually on the one idea of my going to London to see her. I hope with my whole heart that I am wrong; but the rare allusions to her husband, and the constantly repeated desire to see her father (while she has not been yet three months married), seem to me to be bad signs. In brief, my anxiety is too great to be endured. I have so arranged matters with one of my brethren as to be free to travel to London cheaply by steamer; and I begin the journey tomorrow.

My lesser object may be dismissed in two words. Having already decided on going to London, I propose to call on the wealthy nobleman who owns all the land hereabouts, and represent to him the discreditable, and indeed dangerous, condition of the parish kirk for want of means to institute the necessary repairs. If I find myself well received, I shall put in a word for the manse, which is almost in as deplorable a condition as the church. My lord is a wealthy man – may his heart and his purse be opened unto me!

Sister Judith is packing my portmanteau. According to custom, she forebodes the worst. 'Never forget,' she says, 'that I warned you against Marmaduke, on the first night when he entered the house.'

VI

September 10*th* – After more delays than one, on land and sea, I was at last set ashore near the Tower, on the afternoon of yesterday. God help us, my worst anticipations have been realized! My beloved Felicia has urgent and serious need of me.

It is not to be denied that I made my entry into my son-in-law's house in a disturbed and irritated frame of mind. First, my temper was tried by the almost interminable journey, in the noisy and comfortless vehicle which they call a cab, from the river-wharf to the West End of London, where Marmaduke lives. In the second place, I was scandalized and alarmed by an incident which took place – still on the endless journey from east to west – in a street hard by the market of Covent Garden.

We had just approached a large building, most profusely illuminated with gas, and exhibiting prodigious coloured placards having inscribed on them nothing but the name of Barrymore. The cab came suddenly to a standstill; and looking out to see what the obstacle might be, I discovered a huge concourse of men and women, drawn across the pavement and road alike, so that it seemed impossible to pass by them. I enquired of my driver what this assembling of the people meant.

'Oh,' says he, 'Barrymore has made another hit.' This answer being perfectly unintelligible to me, I requested some further explanation, and discovered that 'Barrymore' was the name of a stage-player favoured by the populace; that the building was a theatre; and that all these creatures with immortal souls were waiting, before the doors opened, to get places at the show!

The emotions of sorrow and indignation caused by this discovery so absorbed me, that I failed to notice an attempt the driver made to pass through, where the crowd seemed to be thinner, until the offended people resented the proceeding. Some of them seized the horse's head; others were on the point of pulling the driver off his box, when providentially the police interfered. Under their protection, we drew back, and reached our destination in safety, by another way. I record this otherwise unimportant affair, because it grieved and revolted me (when I thought of the people's souls), and so indisposed my mind to take cheerful views of anything. Under these circumstances, I would fain hope that I have exaggerated the true state of the case, in respect to my daughter's married life.

My good girl almost smothered me with kisses. When I at last got a fair opportunity of observing her, I thought her looking pale and worn and anxious. Query: Should I have arrived at this conclusion if I had met with no example of the wicked dissipations of London, and if I had ridden at my ease in a comfortable vehicle?

They had a succulent meal ready for me, and, what I call, fair enough whisky out of Scotland. Here again I remarked that Felicia ate very little, and Marmaduke nothing at all. He drank wine too – and, good heavens, champagne wine! – a needless waste of money surely when there was whisky on the table. My appetite being satisfied, my son-in-law went out of the room, and returned with his hat in his hand. 'You and Felicia have many things to talk about on your first evening together. I'll leave you for a while – I shall only be in the way.' So he spoke.

It was in vain that his wife and I assured him he was not in the way at all. He kissed his hand, and smiled pleasantly, and left us.

'There, father!' says Felicia. 'For the last ten days, he has gone out like that, and left me alone for the whole evening. When we first returned from Switzerland, he left me in the same mysterious way, only it was after breakfast then. Now he stays at home in the daytime, and goes out at night.'

I enquired if she had not summoned him to give her some explanation.

'I don't know what to make of his explanation,' says Felicia. 'When he went away in the daytime, he told me he had business in the City. Since he took to going out at night, he says he goes to his club.'

'Have you asked where his club is, my dear?'

'He says it's in Pall Mall. There are dozens of clubs in that street – and he has never told me the name of *his* club. I am completely shut out of his confidence. Would you believe it, father? he has not introduced one of his friends to me since we came home. I doubt if they know where he lives, since he took this house.'

What could I say?

I said nothing, and looked round the room. It was fitted up with perfectly palatial magnificence. I am an ignorant man in matters of this sort, and partly to satisfy my curiosity, partly to change the subject, I asked to see the house. Mercy preserve us, the same grandeur everywhere! I wondered if even such an income as eight hundred a year could suffice for it all. In a moment when I was considering this, a truly frightful suspicion crossed my mind. Did these mysterious absences, taken in connection with the unbridled luxury that surrounded us, mean that my son-in-law was a gamester? a shameless shuffler of cards, or a debauched better on horses? While I was still completely overcome by my own previsions of evil, my daughter put her arm in mine to take me to the top of the house.

For the first time I observed a bracelet of dazzling gems on her wrist. 'Not diamonds?' I said. She answered, with as much composure as if she had been the wife of a nobleman, 'Yes, diamonds – a present from Marmaduke.' This was too much for me; my previsions, so to speak, forced their way into words. 'Oh, my poor child!' I burst out, 'I'm in mortal fear that your husband's a gamester!'

She showed none of the horror I had anticipated; she only shook her head and began to cry.

'Worse than that, I'm afraid,' she said.

I was petrified; my tongue refused its office, when I would fain have asked her what she meant. Her besetting sin, poor soul, is a proud spirit. She dried her eyes on a sudden, and spoke out freely, in these words: 'I am not going to cry about it. The other day, father, we were out walking in the park. A horrid, bold, yellow-haired woman passed us in an open carriage. She kissed her hand to Marmaduke, and called out to him, "How are you, Marmy?" I was so indignant that I pushed him away from me, and told him to go and take a drive with his lady. He burst out laughing. "Nonsense!" he said; "she has known me for years – you don't understand our easy London manners." We have made it up since then; but I have my own opinion of the creature in the open carriage.'

Morally speaking, this was worse than all. But, logically viewed, it completely failed as a means of accounting for the diamond bracelet and the splendour of the furniture.

We went on to the uppermost storey. It was cut off from the rest of the house by a stout partition of wood, and a door covered with green baize.

When I tried the door it was locked. 'Ha!' says Felicia, 'I wanted you to see it for yourself!' More suspicious proceedings on the part of my son-in-law! He kept the door constantly locked, and the key in his pocket. When his wife asked him what it meant, he answered: 'My study is up there – and I like to keep it entirely to myself.' After such a reply as that, the preservation of my daughter's dignity permitted but one answer: 'Oh, keep it to yourself, by all means!'

My previsions, upon this, assumed another form.

I now asked myself – still in connection with my son-in-law's extravagant expenditure – whether the clue to the mystery might not haply be the forging of banknotes on the other side of the baize door. My mind was prepared for anything by this time. We descended again to the dining-room. Felicia saw how my spirits were dashed, and came and perched upon my knee. 'Enough of my troubles for tonight, father,' she said. 'I am going to be your little girl again, and we will talk of nothing but Cauldkirk, until Marmaduke comes back.' I am one of the firmest men living, but I could not keep the hot tears out of my eyes when she put her arm round my neck and said those words. By good fortune I was sitting with my back to the lamp; she didn't notice me.

A little after eleven o'clock, Marmaduke returned. He looked pale and weary. But more champagne, and this time something to eat with it, seemed to set him to rights again – no doubt by relieving him from the reproaches of a guilty conscience.

I had been warned by Felicia to keep what had passed between us a secret from her husband for the present; so we had (superficially speaking) a merry end to the evening. My son-in-law was nearly as good company as ever, and wonderfully fertile in suggestions and expedients when he saw they were wanted. Hearing from his wife, to whom I had mentioned it, that I purposed representing the decayed condition of the kirk and manse to the owner of Cauldkirk and the country round about, he strongly urged me to draw up a list of repairs that were most needful, before I waited on my lord. This advice, vicious and degraded as the man who offered it may be, is sound advice nevertheless. I shall assuredly take it.

So far I had written in my Diary, in the forenoon. Returning to my daily record, after a lapse of some hours, I have a new mystery of iniquity to chronicle. My abominable son-in-law now appears (I blush to write it) to be nothing less than an associate of thieves!

After the meal they call luncheon, I thought it well, before recreating myself with the sights of London, to attend first to the crying necessities of the kirk and the manse. Furnished with my written list, I presented myself at his lordship's residence. I was immediately informed that he was otherwise engaged, and could not possibly receive me. If I wished to see my lord's secretary, Mr Helmsley, I could do so. Consenting to this, rather than fail entirely in my errand, I was shown into the secretary's room.

Mr Helmsley heard what I had to say civilly enough; expressing, however, grave doubts whether his lordship would do anything for me, the demands on his purse being insupportably numerous already. However, he undertook to place my list before his employer, and to let me know the result. 'Where are you staying in London?' he asked. I answered, 'With my son-in-law, Mr Marmaduke Falmer.' Before I could add the address, the secretary started to his feet, and tossed my list back to me across the table in the most uncivil manner.

'Upon my word,' says he, 'your assurance exceeds anything I ever heard of. Your son-in-law is concerned in the robbery of her ladyship's diamond bracelet – the discovery was made not an hour ago. Leave the house, sir, and consider yourself lucky that I have no instructions to give you in charge to the police.' I protested against this unprovoked outrage, with a violence of language which I would rather not recall. As a minister I ought, under every provocation, to have preserved my self-control.

The one thing to do next was to drive back to my unhappy daughter.

Her guilty husband was with her. I was too angry to wait for a fit opportunity of speaking. The Christian humility which I have all my life cultivated as the first of virtues sank, as it were, from under me. In terms of burning indignation I told them what had happened. The result was too distressing to be described. It ended in Felicia giving her husband back the bracelet. The hardened reprobate laughed at us. 'Wait till I have seen his lordship and Mr Helmsley,' he said, and left the house.

Does he mean to escape to foreign parts? Felicia, womanlike, believes in him still; she is quite convinced that there must be some mistake. I am myself in hourly expectation of the arrival of the police.

With gratitude to Providence, I note before going to bed the harmless termination of the affair of the bracelet – so far as Marmaduke is concerned. The agent who sold him the jewel has been forced to come forward and state the truth. His lordship's wife is the guilty person; the bracelet was hers – a present from her husband. Harassed by debts that she dare not acknowledge, she sold it; my lord discovered that it was gone; and in terror of his anger the wretched woman took refuge in a lie.

She declared that the bracelet had been stolen from her. Asked for the name of the thief, the reckless woman (having no other name in her mind at the moment) mentioned the man who had innocently bought the jewel of her agent, otherwise my unfortunate son-in-law. Oh, the profligacy of the modern Babylon! It was well I went to the secretary when I did, or we should really have had the police in the house. Marmaduke found them in consultation over the supposed robbery, asking for his address. There was a dreadful exhibition of violence and recrimination at his lordship's residence: in the end he repurchased the bracelet. My son-in-law's money has been returned to him; and Mr Helmsley has sent me a written apology.

In a worldly sense, this would, I suppose, be called a satisfactory ending.

It is not so, to my mind. I freely admit that I too hastily distrusted Marmaduke; but am I, on that account, to give him back immediately the place which he once occupied in my esteem? Again this evening he mysteriously quitted the house, leaving me alone with Felicia, and giving no better excuse for his conduct than that he had an engagement. And this when I have a double claim on his consideration, as his father-in-law and his guest!

September 11*th* – The day began well enough. At breakfast, Marmaduke spoke feelingly of the unhappy result of my visit to his lordship, and asked me to let him look at the list of repairs. 'It's just useless to expect anything from my lord, after what has happened,' I said. 'Besides, Mr Helmsley gave me no hope when I stated my case to him.' Marmaduke still held out his hand for the list. 'Let me try if I can get some subscribers,' he replied. This was kindly meant, at any rate. I gave him the list; and I began to recover some of my old friendly feeling for him. Alas! the little gleam of tranquillity proved to be of short duration.

We made out our plans for the day pleasantly enough. The check came when Felicia spoke next of our plans for the evening. 'My father has only four days more to pass with us,' she said to her husband. 'Surely you won't go out again tonight, and leave him?' Marmaduke's face clouded over directly; he looked embarrassed and annoyed. I sat perfectly silent, leaving them to settle it by themselves.

'You will stay with us this evening, won't you?' says Felicia. No: he was not free for that evening. 'What! another engagement? Surely you can put it off?' No; impossible to put it off. 'Is it a ball, or a party of some kind?' No answer; he changed the subject – he offered Felicia the money repaid to him for the bracelet. 'Buy one for yourself, my dear, this time.' Felicia handed him back the money, rather too haughtily perhaps. 'I don't want a bracelet,' she said; 'I want your company in the evening.'

He jumped up, good-tempered as he was, in something very like a rage – then looked at me, and checked himself on the point (as I believe) of using profane language. 'This is downright persecution!' he burst out, with an angry turn of his head towards his wife. Felicia got up, in her turn. 'Your language is an insult to my father and to me!' He looked thoroughly staggered at this: it was evidently their first serious quarrel.

Felicia took no notice of him. 'I will get ready directly, father; and we will go out together.' He stopped her as she was leaving the room – recovering his good temper with a readiness which it pleased me to see. 'Come, come, Felicia! We have not quarrelled yet, and we won't quarrel now. Let me off this one time more, and I will devote the next three evenings of your father's visit to him and to you: Give me a kiss, and make it up.' My daughter doesn't do things by halves. She gave him a dozen kisses, I should think – and there was a happy end to it.

'But what shall we do tomorrow evening?' says Marmaduke, sitting down by his wife, and patting her hand as it lay in his.

'Take us somewhere,' says she. Marmaduke laughed. 'Your father objects to public amusements. Where does he want to go to?' Felicia took up the newspaper. 'There is an oratorio at Exeter Hall,' she said; 'my father likes music.' He turned to me. 'You don't object to oratorios, sir?' 'I don't object to music,' I answered, 'so long as I am not required to enter a theatre.' Felicia handed the newspaper to me. 'Speaking of theatres, father, have you read what they say about the new play? What a pity it can't be given out of a theatre!' I looked at her in speechless amazement. She tried to explain herself. 'The paper says that the new play is a service rendered to the cause of virtue; and that the great actor, Barrymore, has set an example in producing it which deserves the encouragement of all truly religious people. Do read it, father!' I held up my hands in dismay. My own daughter perverted! pinning her faith on a newspaper! speaking, with a perverse expression of interest, of a stage-play and an actor! Even Marmaduke witnessed this lamentable exhibition of backsliding with some appearance of alarm. 'It's not her fault, sir,' he said, interceding with me. 'It's the fault of the newspaper. Don't blame her!' I held my peace; determining inwardly to pray for her. Shortly afterwards my daughter and I went out. Marmaduke accompanied us part of the way, and left us at a telegraph-office. 'Who are you going to telegraph to?' Felicia asked. Another mystery! He answered, 'Business of my own, my dear' – and went into the office.

September 12*th* – Is my miserable son-in-law's house under a curse? The yellow-haired woman in the open carriage drove up to the door at half-past ten this morning, in a state of distraction. Felicia and I saw her from the drawing-room balcony – a tall woman in gorgeous garments. She knocked with her own hand at the door – she cried out distractedly, 'Where is he? I must see him!' At the sound of her voice, Marmaduke (playing with his little dog in the drawing-room) rushed downstairs, and out into the street. 'Hold your tongue!' we heard him say to her. 'What are you here for?'

What she answered we failed to hear: she was certainly crying. Marmaduke stamped on the pavement like a man beside himself – took her roughly by the arm, and led her into the house.

Before I could utter a word, Felicia left me, and flew headlong down the stairs.

She was in time to hear the dining-room door locked. Following her, I prevented the poor jealous creature from making a disturbance at the door. God forgive me – not knowing how else to quiet her – I degraded myself by advising her to listen to what they said. She instantly opened the door of the back dining-room, and beckoned to me to follow. I naturally hesitated. 'I shall go mad,' she whispered, 'if you leave me by myself!' What could I do? I degraded myself for the second time. For my own child – in pity for my own child!

We heard them, through the flimsy modern folding-doors, at those times when he was most angry, and she most distracted.

That is to say, we heard them when they spoke in their loudest tones.

'How did you find out where I live?' says he. 'Oh, you're ashamed of me?' says she. Mr Helmsley was with us yesterday evening. That's how I found out!' 'What do you mean?' 'I mean that Mr Helmsley had your card and address in his pocket. Ah, you were obliged to give your address when you had to clear up that matter of the bracelet! You cruel, cruel man, what have I done to deserve such a note as you sent me this morning?' 'Do what the note tells you!' 'Do what the note tells me? Did anybody ever hear a man talk so, out of a lunatic asylum? Why, you haven't even the grace to carry out your own wicked deception – you haven't even gone to bed!' There the voices grew less angry, and we missed what followed. Soon the lady burst out again, piteously entreating him this time. 'Oh, Marmy, don't ruin me! Has anybody offended you? Is there anything you wish to have altered? Do you want more money? It is too cruel to treat me in this way – it is indeed!' He made some answer, which we were not able to hear; we could only suppose that he had upset her temper again. She went on louder than ever. 'I've begged and prayed of you – and you're as hard as iron. I've told you about the Prince – and *that* has had no effect on you. I have done now. We'll see what the doctor says.' He got angry, in his turn; we heard him again. 'I won't see the doctor!' 'Oh, you refuse to see the doctor? I shall make your refusal known – and if there's law in England, you shall feel it!' Their voices dropped again; some new turn seemed to be taken by the conversation. We heard the lady once more, shrill and joyful this time. 'There's a dear! You see it, don't you, in the right light? And you haven't forgotten the old times, have you? You're the same dear, honourable, kind-hearted fellow that you always were!'

I caught hold of Felicia, and put my hand over her mouth.

There was a sound in the next room which might have been – I cannot be certain – the sound of a kiss. The next moment, we heard the door of the room unlocked. Then the door of the house was opened, and the noise of retreating carriage-wheels followed. We met him in the hall, as he entered the house again.

My daughter walked up to him, pale and determined.

'I insist on knowing who that woman is, and what she wants here.' Those were her first words. He looked at her like a man in utter confusion. 'Wait till this evening; I am in no state to speak to you now!' With that, he snatched his hat off the hall table, and rushed out of the house.

It is little more than three weeks since they returned to London from their happy wedding-tour – and it has come to this!

The clock has just struck seven; a letter has been left by a messenger, addressed to my daughter. I had persuaded her, poor soul, to lie down in her own room. God grant that the letter may bring her some tidings of her husband! I please myself in the hope of hearing good news.

My mind has not been kept long in suspense. Felicia's waiting-woman has brought me a morsel of writing-paper, with these lines pencilled on it in my daughter's handwriting: 'Dearest father, make your mind easy. Everything is explained. I cannot trust myself to speak to you about it tonight – and *he* doesn't wish me to do so. Only wait till tomorrow, and you shall know all. He will be back about eleven o'clock. Please don't wait up for him – he will come straight to me.'

September 13*th* – The scales have fallen from my eyes; the light is let in on me at last. My bewilderment is not to be uttered in words – I am like a man in a dream.

Before I was out of my room in the morning, my mind was upset by the arrival of a telegram addressed to myself. It was the first thing of the kind I ever received; I trembled under the prevision of some new misfortune as I opened the envelope.

Of all the people in the world, the person sending the telegram was sister Judith! Never before did this distracting relative confound me as she confounded me now. Here is her message: 'You can't come back. An architect from Edinburgh asserts his resolution to repair the kirk and the manse. The man only waits for his lawful authority to begin. The money is ready – but who has found it? Mr Architect is forbidden to tell. We live in awful times. How is Felicia?'

Naturally concluding that Judith's mind must be deranged, I went downstairs to meet my son-in-law (for the first time since the events of yesterday) at the late breakfast which is customary in this house. He was waiting for me – but Felicia was not present. 'She breakfasts in her room this morning,' says Marmaduke; 'and I am to give you the explanation which has already satisfied your daughter. Will you take it at great length, sir? or will you have it in one word?' There was something in his manner that I did not at all like – he seemed to be setting me at defiance. I said, stiffly, 'Brevity is best; I will have it in one word.'

'Here it is then,' he answered. 'I am Barrymore.'

POSTSCRIPT ADDED BY FELICIA

If the last line extracted from my dear father's Diary does not contain explanation enough in itself, I add some sentences from Marmaduke's letter to me, sent from the theatre last night. (N.B. – I leave out the expressions of endearment: they are my own private property.)

> . . . Just remember how your father talked about theatres and actors, when I was at Cauldkirk, and how you listened in dutiful agreement with him. Would he have consented to your marriage if he had known that I was one of the 'spouting rogues', associated with the 'painted Jezebels' of the play-house? He would never have consented – and you

yourself, my darling, would have trembled at the bare idea of marrying an actor.

Have I been guilty of any serious deception? and have my friends been guilty in helping to keep my secret? My birth, my name, my surviving relatives, my fortune inherited from my father – all these important particulars have been truly stated. The name of Barrymore is nothing but the name that I assumed when I went on the stage.

As to what has happened, since our return from Switzerland, I own that I ought to have made my confession to you. Forgive me if I weakly hesitated. I was so fond of you; and I so distrusted the Puritanical convictions which your education had rooted in your mind, that I put it off from day to day. Oh, my angel! . . .

Yes, I kept the address of my new house a secret from all my friends, knowing they would betray me if they paid us visits. As for my mysteriously-closed study, it was the place in which I privately rehearsed my new part. When I left you in the mornings, it was to go to the theatre rehearsals. My evening absences began of course with the first performance.

Your father's arrival seriously embarrassed me. When you (most properly) insisted on my giving up some of my evenings to him, you necessarily made it impossible for me to appear on the stage. The one excuse I could make to the theatre was, that I was too ill to act. It did certainly occur to me to cut the Gordian knot by owning the truth. But your father's horror, when you spoke of the newspaper review of the play, and the shame and fear you showed at your own boldness, daunted me once more.

The arrival at the theatre of my written excuse brought the manageress down upon me, in a state of distraction. Nobody could supply my place; all the seats were taken; and the Prince was expected. There was what we call a scene between the poor lady and myself. I felt I was in the wrong; I saw that the position in which I had impulsively placed myself was unworthy of me – and it ended in my doing my duty to the theatre and the public. But for the affair of the bracelet, which obliged me as an honourable man to give my name and address, the manageress would not have discovered me. She, like everyone else, only knew of my address at my bachelor chambers. How could you be jealous of the old theatrical comrade of my first days on the stage? Don't you know yet that you are the one woman in the world? . . .

A last word relating to your father, and I have done.

Do you remember my leaving you at the telegraph-office? It was to send a message to a friend of mine, an architect in Edinburgh, instructing him to go immediately to Cauldkirk, and provide for the repairs at my expense. The theatre, my dear, more than trebles my paternal income, and I can well afford it. Will your father refuse to accept a tribute of respect to a Scottish minister, because it is paid out of an actor's pocket? You shall ask him the question.

And, I say, Felicia – will you come and see me act? I don't expect your father to enter a theatre; but, by way of further reconciling him to his son-in-law, suppose you ask him to hear me read the play?

The Vicar's Conversion

A. E. W. Mason

'These are fancies,' said the vicar.

The vicar had just come to the parish, and had come straight from a college lecture-room. The peasant with whom he was walking on the trim gravel-path between the lych-gate and the church-door had heard that church-clock strike six on every morning of his seventy-two years.

'These are fancies, Jan, and reprehensible. It is disheartening to notice how the traditions of ignorance still live in distant villages. In olden times there was more excuse, and to be sure instances were more common. An unexpected draught of wind on a calm day and a rustle of the trees, and at once it was the fairies calling "Horse and Hattock", as they were transported from place to place. To see one's self in a dream divided into a two-fold person was a sign of death, doubtless because such a vision had happened to a man in a delirium and near his end. Superstition was an excuse, too, for quacks, and by them encouraged. There was a miller in Norfolk who owned a beryl set in a circle of silver, on which were engraved the names of four angels – Ariel, Raphael, Michael, and Gabriel – and in this beryl he professed to see prescriptions written on the images of herbs, and so to cure the sick.'

Jan shook his head in admiration of the vicar's harangue.

'There's book-larnin' in every word,' said he.

'Then there are the phantasmata proper,' continued the vicar,

179

'such as corpse-candles, which, rightly understood, are no more than Will-o'-the-wisps or marsh fires and exhalations of the soil, and when seen in churchyards are indeed an argument for cremation.'

The vicar was enjoying his lecture too much to remark the look of dismay on Jan's old, wrinkled face, or to pay any heed to his expostulation against that or any argument for cremation. He bore Jan down with knowledge.

'Besides these, there are the apparitions, reserved, it would seem,' he continued, with a severe look at Jan, 'to those who have the second sight. The Scotch are the chief offenders in claiming that gift, and they tell many ridiculous stories about meeting people on the high road with winding-sheets up to their knees or necks according as they are to die, immediately or only soon. There is a legend told of the Macleans, whose child's nurse began suddenly to weep when she saw Maclean and his lady entering together. She wept, it seems, because she saw between them a man in a scarlet cloak and a white hat, who gave the lady a kiss. And the meaning of that rubbish was that Maclean would die and his lady marry again, and marry a man in a scarlet cloak and a white hat.'

'An' did she?' interrupted Jan.

'Did she?' said the vicar, with scorn. 'Would any woman marry a man in a scarlet cloak and a white hat?'

'She might be daft loike,' said Jan.

The vicar waved the suggestion aside.

'The Scotch, indeed, make the most absurd pretensions. Aubrey writes that in the Island of Skye they offered in his day to teach second sight for a pound of tobacco.'

'They couldn't du that,' said Jan. ''Tisn't to be larned. 'Tis born in a body, so to speak. My feyther had it afore me –'

'Now, Jan,' interrupted the vicar, 'I cannot listen to you. It is mere presumption for you to speak in that way.'

'Be sure, vicar,' replied Jan. 'Oi aren't proud o' the gift.

Would git rid of it if Oi cud. Tain't pleasant to sit supping your yale with them as you knows are corpses already, so to say, and many years Oi've never been near churchyard at all on New Year's Eve, so as Oi moightn't knaw. But when Oi du come, sure enough all who are goin' to doi durin' the year comes down the lane, through the gate, and up the path into church. An' those who'll doi first comes first. They don't wear no sheets or trappin's, but they comes in their cloathes, opens gate, and so into church. An' Oi'll prove it to you, vicar.'

'How?'

'Oi'll watch tomorrow, bein' New Year's Eve, and Oi'll wroite down the names of the three who first go through the gate. Then Oi'll put the names in envelopes and mark 'em outside "one", "two", "three", and give you the envelopes. Then, when the first person doies you open the first envelope, and there you'll find the name, and same wi' the second and the third.'

The vicar was in a quandary. It was undignified to accept the challenge: it would seem cowardly to refuse it. He compounded with his dignity and accepted.

'Not because I have any doubts myself,' he said to Jan, 'but in order to convince you of the absurdity of your pretension.'

On the first of January the three envelopes were delivered to him by Jan. They were sealed and numbered. The vicar tossed them contemptuously into a drawer and locked them up. He forgot them altogether until the end of the month, when he was summoned hastily to the bedside of a labourer who was ill with influenza. The man was very old – eighty-four, the doctor said.

'Is there a chance of his living?' asked the vicar when he came out of the cottage with the doctor.

'Not one in ten thousand. He has been breaking for months. Last autumn I didn't think he would see another summer.'

The vicar met Jan in the street and remembered the envelopes. He shrugged his shoulders at the recollection of the ridiculous challenge and went home to his study. His uncompleted sermon lay on his desk and he sat down to it. In a minute or two he went to his book-case for a reference and, standing before his shelves, forgot why he had risen from his chair. He was thinking. 'After all, old Peter Stewer's death was an easy guess.' He went back to his table and unlocked the drawer. 'It wouldn't be a proof if Peter Stewer's name was in envelope No. 1.' He took out envelope No. 1. 'Anyone, it seemed, might have known in the autumn that Peter Stewer was breaking.' And his next thought was, 'These envelopes are very thick.' He woke up with a start to realize that he was holding the envelope up to the light of the window, and he tossed it back impatiently and snapped the drawer to.

Peter Stewer died at three o'clock in the morning. The vicar heard the news at nine as he was walking to the cottage, and he suddenly turned back as though he were going home. He changed his mind, however, and turned again, continuing his walk to the cottage.

'He was eighty-four,' said Peter's daughter, phlegmatically.

'A ripe age,' replied the vicar.

He repeated 'Eighty-four' to himself more than once as he went home. 'Eighty-four. Very likely his name's in the envelope. There's no proof in that'; and he felt himself grabbed by the arm. It was the doctor who had caught hold of him.

'You're in a great hurry,' said the doctor.

'Am I?' said the vicar, colouring red. 'I did not notice. My thoughts were busy.'

'On tomorrow's sermon, eh? Well, I won't spoil it.'

The vicar, however, now, would not let the doctor go; he loitered, he had a word for everybody he passed in the street, and it was not until the evening that he opened the envelope. He opened it with a great show of carelessness, all the greater because he was conscious that his heart was beating a little quicker than usual. He was prepared for the name, and yet the sight of it written there in black and white, 'Peter Stewer', was a shock to him. He tore the paper into fragments and tried to thrust the matter from his mind.

But Jan was at the funeral, and after the ceremony he said:

'What did I tell 'ee, vicar?'

'Peter was old,' said the vicar, 'and breaking fast. It was easy to guess his name.'

'Wait to the next, vicar,' said Jan. 'Oi'm not proud o' the gift – Oi wish Oi hadn't it; but wait for the next.'

Now, the parish was situated in a healthy, upland district, and the winter was mild. One or two of the elder people suffered the usual ailments of February and March, but there was no serious illness. More than once the vicar was inclined to tear up his envelopes during that time, for he had come to live in an expectation of a summons to a death-bed. But it would have seemed almost a confession that he gave in, that he admitted the possibility of second sight and the possession of it by Jan. He did not. He assured himself often that he did not. Indeed, it would after all prove nothing if all three envelopes contained the correct names. For there were extraordinary flukes: they happened every day. The vicar had read in his newspaper of them happening at gambling saloons. Jan was just gambling on the names as a player gambles on numbers. No, the vicar did not object to the letters because he shirked the challenge but because they kept him in spite of himself speculating who of his parishioners would be the next to go.

Half-way through March he knew. A servant from the great house on the hanger above the village came to fetch him. A runaway horse, a collision with a cart, and the daughter of the house seriously hurt – this was the footman's story. The vicar hurried up the hill. The envelopes in his drawer were at that time swept clean out of his mind; he had no thoughts but thoughts of dread and pity. The girl who had been injured was barely nineteen, and she had all her acquaintances for her friends.

The doctor was already upstairs; the vicar waited in the great hall with the girl's father, hearing over and over again a broken narrative of the accident. At last the doctor descended, and neither of the two men waiting below had the courage to put a question. The doctor replied to their looks, and replied cheerfully. He recommended that a telegram should be sent for a specialist.

'There is a chance, then?' asked the father, in a voice he could not raise above a whisper.

'More than a chance,' replied the doctor, and the vicar was at once, in spite of himself, and against his will, certain that there was no chance – not one in ten thousand. Perhaps it was that he remembered a similar question put by him outside old Peter Stewer's gate. At all events, the envelopes were recalled to his mind. Jan had as much as told him that the next of his parishioners to go would be young. And a conviction which he could not shake off stood fixed in his mind, that 'Gertrude Leslie' was the name written within the envelope. He seemed, as he stood in the hall listening to the interchange of hopeful words, to be actually reading the name through the envelope, and it was with a start almost of guilt that he roused himself to take his leave. In three days' time he had occasion to open the second envelope. 'Gertrude Leslie' was the name inscribed in it, and he opened it on the day of Gertrude Leslie's death.

'What did I tell 'ee, vicar?' said Jan.

The vicar turned away without answering. He could not argue that Jan had merely made a likely guess. Apart from the other circumstances, it hardly seemed natural that Jan should have guessed at the Squire's daughter at all, when there were all his cronies and acquaintances to select from. The vicar from that moment took an aversion to Jan as to something repellent and uncanny; and it became a surprise to him that the villagers regarded the peasant with indifference and almost with pity as a being endowed with a commonplace but uncomfortable gift.

The vicar no longer disbelieved in Jan's second sight. He owned as much frankly to himself one evening, and took the third envelope from the drawer. 'I may as well burn this, then,' he debated, 'since I am already convinced'; and even while he was debating he replaced it in the drawer. His disbelief was replaced by curiosity – curiosity to know not so much whose name was in the envelope, but rather which of his parishioners would be the next to die – a point upon which the breaking of the seal would surely illumine him. He felt that it would be weak, however, to break the seal. He had a sense, too, that it would be wrong: it seemed to him almost that it would be an acknowledgement of a submission to the powers of darkness.

But he kept the envelope; and it tempted him like a forbidden thing, it called to him to break the seal and read, it became permanent in his thoughts. His parishioners began to notice a curious, secret look of inquiry, which came into his eyes whenever he met or spoke with them. He was speculating, 'Is it you?' And the spring came.

The vicar threw up his window one morning and felt his blood renewed. He drew in the fresh morning air, with a consciousness that of late he had been living in and breathing a miasma. The trees in his garden were lively and musical with birds; there were sprouts of tender green upon the branches; the blackbirds were pecking at his lawn, and between the blades of grass he saw the shy white bells of snowdrops. He determined to brush all this oppressive curiosity from his mind, to forget the envelope lurking in his drawer.

He breakfasted, and went out to make a call. On his way to the cottage he was visiting he passed the post-office. By the letter-box the schoolmistress was standing with some letters in her hand. She raised her hand and slipped one of the letters into the box just as the vicar came up to her. The vicar was a keen-sighted man, and it chanced that his eyes fell upon the envelope. He read the superscription and recognized the handwriting. The envelope was addressed to Jan's son, a yeoman with the South African Field Force, and the address was written in the same handwriting as the names in the envelopes marked 1 and 2 which he had opened.

'So you are posting Jan's letters?' said the vicar, who was a trifle puzzled.

'Yes,' explained the schoolmistress. 'Jan's an old man, and there was no school here when he was a boy. So he never learnt to read or write. He tells me what he wants to say to his boy, and I write it for him.'

'Then you know the name in the third envelope?' cried the vicar. The question was out and spoken before he was aware of what he said. Then he flushed with shame. It was humiliating, it was most undignified to betray such vehement curiosity. The vicar was so disconcerted that he hardly paid heed to the confusion and excuses of the schoolmistress.

'I did not know why Jan wanted the names written,' she pleaded. 'He never told me. I would never have done it if I had known that this was one of his heathenish tricks. I did not guess until the Squire's daughter died. I don't believe it, sir, even now, any more than you do.'

'Well, well!' The vicar cut her short, anxious to escape from his undignified position. 'You were not to blame, since you did not know. But it is not right to encourage Jan in these' – he cast about for an ambiguous word and found it – 'in these devices.'

The vicar hurried home in a turmoil of indignation against Jan, and more particularly against himself. He would put an end to the obsession of this sealed envelope which was daily engrossing more and more of his life. He went straight to his study, unlocked the drawer, and pulled out the envelope. He tore it, open, shutting his eyes the while unconsciously, so that he might read the name at once, and have done with it. Then he opened his eyes, and read. The name was his own!

The vicar looked out of his window upon his garden, but the spring morning had lost its charm for him.

Autumn Sunshine

William Trevor

The rectory was in County Wexford, eight miles from Enniscorthy. It was a handsome eighteenth-century house, with Virginia creeper covering three sides and a tangled garden full of buddleia and struggling japonica which had always been too much for its incumbents. It stood alone, seeming lonely even, approximately at the centre of the country parish it served. Its church – St Michael's Church of Ireland – was two miles away, in the village of Boharbawn.

For twenty-six years the Morans had lived there, not wishing to live anywhere else. Canon Moran had never been an ambitious man; his wife, Frances, had found contentment easy to attain in her lifetime. Their four girls had been born in the rectory, and had become a happy family there. They were grown up now, Frances's death was still recent: like the rectory itself, its remaining occupant was alone in the countryside. The death had occurred in the spring of the year, and the summer had somehow been bearable. The clergyman's eldest daughter had spent May and part of June at the rectory with her children. Another one had brought her family for most of August, and a third was to bring her newly married husband in the winter. At Christmas nearly all of them would gather at the rectory and some would come at Easter. But that September, as the days drew in, the season was melancholy.

Then, one Tuesday morning, Slattery brought a letter from

Canon Moran's youngest daughter. There were two other letters as well, in unsealed buff envelopes which meant that they were either bills or receipts. Frail and grey-haired in his elderliness, Canon Moran had been wondering if he should give the lawn in front of the house a last cut when he heard the approach of Slattery's van. The lawn-mower was the kind that had to be pushed, and in the spring the job was always easier if the grass had been cropped close at the end of the previous summer.

'Isn't that a great bit of weather, Canon?' Slattery remarked, winding down the window of the van and passing out the three envelopes. 'We're set for a while, would you say?'

'I hope so, certainly.'

'Ah, we surely are, sir.'

The conversation continued for a few moments longer, as it did whenever Slattery came to the rectory. The postman was young and easy-going, not long the successor to old Mr O'Brien, who'd been making the round on a bicycle when the Morans first came to the rectory in 1952. Mr O'Brien used to talk about his garden; Slattery talked about fishing, and often brought a share of his catch to the rectory.

'It's a great time of year for it,' he said now, 'except for the darkness coming in.'

Canon Moran smiled and nodded; the van turned round on the gravel, dust rising behind it as it moved swiftly down the avenue to the road. Everyone said Slattery drove too fast.

He carried the letters to a wooden seat on the edge of the lawn he'd been wondering about cutting. Deirdre's handwriting hadn't changed since she'd been a child; it was round and neat, not at all a reflection of the girl she was. The blue English stamp, the Queen in profile blotched a bit by the London postmark, wasn't on its side or half upside down, as you might possibly expect with Deirdre. Of all the Moran children, she'd grown up to be the only difficult one. She hadn't come to the funeral and hadn't written about her mother's death. She hadn't been to the rectory for three years.

I'm sorry, she wrote now. *I couldn't stop crying actually. I've never known anyone as nice or as generous as she was. For ages I didn't even want to believe she was dead. I went on imagining her in the rectory and doing the flowers in church and shopping in Enniscorthy.*

Deirdre was twenty-one now. He and Frances had hoped she'd go to Trinity and settle down, but although at school she'd seemed to be the cleverest of their children she'd had no desire to become a student. She'd taken the Rosslare boat to Fishguard one night, having said she was going to spend a week with her friend Maeve Coles in Cork. They hadn't known she'd gone to England until they received a picture postcard from London telling them not to worry, saying she'd found work in an egg-packing factory.

Well, I'm coming back for a little while now, she wrote, *if you could put up with me and if you wouldn't find it too much. I'll cross over to Rosslare on the 29th, the morning crossing, and then I'll come on to Enniscorthy on the bus. I don't know what time it will be but there's a pub just by where the bus drops you so could we meet in the small bar there at six o'clock and then I won't have to lug my cases too far? I hope you won't mind going into such a place. If you can't make it, or don't want to see me, it's understandable, so if you don't turn up by half six I'll see if I can get a bus on up to Dublin. Only I need to get back to Ireland for a while.*

It was, as he and Slattery had agreed, a lovely autumn. Gentle sunshine mellowed the old garden, casting an extra sheen of gold on leaves that were gold already. Roses that had been ebullient in June and July bloomed modestly now. Michaelmas daisies were just beginning to bud. Already the crab-apples were falling, hydrangeas had a forgotten look. Canon Moran carried the letter from his daughter into the walled vegetable garden and leaned against the side of the greenhouse, half sitting on a protruding ledge, reading the letter again. Panes of glass were broken in the greenhouse, white paint and putty needed to be renewed, but inside a vine still thrived, and was heavy now with black ripe fruit. Later that morning he would pick some and drive into Enniscorthy, to sell the grapes to Mrs Neary in Slaney Street.

Love, Deirdre: the letter was marvellous. Beyond the rectory the fields of wheat had been harvested, and the remaining stubble had the same tinge of gold in the autumn light; the beech trees and the chestnuts were triumphantly magnificent. But decay and rotting were only weeks away, and the letter from Deirdre was full of life. '*Love, Deirdre*' were words more beautiful than all the season's glories. He prayed as he leaned against the sunny greenhouse, thanking God for this salvation.

For all the years of their marriage Frances had been a help. As a younger man, Canon Moran hadn't known quite what to do. He'd been at a loss among his parishioners, hesitating in the face of this weakness or that: the pregnancy of Alice Pratt in 1954, the argument about grazing rights between Mr Willoughby and Eugene Dunlevy in 1960, the theft of an altar cloth from St Michael's and reports that Mrs Tobin had been seen wearing it as a skirt. Alice Pratt had been going out with a Catholic boy, one of Father Gowan's flock, which made the matter more difficult than ever. Eugene Dunlevy was one of Father Gowan's also, and so was Mrs Tobin.

'Father Gowan and I had a chat,' Frances had said, and she'd had a chat as well with Alice Pratt's mother. A month later Alice Pratt married the Catholic boy, but to this day attended St

Michael's every Sunday, the children going to Father Gowan. Mrs Tobin was given Hail Marys to say by the priest; Mr Willoughby agreed that his father had years ago granted Eugene Dunlevy the grazing rights. Everything, in these cases and in many others, had come out all right in the end: order emerged from the confusion that Canon Moran so disliked, and it was Frances who had always begun the process, though no one ever said in the rectory that she understood the mystery of people as well as he understood the teachings of the New Testament. She'd been a freckle-faced girl when he'd married her, pretty in her way. He was the one with the brains.

Frances had seen human frailty everywhere: it was weakness in people, she said, that made them what they were as much as strength did. And she herself had her own share of such frailty, falling short in all sorts of ways of the God's image her husband preached about. With the small amount of housekeeping money she could be allowed she was a spendthrift, and she said she was lazy. She loved clothes and often overreached herself on visits to Dublin; she sat in the sun while the rectory gathered dust and the garden became rank; it was only where people were concerned that she was practical. But for what she was her husband had loved her with unobtrusive passion for fifty years, appreciating her conversation and the help she'd given him because she could so easily sense the truth. When he'd found her dead in the garden one morning he'd felt he had lost some part of himself.

Though many months had passed since then, the trouble was that Frances hadn't yet become a ghost. Her being alive was still too recent, the shock of her death too raw. He couldn't distance himself; the past refused to be the past. Often he thought that her fingerprints were still in the rectory, and when he picked the grapes or cut the grass of the lawn it was impossible not to pause and remember other years. Autumn had been her favourite time.

* * *

'Of course I'd come,' he said. 'Of course, dear. Of course.'

'I haven't treated you very well.'

'It's over and done with, Deirdre.'

She smiled, and it was nice to see her smile again, although it was strange to be sitting in the back bar of a public house in Enniscorthy. He saw her looking at him, her eyes passing over his clerical collar and black clothes, and his quiet face. He could feel her thinking that he had aged, and putting it down to the death of the wife he'd been so fond of.

'I'm sorry I didn't write,' she said.

'You explained in your letter, Deirdre.'

'It was ages before I knew about it. That was an old address you wrote to.'

'I guessed.'

In turn he examined her. Years ago she'd had her long hair cut. It was short now, like a black cap on her head. And her face had lost its chubbiness; hollows where her cheeks had been made her eyes more dominant, pools of seaweed green. He remembered her child's stocky body, and the uneasy adolescence that had spoilt the family's serenity. Her voice had lost its Irish intonation.

'I'd have met you off the boat, you know.'

'I didn't want to bother you with that.'

'Oh, now, it isn't far, Deirdre.'

She drank Irish whiskey, and smoked a brand of cigarettes called Three Castles. He'd asked for a mineral himself, and the woman serving them had brought him a bottle of something that looked like water but which fizzed up when she'd poured it. A kind of lemonade he imagined it was, and didn't much care for it.

'I have grapes for Mrs Neary,' he said.

'Who's that?'

'She has a shop in Slaney Street. We always sold her the grapes. You remember?'

She didn't, and he reminded her of the vine in the greenhouse.

A shop surely wouldn't be open at this hour of the evening, she said, forgetting that in a country town of course it would be. She asked if the cinema was still the same in Enniscorthy, a cement building half-way up a hill. She said she remembered bicycling home from it at night with her sisters, not being able to keep up with them. She asked after her sisters and he told her about the two marriages that had taken place since she'd left: she had in-laws she'd never met, and nephews and a niece.

They left the bar, and he drove his dusty black Vauxhall straight to the small shop he'd spoken of. She remained in the car while he carried into the shop two large chip-baskets full of grapes. Afterwards Mrs Neary came to the door with him.

'Well, is that Deirdre?' she said as Deirdre wound down the window of the car. 'I'd never know you, Deirdre.'

'She's come back for a little while,' Canon Moran explained, raising his voice a little because he was walking round the car to the driver's seat as he spoke.

'Well, isn't that grand?' said Mrs Neary.

Everyone in Enniscorthy knew Deirdre had just gone off, but it didn't matter now. Mrs Neary's husband, who was a red-cheeked man with a cap, much smaller than his wife, appeared beside her in the shop doorway. He inclined his head in greeting, and Deirdre smiled and waved at both of them. Canon Moran thought it was pleasant when she went on waving while he drove off.

In the rectory he lay wakeful that night, his mind excited by Deirdre's presence. He would have loved Frances to know, and guessed that she probably did. He fell asleep at half-past two and dreamed that he and Frances were young again, that Deirdre was still a baby. The freckles on Frances's face were out in profusion, for they were sitting in the sunshine in the garden, tea things spread about them, the children playing some game among the shrubs. It was autumn then also, the last of the September heat. But because he was younger in his dream he didn't feel part of the season himself, or sense its melancholy.

* * *

A week went by. The time passed slowly because a lot was happening, or so it seemed. Deirdre insisted on cooking all the meals and on doing the shopping in Boharbawn's single shop or in Enniscorthy. She still smoked her endless cigarettes, but the peakiness there had been in her face when she'd first arrived wasn't quite so pronounced – or perhaps, he thought, he'd become used to it. She told him about the different jobs she'd had in London and the different places she'd lived in, because on the postcards she'd occasionally sent there hadn't been room to go into detail. In the rectory they had always hoped she'd managed to get a training of some sort, though guessing she hadn't. In fact, her jobs had been of the most rudimentary kind: as well as her spell in the egg-packing factory, there'd been a factory that made plastic earphones, a cleaning job in a hotel near Euston, and a year working for the Use-Us Office Cleansing Service. 'But you can't have liked any of that work, Deirdre?' he suggested, and she agreed she hadn't.

From the way she spoke he felt that that period of her life was over: adolescence was done with, she had steadied and taken stock. He didn't suggest to her that any of this might be so, not wishing to seem either too anxious or too pleased, but he felt she had returned to the rectory in a very different frame of mind from the one in which she'd left it. He imagined she would remain for quite a while, still taking stock, and in a sense occupying her mother's place. He thought he recognized in her a loneliness that matched his own, and he wondered if it was a feeling that their loneliness might be shared which had brought her back at this particular time. Sitting in the drawing-room while she cooked or washed up, or gathering grapes in the greenhouse while she did the shopping, he warmed delightedly to this theme. It seemed like an act of God that their circumstances should interlace this autumn. By Christmas she would know what she wanted to do with her life, and in the spring that followed she would perhaps be ready to set forth again. A year would have passed since the death of Frances.

'I have a friend,' Deirdre said when they were having a cup of coffee together in the middle of one morning. 'Someone who's been good to me.'

She had carried a tray to where he was composing next week's sermon, sitting on the wooden seat by the lawn at the front of the house. He laid aside his exercise book, and a pencil and a rubber. 'Who's that?' he enquired.

'Someone called Harold.'

He nodded, stirring sugar into his coffee.

'I want to tell you about Harold, Father. I want you to meet him.'

'Yes, of course.'

She lit a cigarette. She said, 'We have a lot in common. I mean, he's the only person . . .'

She faltered and then hesitated. She lifted her cigarette to her lips and drew on it.

He said, 'Are you fond of him, Deirdre?'

'Yes, I am.'

Another silence gathered. She smoked and drank her coffee. He added more sugar to his.

'Of course I'd like to meet him,' he said.

'Could he come to stay with us, Father? Would you mind? Would it be all right?'

'Of course I wouldn't mind. I'd be delighted.'

Harold was summoned, and arrived at Rosslare a few days later. In the meantime Deirdre had explained to her father that her friend was an electrician by trade and had let it fall that he was an intellectual kind of person. She borrowed the old Vauxhall and drove it to Rosslare to meet him, returning to the rectory in the early evening.

'How d'you do?' Canon Moran said, stretching out a hand in

the direction of an angular youth with a birthmark on his face. His dark hair was cut very short, cropped almost. He was wearing a black leather jacket.

'I'm fine,' Harold said.

'You've had a good journey?'

'Lousy, 'smatter of fact, Mr Moran.'

Harold's voice was strongly Cockney, and Canon Moran wondered if Deirdre had perhaps picked up some of her English vowel sounds from it. But then he realized that most people in London would speak like that, as people did on the television and the wireless. It was just a little surprising that Harold and Deirdre should have so much in common, as they clearly had from the affectionate way they held one another's hand. None of the other Moran girls had gone in so much for holding hands in front of the family.

He was to sit in the drawing-room, they insisted, while they made supper in the kitchen, so he picked up the *Irish Times* and did as he was bidden. Half an hour later Harold appeared and said that the meal was ready: fried eggs and sausages and bacon, and some tinned beans. Canon Moran said grace.

Having stated that County Wexford looked great, Harold didn't say much else. He didn't smile much, either. His afflicted face bore an edgy look, as if he'd never become wholly reconciled to his birthmark. It was like a scarlet map on his left cheek, a shape that reminded Canon Moran of the toe of Italy. Poor fellow, he thought. And yet a birthmark was so much less to bear than other afflictions there could be.

'Harold's fascinated actually,' Deirdre said, 'by Ireland.'

Her friend didn't add anything to that remark for a moment, even though Canon Moran smiled and nodded interestedly. Eventually Harold said, 'The struggle of the Irish people.'

'I didn't know a thing about Irish history,' Deirdre said. 'I mean, not anything that made sense.'

The conversation lapsed at this point, leaving Canon Moran

greatly puzzled. He began to say that Irish history had always been of considerable interest to him also, that it had a good story to it, its tragedy uncomplicated. But the other two didn't appear to understand what he was talking about and so he changed the subject. It was a particularly splendid autumn, he pointed out.

'Harold doesn't go in for anything like that,' Deirdre replied.

During the days that followed Harold began to talk more, surprising Canon Moran with almost everything he said. Deirdre had been right to say he was fascinated by Ireland, and it wasn't just a tourist's fascination. Harold had read widely: he spoke of ancient battles, and of the plantations of James I and Elizabeth, of Robert Emmet and the Mitchelstown martyrs, of Pearse and de Valera. 'The struggle of the Irish people' was the expression he most regularly employed. It seemed to Canon Moran that the relationship between Harold and Deirdre had a lot to do with Harold's fascination, as though his interest in Deirdre's native land had somehow caused him to become interested in Deirdre herself.

There was something else as well. Fascinated by Ireland, Harold hated his own country. A sneer whispered through his voice when he spoke of England: a degenerate place, he called it, destroyed by class-consciousness and the unjust distribution of wealth. He described in detail the city of Nottingham, to which he appeared to have a particular aversion. He spoke of unnecessary motorways and the stupidity of bureaucracy, the stifling presence of a Royal family. 'You could keep an Indian village,' he claimed, 'on what those corgis eat. You could house five hundred homeless in Buckingham Palace.' There was brainwashing by television and the newspaper barons. No ordinary person had a chance because pap was fed to the ordinary person, a deliberate policy going back into Victorian times when education and religion had been geared to the enslavement of minds. The English people had brought it on themselves, having lost their spunk, settling instead for consumer durables. 'What better can you expect,' Harold demanded, 'after the hypocrisy of that empire the bosses ran?'

Deirdre didn't appear to find anything specious in this line of talk, which surprised her father. 'Oh, I wonder about that,' he said himself from time to time, but he said it mildly, not wishing to cause an argument, and in any case his interjections were not acknowledged. Quite a few of the criticisms Harold levelled at his own country could be levelled at Ireland also and, Canon Moran guessed, at many countries throughout the world. It was strange that the two neighbouring islands had been so picked out, although once Germany was mentioned and the point made that developments beneath the surface there were a hopeful sign, that a big upset was on the way.

'We're taking a walk,' Harold said one afternoon. 'She's going to show me Kinsella's Barn.'

Canon Moran nodded, saying to himself that he disliked Harold. It was the first time he had admitted it, but the feeling was familiar. The less generous side of his nature had always emerged when his daughters brought to the rectory the men they'd become friendly with or even proposed to marry. Emma, the eldest girl, had brought several before settling in the end for Thomas. Linda had brought only John, already engaged to him. Una had married Carley not long after the death, and Carley had not yet visited the rectory: Canon Moran had met him in Dublin, where the wedding had taken place, for in the circumstances Una had not been married from home. Carley was an older man, an importer of tea and wine, stout and flushed, certainly not someone Canon Moran would have chosen for his second-youngest daughter. But, then, he had thought the same about Emma's Thomas and about Linda's John.

Thomas was a farmer, sharing a sizeable acreage with his father in Co. Meath. He always brought to mind the sarcasm of an old schoolmaster who in Canon Moran's distant schooldays used to refer to a gang of boys at the back of the classroom as 'farmers' sons', meaning that not much could be expected of them. It was an inaccurate assumption but even now, whenever Canon Moran found himself in the company of Thomas, he couldn't help recalling it. Thomas was mostly silent, with a good-natured smile that came slowly and lingered too long. According to his father, and there was no reason to doubt the claim, he was a good judge of beef cattle.

Linda's John was the opposite. Wiry and suave, he was making his way in the Bank of Ireland, at present stationed in Waterford. He had a tiny orange-coloured moustache and was good at golf. Linda's ambition for him was that he should become the Bank of Ireland's manager in Limerick or Galway, where the insurances that went with the position were particularly lucrative. Unlike Thomas, John talked all the time, telling jokes and stories about the Bank of Ireland's customers.

'Nothing is perfect,' Frances used to say, chiding her husband for an uncharitableness he did his best to combat. He disliked being so particular about the men his daughters chose, and he was aware that other people saw them differently: Thomas would do anything for you, John was fun, the middle-aged Carley laid his success at Una's feet. But whoever the husbands of his daughters had been, Canon Moran knew he'd have felt the same. He was jealous of the husbands because ever since his daughters had been born he had loved them unstintingly. When he had prayed after Frances's death he'd felt jealous of God, who had taken her from him.

'There's nothing much to see,' he pointed out when Harold announced that Deirdre was going to show him Kinsella's Barn. 'Just the ruin of a wall is all that's left.'

'Harold's interested, Father.'

They set off on their walk, leaving the old clergyman ashamed that he could not like Harold more. It wasn't just his griminess: there was something sinister about Harold, something furtive about the way he looked at you, peering at you cruelly out of his afflicted face, not meeting your eye. Why was he so fascinated about a country that wasn't his own? Why did he refer so often to 'Ireland's struggle' as if that struggle particularly concerned him? He hated walking, he had said, yet he'd just set out to walk six miles through woods and fields to examine a ruined wall.

Canon Moran had wondered as suspiciously about Thomas and John and Carley, privately questioning every statement they made, finding hidden motives everywhere. He'd hated the thought of his daughters being embraced or even touched, and had forced himself not to think about that. He'd prayed, ashamed of himself then, too. 'It's just a frailty in you,' Frances had said, her favourite way of cutting things down to size.

He sat for a while in the afternoon sunshine, letting all of it hang in his mind. It would be nice if they quarrelled on their walk. It would be nice if they didn't speak when they returned, if Harold simply went away. But that wouldn't happen, because they had come to the rectory with a purpose. He didn't know why he thought that, but he knew it was true: they had come for a reason, something that was all tied up with Harold's fascination and with the kind of person Harold was, with his cold eyes and his afflicted face.

In March 1798 an incident had taken place in Kinsella's Barn, which at that time had just been a barn. Twelve men and women, accused of harbouring insurgents, had been tied together with ropes at the command of a Sergeant James. They had been led through the village of Boharbawn, the Sergeant's soldiers on horseback on either side of the procession, the Sergeant himself bringing up the rear. Designed as an act of education, an example to the inhabitants of Boharbawn and the country people around, the twelve had been herded into a barn owned by a farmer called Kinsella and there burned to death. Kinsella, who had played no part either in the harbouring of insurgents or in the execution of the twelve, was afterwards murdered by his own farm-labourers.

'Sergeant James was a Nottingham man,' Harold said that evening at supper. 'A soldier of fortune who didn't care what he did. Did you know he acquired great wealth, Mr Moran?'

'No, I wasn't at all aware of that,' Canon Moran replied.

'Harold found out about him,' Deirdre said.

'He used to boast he was responsible for the death of a thousand Irish people. It was in Boharbawn he reached the thousand. They rewarded him well for that.'

'Not much is known about Sergeant James locally. Just the legend of Kinsella's Barn.'

'No way it's a legend.'

Deirdre nodded; Canon Moran did not say anything. They were eating cooked ham and salad. On the table there was a cake which Deirdre had bought in McGovern's in Enniscorthy, and a pot of tea. There were several bunches of grapes from the greenhouse, and a plate of wafer biscuits. Harold was fond of salad cream, Canon Moran had noticed; he had a way of hitting the base of the jar with his hand, causing large dollops to spurt all over his ham. He didn't place his knife and fork together on the plate when he'd finished, but just left them anyhow. His fingernails were edged with black.

'You'd feel sick,' he was saying now, working the salad cream again. 'You'd stand there looking at that wall and you'd feel a revulsion in your stomach.'

'What I meant,' Canon Moran said, 'is that it has passed into local legend. No one doubts it took place; there's no question about that. But two centuries have almost passed.'

'And nothing has changed,' Harold interjected. 'The Irish people still share their bondage with the twelve in Kinsella's Barn.'

'Round here of course –'

'It's not round here that matters, Mr Moran. The struggle's worldwide; the sickness is everywhere actually.'

Again Deirdre nodded. She was like a zombie, her father

201

thought. She was being used because she was an Irish girl; she was Harold's Irish connection, and in some almost frightening way she believed herself in love with him. Frances had once said they'd made a mistake with her. She had wondered if Deirdre had perhaps found all the love they'd offered her too much to bear. They were quite old when Deirdre was a child, the last expression of their own love. She was special because of that.

'At least Kinsella got his chips,' Harold pursued, his voice relentless. 'At least that's something.'

Canon Moran protested. The owner of the barn had been an innocent man, he pointed out. The barn had simply been a convenient one, large enough for the purpose, with heavy stones near it that could be piled up against the door before the conflagration. Kinsella, that day, had been miles away, ditching a field.

'It's too long ago to say where he was,' Harold retorted swiftly. 'And if he was keeping a low profile in a ditch it would have been by arrangement with the imperial forces.'

When Harold said that, there occurred in Canon Moran's mind a flash of what appeared to be the simple truth. Harold was an Englishman who had espoused a cause because it was one through which the status quo in his own country might be damaged. Similar such Englishmen, read about in newspapers, stirred in the clergyman's mind: men from Ealing and Liverpool and Wolverhampton who had changed their names to Irish names, who had even learned the Irish language, in order to ingratiate themselves with the new Irish revolutionaries. Such men dealt out death and chaos, announcing that their conscience insisted on it.

'Well, we'd better wash the dishes,' Deirdre said, and Harold rose obediently to help her.

The walk to Kinsella's Barn had taken place on a Saturday afternoon. The following morning Canon Moran conducted his services in St Michael's, addressing his small Protestant congregation, twelve at Holy Communion, eighteen at morning service. He had prepared a sermon about repentance, taking as his text St Luke, 15:32: . . . *for this thy brother was dead, and is alive again; and was lost, and is found.* But at the last moment he changed his mind and spoke instead of the incident in Kinsella's Barn nearly two centuries ago. He tried to make the point that one horror should not fuel another, that passing time contained its own forgiveness. Deirdre and Harold were naturally not in the church, but they'd been present at breakfast, Harold frying eggs on the kitchen stove, Deirdre pouring tea. He had looked at them and tried to think of them as two young people on holiday. He had tried to tell himself they'd come to the rectory for a rest and for his blessing, that he should be grateful instead of fanciful. It was for his blessing that Emma had brought Thomas to the rectory, that Linda had brought John. Una would bring Carley in November. 'Now, don't be silly,' Frances would have said.

'The man Kinsella was innocent of everything,' he heard his voice insisting in his church. 'He should never have been murdered also.'

Harold would have delighted in the vengeance exacted on an innocent man. Harold wanted to inflict pain, to cause suffering and destruction. The end justified the means for Harold, even if the end was an artificial one, a pettiness grandly dressed up. In his sermon Canon Moran spoke of such matters without mentioning Harold's name. He spoke of how evil drained people of their humour and compassion, how people pretended even to themselves. It was worse than Frances's death, he thought, as his voice continued in the church: it was worse that Deirdre should be part of wickedness.

He could tell that his parishioners found his sermon odd, and he didn't blame them. He was confused, and naturally distressed. In the rectory Deirdre and Harold would be waiting for him. They would all sit down to Sunday lunch while plans for atrocities filled Harold's mind, while Deirdre loved him.

'Are you well again, Mrs Davis?' he enquired at the church door of a woman who suffered from asthma.

'Not too bad, Canon. Not too bad, thank you.'

He spoke to all the others, enquiring about health, remarking on the beautiful autumn. They were farmers mostly and displayed a farmer's gratitude for the satisfactory season. He wondered suddenly who'd replace him among them when he retired or died. Father Gowan had had to give up a year ago. The young man, Father White, was always in a hurry.

'Goodbye so, Canon,' Mr Willoughby said, shaking hands as he always did, every Sunday. It was a long time since there'd been the trouble about Eugene Dunlevy's grazing rights; three years ago Mr Willoughby had been left a widower himself. 'You're managing all right, Canon?' he asked, as he also always did.

'Yes, I'm all right, thank you, Mr Willoughby.'

Someone else enquired if Deirdre was still at the rectory, and he said she was. Heads nodded, the unspoken thought being that that was nice for him, his youngest daughter at home again after all these years. There was forgiveness in several faces, forgiveness of Deirdre, who had been thoughtless to go off to an egg-packing factory. There was the feeling, also unexpressed, that the young were a bit like that.

'Goodbye,' he said in a general way. Car doors banged, engines started. In the vestry he removed his surplice and his cassock and hung them in a cupboard.

'We'll probably go tomorrow,' Deirdre said during lunch.

'Go?'

'We'll probably take the Dublin bus.'

'I'd like to see Dublin,' Harold said.

'And then you're returning to London?'

'We're easy about that,' Harold interjected before Deirdre

could reply. 'I'm a tradesman, Mr Moran, an electrician.'

'I know you're an electrician, Harold.'

'What I mean is, I'm on my own; I'm not answerable to the bosses. There's always a bob or two waiting in London.'

For some reason Canon Moran felt that Harold was lying. There was a quickness about the way he'd said they were easy about their plans, and it didn't seem quite to make sense, the logic of not being answerable to bosses and a bob or two always waiting for him. Harold was being evasive about their movements, hiding the fact that they would probably remain in Dublin for longer than he implied, meeting other people like himself.

'It was good of you to have us,' Deirdre said that evening, all three of them sitting around the fire in the drawing-room because the evenings had just begun to get chilly. Harold was reading a book about Che Guevara and hadn't spoken for several hours. 'We've enjoyed it, Father.'

'It's been nice having you, Deirdre.'

'I'll write to you from London.'

It was safe to say that: he knew she wouldn't because she hadn't before, until she'd wanted something. She wouldn't write to thank him for the rectory's hospitality, and that would be quite in keeping. Harold was the same kind of man as Sergeant James had been: it didn't matter that they were on different sides. Sergeant James had maybe borne an affliction also, a humped back or a withered arm. He had ravaged a country that existed then for its spoils, and his most celebrated crime was neatly at hand so that another Englishman could make matters worse by attempting to make amends. In Harold's view the trouble had always been that these acts of war and murder died beneath the weight of print in history books, and were forgotten. But history could be rewritten, and for that Kinsella's Barn was an inspiration: Harold had journeyed to it as people make journeys to holy places.

'Yes?' Deirdre said, for while these reflections had passed

through his mind he had spoken her name, wanting to ask her to tell him the truth about her friend.

He shook his head. 'I wish you could have seen your mother again,' he said instead. 'I wish she were here now.'

The faces of his three sons-in-law irrelevantly appeared in his mind: Carley's flushed cheeks, Thomas's slow good-natured smile, John's little moustache. It astonished him that he'd ever felt suspicious of their natures, for they would never let his daughters down. But Deirdre had turned her back on the rectory, and what could be expected when she came back with a man? She had never been like Emma or Linda or Una, none of whom smoked Three Castles cigarettes and wore clothes that didn't seem quite clean. It was impossible to imagine any of them becoming involved with a revolutionary, a man who wanted to commit atrocities.

'He was just a farmer, you know,' he heard himself saying. 'Kinsella.'

Surprise showed in Deirdre's face. 'It was Mother we were talking about,' she reminded him, and he could see her trying to connect her mother with a farmer who had died two hundred years ago, and not being able to. Elderliness, he could see her thinking. 'Only time he wandered,' she would probably say to her friend.

'It was good of you to come, Deirdre.'

He looked at her, far into her eyes, admitting to himself that she had always been his favourite. When the other girls were busily growing up she had still wanted to sit on his knee. She'd had a way of interrupting him no matter what he was doing, arriving beside him with a book she wanted him to read to her.

'Goodbye, Father,' she said the next morning while they waited in Enniscorthy for the Dublin bus. 'Thank you for everything.'

'Yeah, thanks a ton, Mr Moran,' Harold said.

'Goodbye, Harold. Goodbye, my dear.'

He watched them finding their seats when the bus arrived and

206

then he drove the old Vauxhall back to Boharbawn, meeting Slattery in his postman's van and returning his salute. There was shopping he should have done, meat and potatoes, and tins of things to keep him going. But his mind was full of Harold's afflicted face and his black-rimmed fingernails, and Deirdre's hand in his. And then flames burst from the straw that had been packed around living people in Kinsella's Barn. They burned through the wood of the barn itself, revealing the writhing bodies. On his horse the man called Sergeant James laughed.

Canon Moran drove the car into the rectory's ramshackle garage, and walked around the house to the wooden seat on the front lawn. Frances should come now with two cups of coffee, appearing at the front door with the tray and then crossing the gravel and the lawn. He saw her as she had been when first they came to the rectory, when only Emma had been born; but the grey-haired Frances was somehow there as well, shadowing her youth. 'Funny little Deirdre,' she said, placing the tray on the seat between them.

It seemed to him that everything that had just happened in the rectory had to do with Frances, with meeting her for the first time when she was eighteen, with loving her and marrying her. He knew it was a trick of the autumn sunshine that again she crossed the gravel and the lawn, no more than pretence that she handed him a cup and saucer. 'Harold's just a talker,' she said. 'Not at all like Sergeant James.'

He sat for a while longer on the wooden seat, clinging to these words, knowing they were true. Of course it was cowardice that ran through Harold, inspiring the whisper of his sneer when he spoke of the England he hated so. In the presence of a befuddled girl and an old Irish clergyman England was an easy target, and Ireland's troubles a kind of target also.

Frances laughed, and for the first time her death seemed far away, as her life did too. In the rectory the visitors had blurred her fingerprints to nothing, and had made of her a ghost that could come back. The sunshine warmed him as he sat there, the garden was less melancholy than it had been.

The Traveller

R. H. Benson

'I am amazed, not that the Traveller returns from that
Bourne, but that he returns so seldom.'

The Pilgrim's Way

On one of these evenings as we sat together after dinner in front
of the wide open fireplace in the central room of the house, we
began to talk on that old subject – the relation of Science to
Faith.

'It is no wonder,' said the priest, 'if their conclusions appear
to differ, to shallow minds who think that the last words are
being said on both sides; because their standpoints are so
different. The scientific view is that you are not justified in
committing yourself one inch ahead of your intellectual evidence:
the religious view is that in order to find out anything worth
knowing your faith must always be a little in advance of your
evidence; you must advance *en échelon*. There is the principle of
our Lord's promises. "Act as if it were true, and light will be
given." The scientist on the other hand says, "Do not presume to
commit yourself until light is given." The difference between the
methods lies, of course, in the fact that Religion admits the heart
and the whole man to the witness-box, while Science only admits
the head – scarcely even the senses. Yet surely the evidence of
experience is on the side of Religion. Every really great
achievement is inspired by motives of the heart, and not of the

head; by feeling and passion, not by a calculation of probabilities. And so are the mysteries of God unveiled by those who carry them first by assault: "The Kingdom of Heaven suffereth violence; and the violent take it by force."

'For example,' he continued after a moment, 'the scientific view of haunted houses is that there is no evidence for them beyond that which may be accounted for by telepathy, a kind of thought-reading. Yet if you can penetrate that veneer of scientific thought that is so common now, you find that by far the larger part of mankind still believes in them. Practically not one of us really accepts the scientific view as an adequate one.'

'Have you ever had an experience of that kind yourself?' I asked.

'Well,' said the priest, smiling, 'you are sure you will not laugh at it? There is nothing commoner than to think such things a subject for humour; and that I cannot bear. Each such story is sacred to one person at the very least, and therefore should be to all reverent people.'

I assured him that I would not treat his story with disrespect.

'Well,' he answered, 'I do not think you will, and I will tell you. It only happened a very few years ago. This was how it began:

'A friend of mine was, and is still, in charge of a church in Kent, which I will not name; but it is within twenty miles of Canterbury. The district fell into Catholic hands a good many years ago. I received a telegram, in this house, a day or two before Christmas, from my friend, saying that he had been suddenly seized with a very bad attack of influenza, which was devastating Kent at that time; and asking me to come down, if possible at once, and take his place over Christmas. I had only lately given up active work owing to growing infirmity, but it was impossible to resist this appeal; so Parker packed my things and we went together by the next train.

'I found my friend really ill, and quite incapable of doing

anything; so I assured him that I could manage perfectly, and that he need not be anxious.

'On the next day, a Wednesday, and Christmas Eve, I went down to the little church to hear confessions. It was a beautiful old church, though tiny, and full of interesting things: the old altar had been set up again; there was a rood-loft with a staircase leading on to it; and an awmbry on the north of the sanctuary had been fitted up as a receptacle for the Most Holy Sacrament, instead of the old hanging pyx. One of the most interesting discoveries made in the church was that of the old confessional. In the lower half of the rood-screen, on the south side, a square hole had been found, filled up with an insertion of oak; but an antiquarian of the Alcuin Club, whom my friend had asked to examine the church, declared that this without doubt was the place where in the pre-Reformation times confessions were heard. So it had been restored, and put to its ancient use; and now on this Christmas Eve I sat within the chancel in the dim fragrant light, while penitents came and knelt outside the screen on the single step, and made their confessions through the old opening.

'I know this is a great platitude, but I never can look at a piece of old furniture without a curious thrill at a thing that has been so much saturated with human emotion; but, above all that I have ever seen, I think that this old confessional moved me. Through that little opening had come so many thousands of sins, great and little, weighted with sorrow; and back again, in Divine exchange for those burdens, had returned the balm of the Saviour's blood. "Behold! a door opened in heaven", through which that strange commerce of sin and grace may be carried on – grace pressed down and running over, given into the bosom in exchange for sin. *O bonum commercium!*'

The priest was silent for a moment, his eyes glowing. Then he went on.

'Well, Christmas Day and the three following festivals passed away very happily. On the Sunday night after service, as I came out of the vestry, I saw a child waiting. She told me, when I asked her if she wanted me, that her father and others of her family wished to make their confessions on the following evening about six o'clock. They had had influenza in the house, and had not been able to come out before; but the father was going to work next day, as he was so much better, and would come, if it pleased me, and some of his children to make their confessions in the evening and their communions the following morning.

'Monday dawned, and I offered the Holy Sacrifice as usual, and spent the morning chiefly with my friend, who was now able to sit up and talk a good deal, though he was not yet allowed to leave his bed.

'In the afternoon I went for a walk.

'All the morning there had rested a depression on my soul such as I have not often felt; it was of a peculiar quality. Every soul that tries, however poorly, to serve God, knows by experience those heavinesses by which our Lord tests and confirms His own; but it was not like that. An element of terror mingled with it, as of impending evil.

'As I started for my walk along the high road this depression deepened. There seemed no physical reason for it that I could perceive. I was well myself, and the weather was fair; yet air and exercise did not affect it. I turned at last, about half-past three o'clock, at a milestone that marked sixteen miles to Canterbury.

'I rested there for a moment, looking to the south-east, and saw that far on the horizon heavy clouds were gathering; and then I started homewards. As I went I heard a far-away boom, as of distant guns, and I thought at first that there was some sea-fort to the south where artillery practice was being held; but presently I noticed that it was too irregular and prolonged for the report of a gun; and then it was with a sense of relief that I came to the conclusion it was a far-away thunderstorm, for I felt that the state of the atmosphere might explain away this depression that so troubled me. The thunder seemed to come nearer, pealed more loudly three or four times and ceased.

'But I felt no relief. When I reached home a little after four Parker brought me in some tea, and I fell asleep afterwards in a chair before the fire. I was wakened after a troubled and unhappy dream by Parker bringing in my coat and telling me it was time to keep my appointment at the church. I could not remember what my dream was, but it was sinister and suggestive of evil, and, with the shreds of it still clinging to me, I looked at Parker with something of fear as he stood silently by my chair holding the coat.

'The church stood only a few steps away, for the garden and churchyard adjoined one another. As I went down carrying the lantern that Parker had lighted for me, I remember hearing far away to the south, beyond the village, the beat of a horse's hoofs. The horse seemed to be in a gallop, but presently the noise died away behind a ridge.

'When I entered the church I found that the sacristan had lighted a candle or two as I had asked him, and I could just make out the kneeling figures of three or four people in the north aisle.

'When I was ready I took my seat in the chair set beyond the screen, at the place I have described; and then, one by one, the labourer and his children came up and made their confessions. I remember feeling again, as on Christmas Eve, the strange charm of this old place of penitence, so redolent of God and man, each in his tenderest character of Saviour and penitent; with the red light burning like a luminous flower in the dark before me, to remind me of how God was indeed tabernacling with men, and was their God.

'Now I do not know how long I had been there, when again I heard the beat of a horse's hoofs, but this time in the village just below the churchyard; then again there fell a sudden silence. Then presently a gust of wind flung the door wide, and the candles began to gutter and flare in the draught. One of the girls went and closed the door.

'Presently the boy who was kneeling by me at that time finished his confession, received absolution and went down the church, and I waited for the next, not knowing how many there were.

'After waiting a minute or two I turned in my seat, and was about to get up, thinking there was no one else, when a voice whispered sharply through the hole a single sentence. I could not catch the words, but I supposed they were the usual formula for asking a blessing, so I gave the blessing and waited, a little astonished at not having heard the penitent come up.

'Then the voice began again.'

The priest stopped a moment and looked round, and I could see that he was trembling a little.

'Would you rather not go on?' I said. 'I think it disturbs you to tell me.'

'No; no,' he said; 'it is all right, but it was very dreadful – very dreadful.

'Well, the voice began again in a loud quick whisper, but the odd thing was that I could hardly understand a word; there were just phrases here and there, like the name of God and of our Lady, that I could catch. Then there were a few old French words that I knew; *le roy* came over and over again. Just at first I thought it must be some extreme form of dialect unknown to me; then I thought it must be a very old man who was deaf, because when I tried, after a few sentences, to explain that I could not understand, the penitent paid no attention, but whispered on quickly without a pause. Presently I could perceive that he was in a terrible state of mind; the voice broke and sobbed, and then almost cried out, but still in this loud whisper; then on the other side of the screen I could hear fingers working and moving uneasily, as if entreating admittance at some barred door. Then at last there was silence for a moment, and then plainly some closing formula was repeated, which gradually grew lower and ceased. Then, as I rose, meaning to come round and explain that I had not been able to hear, a loud moan or two came from the penitent. I stood up quickly and looked through the upper part of the screen, and there was no one there.

'I can give you no idea of what a shock that was to me. I stood there glaring, I suppose, through the screen down at the empty step for a moment or two, and perhaps I said something aloud, for I heard a voice from the end of the church.

'Did you call, sir?' And there stood the sacristan, with his keys and lantern, ready to lock up.

'I still stood without answering for a moment, and then I spoke; my voice sounded oddly in my ears.

' "Is there anyone else, Williams? Are they all gone?" or something like that.

'Williams lifted his lantern and looked round the dusky church.

' "No, sir; there is no one."

'I crossed the chancel to go to the vestry, but as I was half-way, suddenly again in the quiet village there broke out the desperate gallop of a horse.

' "There! there!" I cried, "do you hear that?"

'Williams came up the church towards me.

' "Are you ill, sir?" he said. "Shall I fetch your servant?"

'I made an effort and told him it was nothing; but he insisted on seeing me home: I did not like to ask him whether he had heard the gallop of the horse; for, after all, I thought, perhaps there was no connection between that and the voice that whispered.

'I felt very much shaken and disturbed; and after dinner, which I took alone of course, I thought I would go to bed very soon. On my way up, however, I looked into my friend's room for a few minutes. He seemed very bright and eager to talk, and I stayed very much longer than I had intended. I said nothing of what had happened in the church; but listened to him while he talked about the village and the neighbourhood. Finally, as I was on the point of bidding him good-night, he said something like this:

' "Well, I mustn't keep you, but I've been thinking while you've been in church of an old story that is told by antiquarians about this place. They say that one of St Thomas à Becket's murderers came here on the very evening of the murder. It is his day, today, you know, and that is what put me in mind of it, I suppose."

'While my friend said this, my old heart began to beat furiously; but, with a strong effort of self-control, I told him I should like to hear the story.

' "Oh! there's nothing much to tell," said my friend; "and they don't know who it's supposed to have been; but it is said to have been either one of the four knights, or one of the men-at-arms."

' "But how did he come here?" I asked, "and what for?"

' "Oh! he's supposed to have been in terror for his soul, and that he rushed here to get absolution, which, of course, was impossible."

' "But tell me," I said. "Did he come here alone, or how?"

' "Well, you know, after the murder they ransacked the Archbishop's house and stables; and it is said that this man got one of the fastest horses and rode like a madman, not knowing where he was going; and that he dashed into the village, and into the church where the priest was: and then afterwards, mounted again and rode off. The priest, too, is buried in the chancel somewhere, I believe. You see it's a very vague and improbable story. At the Gatehouse at Malling, too, you know, they say that one of the knights slept there the night after the murder."

'I said nothing more; but I suppose I looked strange, because my friend began to look at me with some anxiety, and then ordered me off to bed: so I took my candle and went.

'Now,' said the priest, turning to me, 'that is the story. I need

216

not say that I have thought about it a great deal ever since: and there are only two theories which appear to me credible, and two others, which would no doubt be suggested, which appear to me incredible.

'First, you may say that I was obviously unwell: my previous depression and dreaming showed that, and therefore that I dreamt the whole thing. If you wish to think that – well, you must think it.

'Secondly, you may say, with the Psychical Research Society, that the whole thing was transmitted from my friend's brain to mine; that his was in an energetic, and mine in a passive state, or something of the kind.

'These two theories would be called "scientific", which term means that they are not a hair's-breadth in advance of the facts with which the intellect, a poor instrument at the best, is capable of dealing. And these two "scientific" theories create in their own turn a new brood of insoluble difficulties.

'Or you may take your stand upon the spiritual world, and use the faculties which God has given you for dealing with it, and then you will no longer be helplessly puzzled, and your intellect will no longer overstrain itself at a task for which it was never made. And you may say, I think, that you prefer one of two theories.

'First, that human emotion has a power of influencing or saturating inanimate nature. Of course this is only the old familiar sacramental principle of all creation. The expressions of your face, for instance, caused by the shifting of the chemical particles of which it is composed, vary with your varying emotions. Thus we might say that the violent passions of hatred, anger, terror, remorse, of this poor murderer, seven hundred years ago, combined to make a potent spiritual fluid that bit so deep into the very place where it was all poured out, that under certain circumstances it is reproduced. A phonograph, for example is a very coarse parallel, in which the vibrations of sound translate themselves first into terms of wax, and then re-emerge again as vibrations when certain conditions are fulfilled.

'Or, secondly, you may be old-fashioned and simple, and say that by some law, vast and inexorable, beyond our perception, the personal spirit of the very man is chained to the place, and forced to expiate his sin again and again, year by year, by attempting to express his grief and to seek forgiveness, without the possibility of receiving it. Of course we do not know who he was; whether one of the knights who afterwards did receive absolution, which possibly was not ratified by God; or one of the men-at-arms who assisted, and who, as an anonymous chronicle says, "*sine confessione et viatico subito rapti sunt*".

'There is nothing materialistic, I think, in believing that spiritual beings may be bound to express themselves within limits of time and space; and that inanimate nature, as well as animate, may be the vehicles of the unseen. Arguments against such possibilities have surely, once for all, been silenced, for Christians at any rate, by the Incarnation and the Sacramental system, of which the whole principle is that the Infinite and Eternal did once, and does still, express itself under forms of inanimate nature, in terms of time and space.

'With regard to another point, perhaps I need not remind you that a thunderstorm broke over Canterbury on the day and hour of the actual murder of the Archbishop.'

The Rector

Margaret Oliphant

CHAPTER I

It is natural to suppose that the arrival of the new Rector was a rather exciting event for Carlingford. It is a considerable town, it is true, nowadays, but then there are no alien activities to disturb the place – no manufactures, and not much trade. And there is a very respectable amount of very good society at Carlingford. To begin with, it is a pretty place – mild, sheltered, not far from town; and naturally its very reputation for good society increases the amount of that much-prized article. The advantages of the town in this respect have already put five per cent upon the house-rents; but this, of course, only refers to the *real* town, where you can go through an entire street of high garden-walls, with houses inside full of the retired exclusive comforts, the dainty economical refinement peculiar to such places; and where the good people consider their own society as a warrant of gentility less splendid, but not less assured, than the favour of Majesty itself. Naturally there are no Dissenters in Carlingford – that is to say, none above the rank of a greengrocer or milkman; and in bosoms devoted to the Church it may be well imagined that the advent of the new Rector was an event full of importance, and even of excitement.

He was highly spoken of, everybody knew; but nobody knew who had spoken highly of him, nor had been able to find out, even by inference, what were his views. The Church had been Low during the last Rector's reign – profoundly Low – lost in the deepest abysses of Evangelicalism. A determined inclination to preach to everybody had seized upon that good man's brain; he had half emptied Salem Chapel, there could be no doubt; but, on the other hand, he had more than half filled the Chapel of St Roque, half a mile out of Carlingford, where the perpetual curate, young, handsome, and fervid, was on the very topmost pinnacle of Anglicanism. St Roque's was not more than a pleasant walk from the best quarter of Carlingford, on the north side of the town, thank heaven! which one could get at without the dread passage of that new horrid suburb, to which young Mr Rider, the young doctor, was devoting himself. But the Evangelical Rector was dead, and his reign was over, and nobody could predict what the character of the new administration was to be. The obscurity in which the new Rector had buried his views was the most extraordinary thing about him. He had taken high honours at college, and was 'highly spoken of'; but whether he was High, or Low, or Broad, muscular or sentimental, sermonizing or decorative, nobody in the world seemed able to tell.

'Fancy if he were just to be a Mr Bury over again! Fancy him going to the canal, and having sermons to the bargemen, and attending to all sorts of people except to us, whom it is his duty to attend to!' cried one of this much-canvassed clergyman's curious parishioners. 'Indeed I do believe he must be one of these people. If he were in society at all, somebody would be sure to know.'

'Lucy dear, Mr Bury christened you,' said another not less curious but more tolerant enquirer.

'Then he did you the greatest of all services,' cried the third member of the little group which discussed the new Rector under Mr Wodehouse's blossomed apple-trees. 'He conferred such a benefit upon you that he deserves all reverence at your hand. Wonderful idea! a man confers this greatest of Christian blessings on multitudes, and does not himself appreciate the boon he conveys!'

'Well, for that matter, Mr Wentworth, you know –' said the elder lady; but she got no farther. Though she was verging upon forty, leisurely, pious, and unmarried, that good Miss Wodehouse was not polemical. She had 'her own opinions', but few people knew much about them. She was seated on a green garden-bench which surrounded the great may-tree in that large, warm, well-furnished garden. The high brick walls, all clothed with fruit-trees, shut in an enclosure of which not a morsel except this velvet grass, with its nests of daisies, was not under the highest and most careful cultivation. It was such a scene as is only to be found in an old country town; the walls jealous of intrusion, yet thrusting tall plumes of lilac and stray branches of apple-blossom, like friendly salutations to the world without; within, the blossoms dropping over the light bright head of Lucy Wodehouse underneath the apple-trees, and impertinently flecking the Rev. Frank Wentworth's Anglican coat. These two last were young people, with that indefinable harmony in their looks which prompts the suggestion of 'a handsome couple' to the bystander. It had not even occurred to them to be in love with each other, so far as anybody knew, yet few were the undiscerning persons who saw them together without instinctively placing the young curate of St Roque's in permanence by Lucy's side. She was twenty, pretty, blue-eyed, and full of dimples, with a broad Leghorn hat thrown carelessly on her head, untied, with broad strings of blue ribbon falling among her fair curls – a blue which was 'repeated', according to painter jargon, in ribbons at her throat and waist. She had great gardening gloves on, and a basket and huge pair of scissors on the grass at her feet, which grass, besides, was strewed with a profusion of all the sweetest spring blossoms – the sweet narcissus, most exquisite of flowers, lilies of the valley, white and blue hyacinths, golden ranunculus globes – worlds of sober, deep-breathing wallflower. If Lucy had been doing what her kind elder sister called her 'duty', she would have been at this moment arranging her flowers in the drawing-room; but the times were rare when Lucy did her duty according to Miss Wodehouse's estimate; so instead of arranging those clusters of narcissus, she clubbed them together in her hands into a fragrant dazzling sheaf, and discussed the new Rector – not unaware, perhaps, in her secret heart, that the sweet morning, the sunshine and flowers, and exhilarating air, were somehow secretly enhanced by the presence of that black Anglican figure under the apple-trees.

'But I suppose,' said Lucy, with a sigh, 'we must wait till we see him; and if I must be very respectful of Mr Bury because he christened me, I am heartily glad the new Rector has no claim upon my reverence. I have been christened, I have been confirmed –'

'But, Lucy, my dear, the chances are he will marry you,' said Miss Wodehouse, calmly; 'indeed, there can be no doubt that it is only natural he should, for he *is* the Rector, you know; and though we go so often to St Roque's, Mr Wentworth will excuse me saying that he is a very young man.'

Miss Wodehouse was knitting; she did not see the sudden look of dismay and amazement which the curate of St Roque's darted down upon her, nor the violent sympathetic blush which blazed over both the young faces. How shocking that elderly quiet people should have such a faculty for suggestion! You may be sure Lucy Wodehouse and young Wentworth, had it not been 'put into their heads' in such an absurd fashion, would never, all their virtuous lives, have dreamt of anything but friendship. Deep silence ensued after this simple but startling speech. Miss Wodehouse knitted on, and took no notice; Lucy began to gather up the flowers into the basket, unable for her life to think of anything to say. For his part, Mr Wentworth gravely picked the apple-blossoms off his coat, and counted them in his hand. That sweet summer snow kept dropping, dropping, falling here and there as the wind carried it, and with a special attraction to Lucy and her blue ribbons; while behind, Miss Wodehouse sat calmly on the green bench, under the may-tree just beginning to bloom, without lifting her eyes from her knitting. Not far off, the bright English house, all beaming with open doors and windows, shone in the sunshine. With the white may peeping out among the green overhead, and the sweet narcissus in a great dazzling sheaf upon the grass, making all the air fragrant around them, can anybody fancy a sweeter domestic out-of-door scene? or else it seemed so to the perpetual curate of St Roque's.

Ah me! and if he was to be perpetual curate, and none of his great friends thought upon him, or had preferment to bestow, how do you suppose he could ever, ever marry Lucy Wodehouse, if they were to wait a hundred years?

Just then the garden gate – the green gate in the wall – opened to the creaking murmur of Mr Wodehouse's own key. Mr Wodehouse was a man who creaked universally. His boots were a heavy infliction upon the good-humour of his household; and like every other invariable quality of dress, the peculiarity became identified with him in every particular of his life. Everything belonging to him moved with a certain jar, except, indeed, his household, which went on noiseless wheels, thanks to Lucy and love. As he came along the garden path, the gravel started all round his unmusical foot. Miss Wodehouse alone turned round to hail her father's approach, but both the young people looked up at her instinctively, and saw her little start, the falling of her knitting-needles, the little flutter of colour which surprise brought to her maidenly, middle-aged cheek. How they both divined it I cannot tell, but it certainly was no surprise to either of them when a tall embarrassed figure, following the portly one of Mr Wodehouse, stepped suddenly from the noisy gravel to the quiet grass, and stood gravely awkward behind the father of the house.

'My dear children, here's the Rector – delighted to see him! we're all delighted to see him!' cried Mr Wodehouse. 'This is my little girl Lucy, and this is my eldest daughter. They're both as good as curates, though I say it, you know, as shouldn't. I suppose you've got something tidy for lunch, Lucy, eh? To be sure, you ought to know – how can I tell? She might have had only cold mutton, for anything I knew – and that won't do, you know, after college fare. Hollo, Wentworth! I beg your pardon – who thought of seeing you here? I thought you had morning service, and all that sort of thing. Delighted to make you known to the Rector so soon. Mr Proctor – Mr Wentworth of St Roque's.'

The Rector bowed. He had no time to say anything, fortunately for him; but a vague sort of colour fluttered over his face. It was his first living; and cloistered in All Souls for fifteen years of his life, how is a man to know all at once how to accost his parishioners? especially when these curious unknown specimens of natural life happen to be female creatures, doubtless accustomed to compliment and civility. If ever anyone was thankful to hear the sound of another man's voice, that person was the new Rector of Carlingford, standing in the bewildering garden-scene into which the green door had so suddenly admitted him, all but treading on the dazzling bundle of narcissus, and turning with embarrassed politeness from the perpetual curate, whose salutation was less cordial than it might have been, to those indefinite flutters of blue ribbon from which Mr Proctor's tall figure divided the ungracious young man.

'But come along to lunch. Bless me! don't let us be too ceremonious,' cried Mr Wodehouse. 'Take Lucy, my dear sir – take Lucy. Though she has her garden-gloves on, she's manager indoors for all that. Molly here is the one we coddle up and take care of. Put down your knitting, child, and don't make an old woman of yourself. To be sure, it's your own concern – you should know best; but that's my opinion. Why, Wentworth, where are you off to? 'Tisn't a fast, surely – is it, Mary? – nothing of the sort; it's Thursday – *Thursday*, do you hear? and the Rector newly arrived. Come along.'

'I am much obliged, but I have an appointment,' began the curate, with restraint.

'Why didn't you keep it, then, before *we* came in,' cried Mr Wodehouse, 'chatting with a couple of girls like Lucy and Mary? Come along, come along – an appointment with some old woman or other, who wants to screw flannels and things out of you – well, I suppose so! I don't know anything else you could have to say to them. Come along.'

'Thank you. I shall hope to wait on the Rector shortly,' said young Wentworth, more and more stiffly; 'but at present I am sorry it is not in my power. Good morning, Miss Wodehouse – good morning; I am happy to have had the opportunity –' and the voice of the perpetual curate died off into vague murmurs of politeness as he made his way towards the green door.

That green door! what a slight, paltry barrier – one plank and no more; but outside a dusty dry road, nothing to be seen but other high brick walls, with here and there an apple-tree or a lilac, or the half-developed flower-turrets of a chestnut looking over – nothing to be seen but a mean little costermonger's cart, with a hapless donkey, and, down in the direction of St Roque's, the long road winding, still drier and dustier. Ah me! was it paradise inside? or was it only a merely mortal lawn dropped over with apple-blossoms, blue ribbons, and other vanities? Who could tell? The perpetual curate wended sulky on his way. I fear the old woman would have made neither flannel nor tea and sugar out of him in that inhuman frame of mind.

'Dreadful young prig that young Wentworth,' said Mr Wodehouse, 'but comes of a great family, you know, and gets greatly taken notice of – to be sure he does, child. I suppose it's for his family's sake: I can't see into people's hearts. It may be higher motives, to be sure, and all that. He's gone off in a huff about something; never mind, luncheon comes up all the same. Now, let's address ourselves to the business of life.'

For when Mr Wodehouse took knife and fork in hand a

singular result followed. He was silent – at least he talked no longer: the mystery of carving, of eating, of drinking – all the serious business of the table – engrossed the good man. He had nothing more to say for the moment; and then a dread unbroken silence fell upon the little company. The Rector coloured, faltered, cleared his throat – he had not an idea how to get into conversation with such unknown entities. He looked hard at Lucy, with a bold intention of addressing her; but, having the bad fortune to meet her eye, shrank back, and withdrew the venture. Then the good man inclined his profile towards Miss Wodehouse. His eyes wandered wildly round the room in search of a suggestion; but, alas! it was a mere dining-room, very comfortable, but not imaginative. In this dreadful dilemma he was infinitely relieved by the sound of somebody's voice.

'I trust you will like Carlingford, Mr Proctor,' said Miss Wodehouse, mildly.

'Yes – oh yes; I trust so,' answered the confused but grateful man; that is, it will depend very much, of course, on the kind of people I find here.'

'Well, we are a little vain. To tell the truth, indeed, we rather pride ourselves a little on the good society in Carlingford,' said his gentle and charitable interlocutor.

'Ah, yes – ladies?' said the Rector: 'hum – that was not what I was thinking of.'

'But, oh, Mr Proctor,' cried Lucy, with a sudden access of fun, 'you don't mean to say that you dislike ladies' society, I hope?'

The Rector gave an uneasy half-frightened glance at her. The creature was dangerous even to a Fellow of All Souls.

'I may say I know very little about them,' said the bewildered clergyman. As soon as he had said the words he thought they sounded rude; but how could he help it? – the truth of his speech was indisputable.

'Come here, and we'll initiate you – come here as often as

you can spare us a little of your time,' cried Mr Wodehouse, who
had come to a pause in his operations. 'You couldn't have a
better chance. They're head people in Carlingford, though I say
it. There's Mary, she's a learned woman; take you up in a false
quantity, sir, a deal sooner than I should. And Lucy, she's in
another line altogether; but there's quantities of people swear by
her. What's the matter, children, eh? I suppose so – people tell
me so. If people tell me so all day long, I'm entitled to believe it,
I presume?'

Lucy answered this by a burst of laughter, not loud but cordial,
which rang sweet and strange upon the Rector's ears. Miss
Wodehouse, on the contrary, looked a little ashamed, blushed a
pretty pink old-maidenly blush, and mildly remonstrated with
papa. The whole scene was astonishing to the stranger. He had
been living out of nature so long that he wondered within himself
whether it was common to retain the habits and words of
childhood to such an age as that which good Miss Wodehouse
put no disguise upon, or if sisters with twenty years of difference
between them were usual in ordinary households. He looked at
them with looks which to Miss Wodehouse appeared disapproving, but which in reality meant only surprise and discomfort. He
was exceedingly glad when lunch was over, and he was at liberty
to take his leave. With very different feelings from those of
young Wentworth the Rector crossed the boundary of that green
door. When he saw it closed behind him he drew a long breath of
relief, and looked up and down the dusty road, and through
those lines of garden walls, where the loads of blossom burst
over everywhere, with a sensation of having escaped and got at
liberty. After a momentary pause and gaze round him in
enjoyment of that liberty, the Rector gave a start and went on
again rapidly. A dismayed, discomfited, helpless sensation came
over him. These parishioners! – these female parishioners! From
out of another of those green doors had just emerged a brilliant
group of ladies, the rustle of whose dress and murmur of whose

voices he could hear in the genteel half-rural silence. The Rector bolted: he never slackened pace nor drew breath till he was safe in the vacant library of the Rectory, among old Mr Bury's book-shelves. It seemed the only safe place in Carlingford to the languishing transplanted Fellow of All Souls.

CHAPTER II

A month later, Mr Proctor had got fairly settled in his new rectory, with a complete modest establishment becoming his means – for Carlingford was a tolerable living. And in the newly furnished sober drawing-room sat a very old lady, lively but infirm, who was the Rector's mother. Nobody knew that this old woman kept the Fellow of All Souls still a boy at heart, nor that the reserved and inappropriate man forgot his awkwardness in his mother's presence. He was not only a very affectionate son, but a dutiful good child to her. It had been his pet scheme for years to bring her from her Devonshire cottage, and make her mistress of his house. That had been the chief attraction, indeed, which drew him to Carlingford; for had he consulted his own tastes, and kept to his college, who would ensure him that at seventy-five his old mother might not glide away out of life without that last gleam of sunshine long intended for her by her grateful son?

This scene, accordingly, was almost the only one which reconciled him to the extraordinary change in his life. There she sat, the lively old lady; very deaf, as you could almost divine by that vivid enquiring twinkle in her eyes; feeble too, for she had a silver-headed cane beside her chair, and even with that assistance seldom moved across the room when she could help it. Feeble in body, but alert in mind, ready to read anything, to hear anything, to deliver her opinions freely; resting in her big chair in the complete repose of age, gratified with her son's attentions, and overjoyed in his company; interested about everything, and as ready to enter into all the domestic concerns of the new people as if she had lived all her life among them. The Rector sighed and smiled as he listened to his mother's questions, and did his best, at the top of his voice, to enlighten her. His mother was, let us say, a hundred years or so younger than the Rector. If she had been his bride, and at the blithe commencement of life, she could not have shown more inclination to know all about Carlingford. Mr Proctor was middle-àged, and preoccupied by right of his years; but his mother had long ago got over that stage of life. She was at that point when some energetic natures, having got to the bottom of the hill, seem to make a fresh start and reascend. Five years ago, old Mrs Proctor had completed the human term; now she had recommenced her life.

But, to tell the very truth, the Rector would very fain, had that been possible, have confined her enquiries to books and public affairs. For to make confidential disclosures, either concerning one's self or other people, in a tone of voice perfectly audible in the kitchen, is somewhat trying. He had become acquainted with those dread parishioners of his during this interval. Already they had worn him to death with dinner-parties – dinner-parties very pleasant and friendly, when one got used to them; but to a stranger frightful reproductions of each other, with the same dishes, the same dresses, the same stories, in which the Rector communicated gravely with his next neighbour, and eluded as long as he could those concluding moments in the drawing-room, which were worst of all. It cannot be said that his parishioners made much progress in their knowledge of the Rector. What his 'views' were, nobody could divine any more than they could before his arrival. He made no innovations whatever; but he did not pursue Mr Bury's Evangelical ways, and never preached a sermon or a word more than was absolutely necessary. When zealous Churchmen discussed the progress of

Dissent, the Rector scarcely looked interested; and nobody could move him to express an opinion concerning all that lovely upholstery with which Mr Wentworth had decorated St Roque's. People asked in vain, what was he? He was neither High nor Low, enlightened nor narrow-minded; he was a Fellow of All Souls.

'But now tell me, my dear,' said old Mrs Proctor, 'who's Mr Wodehouse?'

With despairing calmness, the Rector approached his voice to her ear. 'He's a churchwarden!' cried the unfortunate man, in a shrill whisper.

'He's what? – you forget I don't hear very well. I'm a great deal deafer, Morley, my dear, than I was the last time you were in Devonshire. What did you say Mr Wodehouse was?'

'He's an ass!' exclaimed the baited Rector.

Mrs Proctor nodded her head with a great many little satisfied assenting nods.

'Exactly my own opinion, my dear. What I like in your manner of expressing yourself, Morley, is its conciseness,' said the laughing old lady. 'Just so – exactly what I imagined; but being an ass, you know, doesn't account for him coming here so often. What is he besides, my dear?'

The Rector made spasmodic gestures towards the door, to the great amusement of his lively mother; and then produced, with much confusion and after a long search, his pocketbook, on a leaf of paper in which he wrote – loudly, in big characters – 'He's a churchwarden – they'll hear in the kitchen.'

'He's a churchwarden! And what if they do hear in the kitchen?' cried the old lady, greatly amused; 'it isn't a sin. Well, now, let me hear: has he a family, Morley?'

Again Mr Proctor showed a little discomposure. After a troubled look at the door, and pause, as if he meditated a remonstrance, he changed his mind, and answered, 'Two daughters!' shouting sepulchrally into his mother's ear.

'Oh so!' cried the old lady – '*two daughters* – so, so – that explains it all at once. I know now why he comes to the Rectory so often. And, I declare, I never thought of it before. Why, you're always there! – so, so – and he's got *two daughters*, has he? To be sure; now I understand it all.'

The Rector looked helpless and puzzled. It was difficult to take the initiative and ask why – but the poor man looked so perplexed and ignorant, and so clearly unaware what the solution was, that the old lady burst into shrill, gay laughter as she looked at him.

'I don't believe you know anything about it,' she said. 'Are they old or young? are they pretty or ugly? Tell me all about them, Morley.'

Now Mr Proctor had not the excuse of having forgotten the appearance of the two Miss Wodehouses: on the contrary, though not an imaginative man, he could have fancied he saw them both before him – Lucy lost in noiseless laughter, and her good elder sister deprecating and gentle as usual. We will not even undertake to say that a gleam of something blue did not flash across the mind of the good man, who did not know what ribbons were. He was so much bewildered that Mrs Proctor repeated her question, and, as she did so, tapped him pretty smartly on the arm to recall his wandering thoughts.

'One's one thing,' at last shouted the confused man, 'and t'other's another!' An oracular deliverance which surely must have been entirely unintelligible in the kitchen, where we will not deny that an utterance so incomprehensible awoke a laudable curiosity.

'My dear, you're lucid!' cried the old lady. 'I hope you don't preach like that. T'other's another! – is she so? and I suppose that's the one you're wanted to marry – eh? For shame, Morley, not to tell your mother!'

The Rector jumped to his feet, thunderstruck. Wanted to marry! – the idea was too overwhelming and dreadful – his

231

mind could not receive it. The air of alarm which immediately diffused itself all over him – his unfeigned horror at the suggestion – captivated his mother. She was amused, but she was pleased at the same time. Just making her cheery outset on this second lifetime, you can't suppose she would have been glad to hear that her son was going to jilt her, and appoint another queen in her stead.

'Sit down and tell me about them,' said Mrs Proctor; 'my dear, you're wonderfully afraid of the servants hearing. They don't know who we're speaking of. Aha! and so you didn't know what they meant – didn't you? I don't say you shouldn't marry, my dear – quite the reverse. A man *ought* to marry, one time or another. Only it's rather soon to lay their plans. I don't doubt there's a great many unmarried ladies in your church, Morley. There always is in a country place.'

To this the alarmed Rector answered only by a groan – a groan so expressive that his quick-witted mother heard it with her eyes.

'They will come to call on me,' said Mrs Proctor, with fun dancing in her bright old eyes. 'I'll tell you all about them, and you needn't be afraid of the servants. Trust to me, my dear – I'll find them out. And now, if you wish to take a walk, or go out visiting, don't let me detain you, Morley. I shouldn't wonder but there's something in the papers I would like to see – or I even might close my eyes for a few minutes: the afternoon is always a drowsy time with me. When I was in Devonshire, you know, no one minded what I did. You had better refresh yourself with a nice walk, my dear boy.'

The Rector got up well pleased. The alacrity with which he left the room, however, did not correspond with the horror-stricken and helpless expression of his face, when, after walking very smartly all round the rectory garden, he paused with his hand on the gate, doubtful whether to retreat into his study, or boldly to face that world which was plotting against him. The question was a profoundly serious one to Mr Proctor. He did not feel by any means sure that he was a free agent, or could assert the ordinary rights of an Englishman, in this most unexpected dilemma. How could he tell how much or how little was necessary to prove that a man had 'committed himself'? For anything he could tell, somebody might be calculating upon him as her lover, and settling his future life for him. The Rector was not vain – he did not think himself an Adonis; he did not understand anything about the matter, which indeed was beneath the consideration of a Fellow of All Souls. But have not women been incomprehensible since ever there was in this world a pen with sufficient command of words to call them so? And is it not certain that, whether it may be to their advantage or disadvantage, every soul of them is plotting to marry somebody? Mr Proctor recalled in dim but frightful reminiscences stories which had dropped upon his ear at various times of his life. Never was there a man, however ugly, disagreeable, or penniless, but he could tell of a narrow escape he had had, some time or other. The Rector recollected and trembled. No woman was ever so dismayed by the persecutions of a lover, as was this helpless middle-aged gentleman under the conviction that Lucy Wodehouse meant to marry him. The remembrance of the curate of St Roque's gave him no comfort: her sweet youth, so totally unlike his sober age, did not strike him as unfavourable to her pursuit of him. Who could fathom the motives of a woman? His mother was wise, and knew the world, and understood what such creatures meant. No doubt it was entirely the case – a dreadful certainty – and what was he to do?

At the bottom of all this fright and perplexity must it be owned that the Rector had a guilty consciousness within himself, that if Lucy drove the matter to extremities, he was not so sure of his own powers of resistance as he ought to be? She might marry him before he knew what he was about; and in such a case the Rector could not have taken his oath at his own private confessional that he would have been so deeply miserable as the circumstances might infer. No wonder he was alarmed at the position in which he found himself; nobody could predict how it might end.

When Mr Proctor saw his mother again at dinner, she was evidently full of some subject which would not bear talking of before the servants. The old lady looked at her son's troubled apprehensive face with smiles and nods and gay hints, which he was much too preoccupied to understand, and which only increased his bewilderment. When the good man was left alone over his glass of wine, he drank it slowly, in funereal silence, with profoundly serious looks; and what between eagerness to understand what the old lady meant, and reluctance to show the extent of his curiosity, had a very heavy half-hour of it in that grave solitary dining-room. He roused himself with an effort from this dismal state into which he was falling. He recalled with a sigh the classic board of All Souls. Woe for the day when he was seduced to forsake that dear retirement! Really, to suffer himself to fall into a condition so melancholy, was far from being right. He must rouse himself – he must find some other society than parishioners; and with a glimpse of a series of snug little dinner-parties, undisturbed by the presence of women, Mr Proctor rose and hurried after his mother, to hear what new thing she might have to say.

Nor was he disappointed. The old lady was snugly posted, ready for a conference. She made lively gestures to hasten him when he appeared at the door, and could scarcely delay the utterance of her news till he had taken his seat beside her. She had taken off her spectacles, and laid aside her paper, and cleared off her work into her work-basket. All was ready for the talk in which she delighted.

'My dear, they've been here,' said old Mrs Proctor, rubbing her hands – 'both together, and as kind as could be – exactly as I expected. An old woman gets double the attention when she's got an unmarried son. I've always observed that; though in Devonshire, what with your fellowship and seeing you so seldom, nobody took much notice. Yes, they've been here; and I like them a great deal better than I expected, Morley, my dear.'

The Rector, not knowing what else to say, shouted 'Indeed, mother!' into the old lady's ear.

'Quite so,' continued that lively observer – 'nice young women – not at all like their father, which is a great consolation. That elder one is a very sensible person, I am sure. She would make a nice wife for somebody, especially for a clergyman. She is not in her first youth, but neither are some other people. A very nice creature indeed, I am quite sure.'

During all this speech the Rector's countenance had been falling, falling. If he was helpless before, the utter woe of his expression now was a spectacle to behold. The danger of being married by proxy was appalling certainly, yet was not entirely without alleviations; but Miss Wodehouse! who ever thought of Miss Wodehouse? To see the last remains of colour fade out of his cheek, and his very lip fall with disappointment, was deeply edifying to his lively old mother. She perceived it all, but made no sign.

'And the other is a pretty creature – certainly pretty: shouldn't you say she was pretty, Morley?' said his heartless mother.

Mr Proctor hesitated, hemmed – felt himself growing red – tried to intimate his sentiments by a nod of assent; but that would not do, for the old lady had presented her ear to him, and was blind to all his gestures.

'I don't know much about it, mother,' he made answer at last.

'*Much* about it! it's to be hoped not. I never supposed you did; but you don't mean to say you don't think her pretty?' said Mrs Proctor – 'but, I don't doubt in the least, a sad flirt. Her sister is a very superior person, my dear.'

The Rector's face lengthened at every word – a vision of these two Miss Wodehouses rose upon him every moment clearer and more distinct as his mother spoke. Considering how ignorant he was of all such female paraphernalia, it is extraordinary how correct his recollection was of all the details of their habitual dress and appearance. With a certain dreadful consciousness of the justice of what his mother said, he saw in imagination the mild elder sister in her comely old-maidenhood. Nobody could doubt her good qualities, and could it be questioned that for a man of fifty, if he was to do anything so foolish, a woman not quite forty was a thousand times more eligible than a creature in blue ribbons? Still the unfortunate Rector did not seem to see it: his face grew longer and longer – he made no answer whatever to his mother's address; while she, with a spice of natural female malice against the common enemy triumphing for the moment over the mother's admiration of her son, sat wickedly enjoying his distress, and aggravating it. His dismay and perplexity amused this wicked old woman beyond measure.

'I have no doubt that younger girl takes a pleasure in deluding her admirers,' said Mrs Proctor; 'she's a wicked little flirt, and likes nothing better than to see her power. I know very well how such people do; but, my dear,' continued this false old lady, scarcely able to restrain her laughter, 'if I were you, I would be very civil to Miss Wodehouse. You may depend upon it, Morley, that's a very superior person. She is not very young, to be sure, but you are not very young yourself. She would make a nice wife – not too foolish, you know, nor fanciful. Ah! I like Miss Wodehouse, my dear.'

The Rector stumbled up to his feet hastily, and pointed to a table at a little distance, on which some books were lying. Then he went and brought them to her table. 'I've brought you some new books,' he shouted into her ear. It was the only way his clumsy ingenuity could fall upon for bringing this most distasteful conversation to an end.

The old lady's eyes were dancing with fun and a little mischief, but, notwithstanding, she could not be so false to her nature as to show no interest in the books. She turned them over with lively remarks and comment. 'But for all that, Morley, I would not have you forget Miss Wodehouse,' she said, when her early bedtime came. 'Give it a thought now and then, and consider the whole matter. It is not a thing to be done rashly; but still you know you are settled now, and you ought to be thinking of settling for life.'

With this parting shaft she left him. The troubled Rector, instead of sitting up to his beloved studies, went early to bed that night, and was pursued by nightmares through his unquiet slumbers. Settling for life! Alas! there floated before him vain visions of that halcyon world he had left – that sacred soil at All Souls, where there were no parishioners to break the sweet repose. How different was this discomposing real world!

CHAPTER III

Matters went on quietly for some time without any catastrophe occurring to the Rector. He had shut himself up from all society, and declined the invitations of the parishioners for ten long days at least; but finding that the kind people were only kinder than ever when they understood he was 'indisposed', poor Mr Proctor resumed his ordinary life confiding timidly in some extra precautions which his own ingenuity had invented. He was shyer than ever of addressing the ladies in those parties he was obliged to attend. He was especially embarrassed and uncomfortable in the presence of the two Miss Wodehouses, who, unfortunately, were very popular in Carlingford, and whom he could not help meeting everywhere. Notwithstanding this embarrassment, it is curious how well he knew how they looked, and what they were doing, and all about them. Though he could not for his life have told what these things were called, he knew Miss Wodehouse's dove-coloured dress and her French grey, and all those gleams of blue which set off Lucy's fair curls, and floated about her pretty person under various pretences, had a distinct though inarticulate place in the good man's confused remembrance. But neither Lucy nor Miss Wodehouse had brought matters to extremity. He even ventured to go to their house occasionally without any harm coming of it, and lingered in that blooming fragrant garden, where the blossoms had given place to fruit, and ruddy apples hung heavy on the branches which had once scattered their petals, rosy-white, on Frank Wentworth's Anglican coat. Yet Mr Proctor was not lulled into incaution by this seeming calm. Other people besides his mother had intimated to him that there were expectations current of his 'settling in life'. He lived not in false security, but wise trembling, never knowing what hour the thunderbolt might fall upon his head.

It happened one day, while still in this condition of mind, that the Rector was passing through Grove Street on his way home. He was walking on the humbler side of the street, where there is a row of cottages with little gardens in front of them – cheap houses, which are contented to be haughtily overlooked by the staircase windows and blank walls of their richer neighbours on the other side of the road. The Rector thought, but could not be sure, that he had seen two figures like those of the Miss Wodehouses going into one of these houses, and was making a little haste to escape meeting those enemies of his peace. But as he went hastily on, he heard sobs and screams – sounds which a man who hid a good heart under a shy exterior could not willingly pass by. He made a troubled pause before the door from which these outcries proceeded, and while he stood thus irresolute whether to pass on or to stop and enquire the cause, someone came rushing out and took hold of his arm.

'Please, sir, she's dying – oh, please, sir, she thought a deal o' you. Please, will you come in and speak to her?' cried the little servant-girl who had pounced upon him so. The Rector stared at her in amazement. He had not his prayer-book – he was not prepared; he had no idea of being called upon in such an emergency. In the meantime the commotion rather increased in the house, and he could hear in the distance a voice adjuring someone to go for the clergyman. The Rector stood uncertain and perplexed, perhaps in a more serious personal difficulty than had ever happened to him all his life before. For what did he know about deathbeds? or what had he to say to anyone on that dread verge? He grew pale with real vexation and distress.

'Have they gone for a doctor? that would be more to the purpose,' he said, unconsciously, aloud.

'Please, sir, it's no good,' said the little maidservant. 'Please, the doctor's been, but he's no good – and she's unhappy in her mind, though she's quite resigned to go: and oh, please, if you would say a word to her, it might do her a deal of good.'

Thus adjured, the Rector had no choice. He went gloomily into the house and up the stairs after his little guide. Why did not they send for the minister of Salem Chapel close by? or for Mr Wentworth, who was accustomed to that sort of thing? Why did they resort to him in such an emergency? He would have made his appearance before the highest magnates of the land – before the Queen herself – before the bench of bishops or the Privy Council – with less trepidation than he entered that poor little room.

The sufferer lay breathing heavily in the poor apartment. She did not look very ill to Mr Proctor's inexperienced eyes. Her colour was bright, and her face full of eagerness. Near the door stood Miss Wodehouse, looking compassionate but helpless, casting wistful glances at the bed, but standing back in a corner as confused and embarrassed as the Rector himself. Lucy was standing by the pillow of the sick woman with a watchful readiness visible to the most unskilled eye – ready to raise her, to change her position, to attend to her wants almost before they were expressed. The contrast was wonderful. She had thrown off her bonnet and shawl, and appeared, not like a stranger, but somehow in her natural place, despite the sweet youthful beauty of her looks, and the gay girlish dress with its floating ribbons. These singular adjuncts notwithstanding, no homely nurse in a cotton gown could have looked more alert or serviceable, or more natural to the position, than Lucy did. The poor Rector, taking the seat which the little maid placed for him directly in the centre of the room, looked at the nurse and the patient with a gasp of perplexity and embarrassment. A deathbed, alas! was an unknown region to him.

'Oh, sir, I'm obliged to you for coming – oh, sir, I'm grateful to you,' cried the poor woman in the bed. 'I've been ill, off and on, for years, but never took thought to it as I ought. I've put off and put off, waiting for a better time – and now, God help me, it's perhaps too late. Oh, sir, tell me, when a person's ill and dying is it too late?'

Before the Rector could even imagine what he could answer, the sick woman took up the broken thread of her own words, and continued –

'I don't feel no trust as I ought to – I don't feel no confidence,' she said, in anxious confession. 'Oh, sir, do you think it matters if one feels it? – don't you think things might be right all the same though we *were* uneasy in our minds? My thinking can't change it one way or another. Ask the good gentleman to speak to me, Miss Lucy, dear – he'll mind what *you* say.'

A look from Lucy quickened the Rector's speech, but increased his embarrassments. 'It – it isn't her doctor she has no confidence in?' he said, eagerly.

The poor woman gave a little cry. 'The doctor – the doctor! what can he do to a poor dying creature? Oh, Lord bless you, it's none of them things I'm thinking of; it's my soul – my soul!'

'But my poor good woman,' said Mr Proctor, 'though it is very good and praiseworthy of you to be anxious about your soul, let us hope that there is no such – no such *haste* as you seem to suppose.'

The patient opened her eyes wide, and stared, with the anxious look of disease, in his face.

'I mean,' said the good man, faltering under that gaze, 'that I see no reason for your making yourself so very anxious. Let us hope it is not so bad as that. You are very ill, but not *so* ill – I suppose.'

Here the Rector was interrupted by a groan from the patient, and by a troubled, disapproving, disappointed look from Lucy Wodehouse. This brought him to a sudden standstill. He gazed for a moment helplessly at the poor woman in the bed. If he had known anything in the world which would have given her consolation, he was ready to have made any exertion for it; but he knew nothing to say – no medicine for a mind diseased was in his repositories. He was deeply distressed to see the disappointment which followed his words, but his distress only made him more silent, more helpless, more inefficient than before.

After an interval which was disturbed only by the groans of the patient and the uneasy fidgeting of good Miss Wodehouse in her corner, the Rector again broke silence. The sick woman had turned to the wall, and closed her eyes in dismay and disappointment – evidently she had ceased to expect anything from him.

'If there is anything I can do,' said poor Mr Proctor, 'I am afraid I have spoken hastily. I meant to try to calm her mind a little; if I can be of any use?'

'Ah, maybe I'm hasty,' said the dying woman, turning round again with a sudden effort – 'but, oh, to speak to me of having time when I've one foot in the grave already!'

'Not so bad as that – not so bad as that,' said the Rector, soothingly.

'But I tell you it is as bad as that,' she cried, with the brief blaze of anger common to great weakness. 'I'm not a child to be persuaded different from what I know. If you'd tell me – if you'd say a prayer – ah, Miss Lucy, it's coming on again.'

In a moment Lucy had raised the poor creature in her arms,

and in default of the pillows which were not at hand, had risen herself into their place, and supported the gasping woman against her own breast. It was a paroxysm dreadful to behold, in which every labouring breath seemed the last. The Rector sat like one struck dumb, looking on at that mortal struggle. Miss Wodehouse approached nervously from behind, and went up to the bedside, faltering forth questions as to what she could do. Lucy only waved her hand, as her own light figure swayed and changed, always seeking the easiest attitude for the sufferer. As the elder sister drew back, the Rector and she glanced at each other with wistful mutual looks of sympathy. Both were equally well-disposed, equally helpless and embarrassed. How to be of any use in that dreadful agony of nature was denied to both. They stood looking on, awed and self-reproaching. Such scenes have doubtless happened in sick-rooms before now.

When the fit was over, a hasty step came up the stair, and Mr Wentworth entered the room. He explained in a whisper that he had not been at home when the messenger came, but had followed whenever he heard of the message. Seeing the Rector, he hesitated, and drew back with some surprise, and, even (for he was far from perfect) in that chamber, a little flush of offence. The Rector rose abruptly, waving his hand, and went to join Miss Wodehouse in her corner. There the two elderly spectators looked on silent at ministrations of which both were incapable; one watching with wondering yet affectionate envy how Lucy laid down the weakened but relieved patient upon her pillows; and one beholding with a surprise he could not conceal, how a young man, not half his own age, went softly, with all the confidence yet awe of nature, into those mysteries which he dared not touch upon. The two young creatures by the deathbed acknowledged that their patient was dying; the woman stood by her watchful and affectionate – the man held up before her that cross, not of wood or metal, but of truth and everlasting verity, which is the only hope of man. The spectators looked on, and did not interrupt – looked on, awed and wondering – unaware of how it was, but watching as if it were a miracle wrought before their eyes. Perhaps all the years of his life had not taught the Rector so much as did that half-hour in an unknown poor bed-chamber, where, honest and humble, he stood aside, and, kneeling down, responded to his young brother's prayer. His young brother – young enough to have been his son – not half nor a quarter part so learned as he; but a world further on in that profession which they shared – the art of winning souls.

When those prayers were over, the Rector, without a word to anybody, stole quietly away. When he got into the street, however, he found himself closely followed by Miss Wodehouse, of whom he was not at this moment afraid. That good creature was crying softly under her veil. She was eager to make up to him, to open out her full heart; and indeed the Rector, like herself, in that wonderful sensation of surprised and unenvying discomfiture, was glad at that moment of sympathy too.

'Oh, Mr Proctor, isn't it wonderful?' sighed good Miss Wodehouse.

The Rector did not speak, but he answered by a very emphatic nod of his head.

'It did not use to be so when you and I were young,' said his companion in failure. 'I sometimes take a little comfort from that; but no doubt, if it had been in me, it would have shown itself somehow. Ah, I fear, I fear, I was not well brought up; but, to be sure, that dear child has not been brought up at all, if one may say so. Her poor mother died when she was born. And oh, I'm afraid I never was kind to Lucy's mother, Mr Proctor. You know she was only a year or two older than I was; and to think of that child, that baby! What a world she is, and always was, before me, that might have been her mother, Mr Proctor!' said Miss Wodehouse, with a little sob.

'But things were different in our young days,' said the Rector, repeating her sentiment, without enquiring whether it were true or not, and finding a certain vague consolation in it.

'Ah, that is true,' said Miss Wodehouse – 'that is true; what a blessing things are so changed; and these blessed young creatures,' she added softly, with tears falling out of her gentle old eyes – 'these blessed young creatures are near the Fountainhead.'

With this speech Miss Wodehouse held out her hand to the Rector, and they parted with a warm mutual grasp. The Rector went straight home – straight to his study, where he shut himself in, and was not to be disturbed; that night was one long to be remembered in the good man's history. For the first time in his life he set himself to enquire what was his supposed business in this world. His treatise on the Greek verb, and his new edition of Sophocles, were highly creditable to the Fellow of All Souls; but how about the Rector of Carlingford? What was he doing here, among that little world of human creatures who were dying, being born, perishing, suffering, falling into misfortune and anguish, and all manner of human vicissitudes, every day? Young Wentworth knew what to say to that woman in her distress; and so might the Rector, had her distress concerned a disputed translation, or a disused idiom. The good man was startled in his composure and calm. Today he had visibly failed in a duty which even in All Souls was certainly known to be one of the duties of a Christian priest. Was he a Christian priest, or what was he? He was troubled to the very depths of his soul. To hold an office the duties of which he could not perform, was clearly impossible. The only question, and that a hard one, was, whether he could learn to discharge those duties, or whether he must cease to be Rector of Carlingford. He laboured over this problem in his solitude, and could find no answer. 'Things were different when we were young,' was the only thought that was any comfort to him, and that was poor consolation.

For one thing, it is hard upon the most magnanimous of men to confess that he has undertaken an office for which he has not found himself capable. Magnanimity was perhaps too lofty a word to apply to the Rector; but he was honest to the bottom of his soul. As soon as he became aware of what was included in the duties of his office, he must perform them, or quit his post. But how to perform them? Can one *learn* to convey consolation to the dying, to teach the ignorant, to comfort the sorrowful? Are these matters to be acquired by study, like Greek verbs or intricate measures? The Rector's heart said No. The Rector's imagination unfolded before him, in all its halcyon blessedness, that ancient paradise of All Souls, where no such confounding demands ever disturbed his beatitude. The good man groaned within himself over the mortification, the labour, the sorrow, which this living was bringing upon him. 'If I had but let it pass to Morgan, who wanted to marry,' he said with self-reproach; and then suddenly bethought himself of his own most innocent filial romance, and the pleasure his mother had taken in her new house and new beginning of life. At that touch the tide flowed back again. Could he dismiss her now to another solitary cottage in Devonshire, her old home there being all dispersed and broken up, while the house she had hoped to die in cast her out from its long-hoped-for shelter? The Rector was quite overwhelmed by this new aggravation. If by any effort of his own, any sacrifice to himself, he could preserve this bright new home to his mother, would he shrink from that labour of love?

Nobody, however, knew anything about those conflicting thoughts which rent his sober bosom. He preached next Sunday as usual, letting no trace of the distressed, wistful anxiety to do his duty which now possessed him gleam into his sermon. He looked down upon a crowd of unsympathetic, uninterested faces, when he delivered that smooth little sermon, which nobody cared much about, and which disturbed nobody. The only eyes which in the smallest degree comprehended him were those of good Miss Wodehouse, who had been the witness and the participator of his humiliation. Lucy was not there. Doubtless

Lucy was at St Roque's, where the sermons of the perpetual curate differed much from those of the Rector of Carlingford. Ah me! the rectorship, with all its responsibilities, was a serious business; and what was to become of it yet, Mr Proctor could not see. He was not a hasty man – he determined to wait and see what events might make of it; to consider it ripely – to take full counsel with himself. Every time he came out of his mother's presence, he came affected and full of anxiety to preserve to her that home which pleased her so much. She was the strong point in favour of Carlingford; and it was no small tribute to the good man's filial affection, that for her chiefly he kept his neck under the yoke of a service to which he knew himself unequal, and sighing, turned his back upon his beloved cloisters. If there had been no other sick-beds immediately in Carlingford, Mrs Proctor would have won the day.

CHAPTER IV

Such a blessed exemption, however, was not to be hoped for. When the Rector was solemnly sent for from his very study to visit a poor man who was not expected to live many days, he put his prayer-book under his arm, and went off doggedly, feeling that now was the crisis. He went through it in as exemplary a manner as could have been desired, but it was dreadful work to the Rector. If nobody else suspected him, he suspected himself. He had no spontaneous word of encourage-ment or consolation to offer; he went through it as his duty with a horrible abstractness. That night he went home disgusted beyond all possible power of self-reconciliation. He could not continue this. Good evangelical Mr Bury, who went before him, and by nature loved preaching, had accustomed the people to much of such visitations. It was murder to the Fellow of All Souls.

That night Mr Proctor wrote a long letter to his dear cheery old mother, disclosing all his heart to her. It was written with a pathos of which the good man was wholly unconscious, and finished by asking her advice and her prayers. He sent it up to her next morning on her breakfast tray, which he always furnished with his own hands, and went out to occupy himself in paying visits till it should be time to see her, and ascertain her opinion. At Mr Wodehouse's there was nobody at home but Lucy, who was very friendly, and took no notice of that sad encounter which had changed his views so entirely. The Rector found, on enquiry, that the woman was dead, but not until Mr Wentworth had administered to her fully the consolations of the Church. Lucy did not look superior, or say anything in admiration of Mr Wentworth, but the Rector's conscience supplied all that was wanting. If good Miss Wodehouse had been there with her charitable looks, and her disefficiency so like his own, it would have been a consolation to the good man. He would have turned joyfully from Lucy and her blue ribbons to that distressed dove-coloured woman, so greatly had recent events changed him. But the truth was, he cared nothing for either of them nowadays. He was delivered from those whimsical distressing fears. Something more serious had obliterated those lighter apprehensions. He had no leisure now to think that somebody had planned to marry him; all his thoughts were fixed on matters so much more important that this was entirely forgotten.

Mrs Proctor was seated as usual in the place she loved, with her newspapers, her books, her work-basket, and silver-headed cane at the side of her chair. The old lady, like her son, looked serious. She beckoned him to quicken his steps when she saw him appear at the drawing-room door, and pointed to the chair placed beside her, all ready for this solemn conference. He came in with a troubled face, scarcely venturing to look at her, afraid to see the disappointment which he had brought upon his dearest friend. The old lady divined why it was he did not lift his eyes.

She took his hand and addressed him with all her characteristic vivacity.

'Morley, what is this you mean, my dear? When did I ever give my son reason to distrust me? Do you think I would suffer you to continue in a position painful to yourself for my sake? How dare you think such a thing of me, Morley? Don't say so; you didn't mean it? I can see it in your eyes.'

The Rector shook his head, and dropped into the chair placed ready for him. He might have had a great deal to say for himself could she have heard him. But as it was, he could not shout all his reasons and apologies into her deaf ear.

'As for the change to me,' said the old lady, instinctively seizing upon the heart of the difficulty, 'that's nothing – simply nothing. I've not had time to get attached to Carlingford. I've no associations with the place. Of course I shall be very glad to go back to all my old friends. Put that out of the question, Morley.'

But the Rector only shook his head once more. The more she made light of it, the more he perceived all the painful circumstances involved. Could his mother go back to Devonshire and tell all her old ladies that her son had made a failure in Carlingford? He grieved within himself at the thought. His brethren at All Souls might understand *him*; but what could console the brave old woman for all the condolence and commiseration to which she would be subject? 'It goes to my heart, mother,' he cried in her ear.

'Well, Morley, I am very sorry you find it so,' said the old lady; 'very sorry you can't see your way to all your duties. They tell me the late Rector was very Low Church, and visited about like a Dissenter, so it is not much wonder you, with your different habits, find yourself a good deal put out; but, my dear, don't you think it's only at first? Don't you think after a while the people would get into your ways, and you into theirs? Miss Wodehouse was here this morning, and was telling me a good deal about the late Rector. It's to be expected you should find the difference;

but by-and-by, to be sure, you might get used to it, and the people would not expect so much.'

'Did she tell you where we met the other day?' asked the Rector, with a brevity rendered necessary by Mrs Proctor's infirmity.

'She told me – she's a dear confused good soul,' said the old lady – 'about the difference between Lucy and herself, and how the young creature was twenty times handier than she, and something about young Mr Wentworth of St Roque's. Really, by all I hear, that must be a very presuming young man,' cried Mrs Proctor, with a lively air of offence. 'His interference among your parishioners, Morley, is really more than I should be inclined to bear.'

Once more the good Rector shook his head. He had not thought of that aspect of the subject. He was indeed so free from vanity or self-importance, that his only feeling in regard to the sudden appearance of the perpetual curate was respect and surprise. He would not be convinced otherwise even now. 'He can do his duty, mother,' he answered, sadly.

'Stuff and nonsense!' cried the old lady, 'Do you mean to tell me a boy like that can do his duty better than my son could do it, if he put his mind to it? And if it is your duty, Morley, dear,' continued his mother, melting a little, and in a coaxing persuasive tone, 'of course I know you *will* do it, however hard it may be.'

'That's just the difficulty,' cried the Rector, venturing on a longer speech than usual, and roused to a point at which he had no fear of the listeners in the kitchen; 'such duties require other training than mine has been. I can't! – do you hear me, mother? – I must not hold a false position; that's impossible.'

'You shan't hold a false position,' cried the old lady; 'that's the only thing that *is* impossible – but, Morley, let us consider, dear. You are a clergyman, you know; you ought to understand all that's required of you a great deal better than these people do. My dear, your poor father and I trained you up to be a clergyman,' said Mrs Proctor, rather pathetically, 'and not to be a Fellow of All Souls.'

The Rector groaned. Had it not been advancement, progress, unhoped-for good fortune, that made him a member of that learned corporation? He shook his head. Nothing could change the fact now. After fifteen years' experience of that Elysium, he could not put on the cassock and surplice with all his youthful fervour. He had settled into his life-habits long ago. With the quick perception which made up for her deficiency, his mother read his face, and saw the cause was hopeless; yet with female courage and pertinacity made one effort more.

'And with an excellent hard-working curate,' said the old lady – 'a curate whom, of course, we'd do our duty by, Morley, and who could take a great deal of the responsibility off your hands; for Mr Leigh, though a nice young man, is not, I know, the man *you* would have chosen for such a post; and still more, my dear son – we were talking of it in jest not long ago, but it is perfect earnest, and a most important matter – with a good wife, Morley; a wife who would enter into all the parish work, and give you useful hints, and conduct herself as a clergyman's wife should – with such a wife –'

'Lucy Wodehouse!' cried the Rector, starting to his feet, and forgetting all his proprieties; 'I tell you the thing is impossible. I'll go back to All Souls.'

He sat down again doggedly, having said it. His mother sat looking at him in silence, with tears in her lively old eyes. She was saying within herself that she had seen his father take such a 'turn', and that it was no use arguing with them under such circumstances. She watched him as women often do watch men, waiting till the creature should come to itself again and might be spoken to. The incomprehensibleness of women is an old theory, but what is that to the curious wondering observation with which wives, mothers, and sisters watch the other unreasoning animal in those moments when he has snatched the reins out of their hands, and is not to be spoken to! What he will make of it in those unassisted moments, afflicts the compassionate female understanding. It is best to let him come to, and feel his own helplessness. Such was Mrs Proctor's conclusion, as, vexed, distressed, and helpless, she leant back in her chair, and wiped a few tears of disappointment and vexation out of her bright old eyes.

The Rector saw this movement, and it once more excited him to speech. 'But you shall have a house in Oxford, mother,' he cried – 'you shan't go back to Devonshire – where I can see you every day, and you can hear all that is going on. Bravo! that will be a thousand times better than Carlingford.'

It was now Mrs Proctor's turn to jump up, startled, and put her hand on his mouth and point to the door. The Rector did not care for the door; he had disclosed his sentiments, he had taken his resolution, and now the sooner all was over the better for the emancipated man.

Thus concluded the brief incumbency of the Reverend Morley Proctor. He returned to Oxford before his year of grace was over, and found everybody very glad to see him; and he left Carlingford with universal good wishes. The living fell to Morgan, who wanted to be married, and whose turn was much more to be a working clergyman than a classical commentator. Old Mrs Proctor got a pretty house under shelter of the trees of St Giles's, and half the undergraduates fell in love with the old lady in the freshness of her second lifetime. Carlingford passed away like a dream from the lively old mother's memory, and how could any reminiscences of that uncongenial locality disturb the recovered beatitude of the Fellow of All Souls?

Yet all was not so satisfactory as it appeared. Mr Proctor paid for his temporary absence. All Souls was not the Elysium it had been before that brief disastrous voyage into the world. The good man felt the stings of failure; he felt the mild jokes of his brethren in those Elysian fields. He could not help conjuring up to himself visions of Morgan with his new wife in that pretty rectory. Life, after all, did not consist of books, nor were Greek verbs essential to happiness. The strong emotion into which his own failure had roused him; the wondering silence in which he stood looking at the ministrations of Lucy Wodehouse and the young curate; the tearful sympathetic woman as helpless as himself, who had stood beside him in that sick-chamber, came back upon his recollection strangely, amidst the repose, not so blessed as heretofore, of All Souls. The good man had found out that secret of discontent which most men find out a great deal earlier than he. Something better, though it might be sadder, harder, more calamitous, was in this world. Was there ever human creature yet that had not something in him more congenial to the thorns and briars outside to be conquered, than to that mild paradise for which our primeval mother disqualified all her children? When he went back to his dear cloisters, good Mr Proctor felt that sting: a longing for the work he had rejected stirred in him – a wistful recollection of the sympathy he had not sought.

And if in future years any traveller, if travellers still fall upon adventures, should light upon a remote parsonage in which an elderly embarrassed Rector, with a mild wife in dove-coloured dresses, toils painfully after his duty, more and more giving his heart to it, more and more finding difficult expression for the unused faculty, let him be sure that it is the late Rector of Carlingford, self-expelled out of the uneasy paradise, setting forth untimely, yet not too late, into the laborious world.

Benefit of Clergy

Bertrand Russell

I

Penelope Colquhoun climbed slowly up the stairs and sank wearily into an uncomfortable wicker chair in her tiny sitting-room. 'Oh, I am bored, I am bored, I am bored,' she said out loud with a deep sigh.

It must be confessed that she had reason for this feeling. Her father was the vicar of a remote parish in rural Suffolk, the name of which was Quycombe Magna. The village consisted of the church, the vicarage, a post office, a public house, ten cottages, and – its only redeeming feature – a fine old Manor House. Its only connexion with the outer world at that time, some fifty years since, was a bus which ran three times a week to Quycombe Parva, a much larger village, with a railway station from which (it was said) persons of sufficient longevity might hope to reach Liverpool Street.

Penelope's father, who had been for five years a widower, was of a type now nearly extinct: low-church, bigoted, and opposed to every kind of enjoyment. His wife had been all that, in his opinion, a wife should be: submissive, patient, and indefatigable in parish work. He took it for granted that Penelope would follow unquestioningly in the footsteps of her sainted mother. Having no alternative, she did her best. She decorated the church for Christmas and the Harvest Festival; she presided over the

253

Mothers' Meeting; she visited old women and enquired about their ailments; she scolded the verger if he neglected his duties. No chink of pleasure was allowed to lighten her routine. The vicar frowned upon adornment of the female person. She wore always woollen stockings and a severe coat and skirt, presumably new once, but now shabby. Her hair was pulled tightly back from the forehead. No kind of ornament had ever been imagined, since her father would have thought it the inevitable gateway to hell. Except for a charwoman for two hours in the mornings, she had no domestic help, and had to do the cooking and housework in addition to the parish duties normally performed by vicars' wives.

She had, on occasion, made ineffectual efforts to achieve a little liberty; but in vain. Her father was always able to cite a text proving conclusively that her demands were wicked. He was particularly fond of Ecclesiasticus, which, as he was wont to point out, could be cited for edification though not for doctrine. Once, shortly after her mother's death, an itinerant fair came to Quycombe Magna and she asked if she might be allowed to see it. He replied, 'Whoso taketh pleasure in wickedness shall be condemned: but he that resisteth pleasure crowneth his life.' Once it was discovered that she had exchanged a few words with a passing cyclist who had asked the way to Ipswich. Her father was deeply shocked and said: 'She that is bold dishonoureth both her father and her husband, but they both shall despise her.' When she protested that the conversation had been harmless, he said that unless she reformed he would not allow her to go about the village alone, and reinforced the threat by the text: 'If thy daughter be shameless, keep her in straitly, lest she abuse herself through over much liberty.' She was fond of music and would have liked to have a piano, but her father considered this unnecessary, saying, 'Wine and music will rejoice the heart, but the love of wisdom is above them both.' He was never tired of explaining how much anxiety he had on her account. He would say, 'The father waketh for the daughter, when no man knoweth, and the care for her taketh away sleep . . . For from garments cometh a moth, and from women wickedness.'

The five years that followed her mother's death had driven Penelope to the very verge of what she could endure. At last, when she reached the age of twenty, a tiny crack opened in her prison walls. The Manor House, which had stood empty for some years, was again inhabited by the lady of the Manor, Mrs Menteith. She was American and well-to-do. Her husband, who could not endure vegetating in East Anglia, had gone out to Ceylon. She had returned from Ceylon to find schools for her sons and to see about letting the Manor House. The vicar could not wholly approve of her, as she was gay and well dressed, and what he would consider worldly. But, as the Manor House contributed by far the largest subscription to church expenses, he found a text in Ecclesiasticus about the unwisdom of offending the rich, and did not forbid his daughter to know the lively lady.

No sooner had Penelope finished sighing over her boredom than she heard a knock on the old-fashioned knocker on the front door of the vicarage, and on going down she found Mrs Menteith on the doorstep. A few sympathetic words brought an outburst from Penelope which touched Mrs Menteith's heart. Looking at the girl with the eye of a connoisseur, she perceived possibilities that neither the girl herself nor anybody in the parish had suspected.

'My dear,' she said, 'do you realize that if you were free to take a little trouble, you could be a raving beauty?'

'Oh, Mrs Menteith,' said the girl, 'surely you are joking!'

'No,' said the lady, 'I am not. And, if we can outwit your father, I will prove it.'

After some further conversation, they hatched a plot. At this moment Mr Colquhoun came in and Mrs Menteith said,

'Dear Mr Colquhoun, I wonder if you could spare your daughter to me for just one day. I have a lot of tiresome business to do in Ipswich and I shall find the time intolerably tedious if I have to be alone. You will be doing me a great kindness, if you allow your daughter to accompany me in my car.'

Somewhat reluctantly and after some further blandishment, the vicar consented.

The great day came, and Penelope could hardly contain herself for excitement.

'Your father,' said Mrs Menteith, 'is an old horror, and I am thinking out a scheme by which in time you may be liberated from his tyranny. When we get to Ipswich I will dress you from head to foot in the most becoming clothes that I can find there. I will have your hair done as it should be done. I think the result will surprise you.'

It certainly did. When Penelope saw herself dressed to satisfy Mrs Menteith, she looked in the long mirror and thought, 'Is this really me?' She became completely lost in a daze of nascent vanity. A whole flood of new emotions crowded in upon her. New hopes and undreamt-of possibilities made her determine to be done with the life of a drudge. But the manner of escape still remained an unsolved problem.

While she was still brooding, Mrs Menteith took her to the beauty parlour to have her hair done. She had to wait some time, and her eye fell upon a copy of *The Matrimonial News*.

'Mrs Menteith,' she said, 'you are doing so much for me that I hesitate to ask one further favour – What will be the use of looking beautiful if nobody ever sees me? And at Quycombe Magna, no young men are to be seen from one year's end to another. Will you allow me to put an advertisement in *The Matrimonial News* giving the Manor House as my address, and interviewing there any applicant who seems worth seeing?'

Mrs Menteith, who by this time was thoroughly enjoying the fun, agreed. And Penelope, with her help, drew up the following advertisement:

> *Young woman, of great beauty and impeccable virtue,*
> *but isolated in remote country district, wishes to meet*
> *young man with a view to matrimony. Applicants to*
> *enclose photograph and, if viewed favourably, young*
> *woman's photograph will be sent in return. Reply: Miss*
> *P., Manor House, Quycombe Magna.*
>
>   *P.S. – No clergy need apply.*

Having dispatched this advertisement, she underwent the ministrations of the beauty parlour and was then photographed in all her splendour. For the moment, this ended the dream of glory. She had to take off all her fine clothes and brush her hair back into its previous straight severity. But the fine clothes went back with Mrs Menteith to the Manor House with the promise that she should wear them in interviewing applicants.

When she got home, she put on a weary expression, and told her father how bored she'd been while waiting in the anterooms of solicitors and house agents.

'Penelope,' said her father, 'you were doing a kindness to Mrs Menteith, and the virtuous are never bored when doing a kindness.'

She accepted this observation with becoming meekness, and prepared herself to wait with what patience she could command for such replies as her advertisement might bring forth.

II

The replies to Penelope's advertisement were many and various. Some were earnest, some facetious; some explained that the writer was rich, or else that he was so clever that he soon would be rich; some, it was possible to suspect, hoped that matrimony might be avoided; some emphasized their good nature, others their powers of domination. Penelope, whenever she could, went to the Manor House to collect the answers. But there was only one among them all that she felt to be promising:

Dear Miss P.,

Your advertisement intrigues me. Few women would have the nerve to claim great beauty, and only a small proportion of these would at the same time claim impeccable virtue. I am trying to reconcile this with your aversion from the clerical profession, which permits the glimmer of a hope that your virtue is not more impeccable than becomes a young woman. I am consumed with curiosity, and, if you give me a chance to gratify it, you will increase my felicity.

Yours expectantly,

PHILIP ARLINGTON

P.S. – I enclose my photograph.

This letter intrigued her. The writer's complete silence as to his own merits made her suppose them so great that he could take them for granted. In the photograph, he looked lively and intelligent, with a considerable sense of fun and a not unpleasing dash of roguery. To him alone she replied, enclosing a photograph of herself in all her finery and suggesting a day on which she could meet him for lunch at the Manor House. He accepted. The day came.

The Manor House and Mrs Menteith's presence at lunch gave a favourable impression of Penelope's respectability and social status. After lunch they were left alone to make each other's acquaintance. He began by observing that in the matter of beauty her advertisement had claimed no more than the truth, and he expressed surprise that she had resorted to such a medium in the search for a husband, which (so he was pleased to say) should have been all too easy. This led her to explain her domestic circumstances, including the grounds of her objection to the clergy. With every moment she found his half-humorous sympathy more agreeable, and became more convinced that life as his wife would be in all respects the opposite of life as her father's daughter.

At the end of two hours' *tête-à-tête*, she was already in love with him and, so far as she could judge, he was by no means indifferent to her. She then broached the problem which had been troubling her.

'I am,' she said, 'only twenty years of age and cannot yet marry without my father's consent. He will never consent to my marrying a man who is not in Orders. Do you think that when I introduce you to him, you could convincingly pose as a clergyman?'

At this question, a queer twinkle appeared in his eyes, which she found somewhat puzzling, but he replied reassuringly,

'Yes, I think I can manage that.'

She was delighted to have him as a partner in the hoodwinking of her father, and felt more at one with him than ever. She spoke of him to her father as a friend of Mrs Menteith's whom she had happened to meet at the Manor House. Her father was naturally upset at the thought of losing a domestic drudge who demanded no wages, but Mrs Menteith backed up Penelope in glowing accounts of the young man's exemplary piety and of the chances of future preferment which he owed to several episcopal patrons. At last the old man reluctantly consented to inspect this paragon, and to permit the engagement if the inspection proved satisfactory. Penelope was on tenterhooks for fear her dear Philip should make some slip which would enable her father to discover the deception. But, to her bewildered joy, everything went off without a hitch. The young man spoke of the parish in which he was curate, described his vicar, mentioned that he had taken Orders because of the family living in which the present incumbent was ninety years of age, and wound up with a glowing peroration about the importance and sacredness of the work to which he hoped to dedicate his life. Penelope secretly gasped, but observed with amusement that her father's opinion of Philip grew with leaps and bounds, reaching its acme when the young man actually quoted Ecclesiasticus.

All the difficulties being thus smoothed away, the marriage took place in a few weeks. They went to Paris for their honeymoon, she explaining that she had had enough of the country and, when pleasure was the object, preferred populous gaiety to the beauties of nature. The honeymoon was to her one long dream of delight. Her husband was invariably charming and never objected to the many forms of frivolity which her abstemious years had compelled her hitherto to repress. There was only one cloud on the horizon. He was very reticent about himself, but explained that for financial reasons he was compelled to live in the village of Poppleton in Somerset. And from his talk about the neighbouring grand house, inhabited by Sir Rostrevor and Lady Kenyon, she supposed that he must be their agent. But, although she wondered at times that he was not more explicit, every moment of the honeymoon was so filled with pleasure that she had little time to brood on the matter. He explained that he must reach Poppleton on a certain Saturday. They arrived very late at the Rye House where he lived. It was too dark and she was too weary to wish for anything but sleep at the moment. He led her upstairs and she fell asleep as soon as her head touched the pillow.

III

She awoke next morning to the sound of church bells and to the sight of her husband putting on clerical attire. This sight made her instantly wide awake.

'What *are* you putting on those clothes for!' she exclaimed.

'Well, my dear,' he replied with a smile, 'the time has come to make a little confession. When I first saw your advertisement I felt nothing but curiosity, and it was only for fun that I suggested an interview. But, as soon as I saw you, I loved you. And every moment at the Manor House deepened this feeling. I determined to win you and, since this was impossible by fair means, I used foul ones. I can no longer conceal from you that I am a curate in this parish. That I have basely deceived you is true. My only excuse is the greatness of my love, which could not have won you in any other way.'

At this she leapt from her bed, exclaiming, 'I shall never forgive you! Never! Never! Never! But I will make you repent. I will make you rue the day that you treated a poor girl in this infamous manner. I will make you, and as many as possible of your clerical accomplices, as much of a laughing stock as you have made me.' By this time he was fully dressed. She pushed him out of the door, locked it, and remained in solitary dudgeon throughout the rest of the day.

He gave no sign of his presence until suppertime, when he knocked on her door with a tray saying, 'If you're going to punish me, you must keep alive; and if you're to keep alive, you must eat. So here's a tray. But you needn't speak to me. I'll put it on the floor and go away. *Bon appétit!*' At first she wanted to be proud, but she had had no breakfast and no lunch and no tea. And at last hunger overcame her, and she devoured everything on the tray. Nevertheless, she did not abandon her scheme of revenge.

Refreshed by her supper, she spent the evening composing a dignified letter to him, outlining a *modus vivendi* for the immediate future. She took great pains with this letter, and made several drafts of it. But in the end she was satisfied. In the final draft she said:

Sir,
   You will, of course, realize that, in view of your infamous behaviour, I shall never again speak an unnecessary word

*to you. I shall not tell the world what you have done to me,
for that would be to lay bare my own folly; but I shall make
it clear to all the world that I do not love you, that you
were infatuated, and that any other man would do as well.
I shall delight in causing scandal because it will reflect on
your judgement. And if, in doing so, I can bring clerics into
disrepute, my pleasure will be enhanced. My only aim in
life, henceforth, will be to inflict upon you a humiliation as
profound as that which you have inflicted upon me. Your
wife, henceforth in name only,*

PENELOPE

She put the letter on the supper tray, and put the supper tray
outside her door.

Next morning another tray appeared, containing not only a
delicious breakfast, but also a note. At first she thought she
would tear it into little pieces and throw the little pieces out of
the window. But she could not resist the hope that he would be
overwhelmed with sorrow and shame, and would make such
apology as the circumstances allowed. She tore open the letter
and read:

*Bravo, dearest Penelope! Your letter is a masterpiece in
dignified reproach. I doubt if I could have improved it if
you had asked my advice. But as for revenge, my dear, we
shall see. It may not work out quite as you are thinking.
Still your clerical admirer,*

PHILIP

P.S. – Don't forget the garden party.

The garden party in question, of which Philip had spoken during
the honeymoon, was to be given that day by Sir Rostrevor and
Lady Kenyon at their lovely Elizabethan mansion, Mendip Place.
The date had been fixed partly with a view to introducing the

bride to the county. For some time she hesitated as to whether she should go, her husband's postscript inclining her towards the negative. But after some deliberation she decided that the party would afford her an opportunity of inaugurating her revenge. She dressed with the utmost care. Indignation lent a sparkle to her looks, which made them even more irresistible than usual. She decided that it would further her ends to conceal her quarrel with her husband, and they arrived together with the utmost correctness. Her beauty was so dazzling that all the men who saw her forgot everything else. She, however, put on a demure and simple demeanour, and, ignoring the grand people who sought introductions to her, devoted her attentions almost exclusively to the vicar. The vicar, whose name was Mr Reverdy, was a man of young middle age, and Penelope discovered within a few minutes that he had a passion for local archaeology. He told her with great earnestness that there was in the neighbourhood a Long Barrow probably full of the most valuable prehistoric relics, but that he alone was interested in it, and no one could be induced to dig it up. She looked at him with great eyes and said, 'Oh, Mr Reverdy, what a shame!' He was so impressed that he congratulated his curate upon having found such a perfect soul-mate.

He managed to persuade Penelope (though, as he supposed, with some difficulty) to go next day in his carriage to view certain interesting archaeological remains at a distance of about ten miles from Poppleton. They were seen driving together through the village, he in very earnest conversation and she with an air of rapt attention. They were, of course, seen by everybody. But especially by a certain old lady named Mrs Quigley, who made the purveying of gossip her business. Mrs Quigley had a daughter whom she had destined for dear Mr Arlington, and she began to see reason to doubt the wisdom of his neglect of this excellent spinster. As the vicar and Penelope drove by, Mrs Quigley said, 'Humph!' And all those who heard her understood the meaning of this monosyllable. But worse was to follow. Next morning, at a moment when Mr Arlington was known to be occupied with parish duties, the vicar was seen marching up to the Rye House, carrying a large tome on the archaeology of Somerset. And he was observed to stay for a considerably longer time than the mere delivery of the volume would require. Backstairs gossip revealed to Mrs Quigley, and therefore to the whole village, that the newly married couple occupied separate rooms.

The poor vicar, meanwhile, not yet aware of Mrs Quigley's activities, babbled to everybody about the beauty, intelligence, and virtue of his curate's wife. And with every word that he uttered, he increased the gravamen of the charges against himself as well as her. At last Mrs Quigley could bear it no longer and felt it her duty to write to Mr Glasshouse, the Rural Dean, suggesting that for the sake of the dear vicar it would be well if a cure could be found elsewhere for the curate. Mr Glasshouse, who knew Mrs Quigley, was not inclined to take the matter very seriously, and thought that a word in season to the vicar was all that would be necessary. He visited the vicar, who assured him that nothing in the world could be more innocent than the few dealings that he had had with Mrs Arlington. He, however, praised her innocence somewhat more warmly than the Rural Dean thought quite fitting. And Mr Glasshouse decided to view the lady for himself.

He arrived at the Rye House at tea-time, and was warmly welcomed by Penelope, who was beginning to get a little tired of archaeology and the vicar. It must, however, be confessed that when Mr Glasshouse, with great delicacy, approached the subject of the scandalous rumours retailed to him by Mrs Quigley, Penelope, though she denied everything, did it in such a manner as to convince Mr Glasshouse that the vicar had been at least indiscreet. Mr Glasshouse by this time had confessed that archaeology was too much concerned with the dead past to suit his taste, and that for his part he preferred life to dead stones.

'Oh, Mr Glasshouse,' she replied, 'how right you are, and how wholly I agree with you. Do tell me, dear Dean, what forms of life particularly interest you.'

'Rare birds,' he replied, 'especially those that frequent the fens of Sedgemoor, where not only are kingfishers common, but even yellow water-wagtails reward the patient watcher.'

Clasping her hands together, and looking up at him enthusiastically, she explained that in spite of living in the neighbourhood of the Norfolk fens, and in spite of many journeys of exploration, she had never yet been gratified in her longing to see a yellow water-wagtail.

The Rural Dean, sad as it is to relate, forgot his mission, forgot his duty to the diocese, forgot his sacred calling, and invited her to join him in watching for the yellow water-wagtail in a lonely spot that he knew to be one of its favourite haunts.

'Oh, Mr Dean,' she replied, 'what *will* Mrs Quigley say?'

He did his best to put on the airs of the man of the world, and brushed aside that virtuous matron as a woman of no account. Before he could finish the second cup of tea, Penelope had yielded to his vehemence and agreed to join him in an expedition on the first fine day.

They went. But, lonely as the spot was, Mrs Quigley's spies were at work. Before long she knew the worst, and more. Seeing that the Church had failed her, she attempted to secure the help of Lady Kenyon, assuring her that from the reports she had received it was not only birds that the Rural Dean had observed.

'I will not say more,' she added, 'for that is too easy to imagine. Can you, dear Lady, exorcize this Siren who is turning from the path of duty even the most staid and highly respected of our religious mentors?' Lady Kenyon replied that she would think it over and see what she could do. Knowing Mrs Quigley, she thought that it might be wise to get a more first-hand report as to the facts, so she called on Penelope and asked what all the fuss was about.

After a little coaxing, she got the whole story out of Penelope. But, instead of taking the story tragically, Lady Kenyon merely laughed.

'Oh, my dear girl,' she said, 'what you're doing is really too easy. How can you expect these stuffy old men to resist you? Why, they'd never seen a really beautiful woman in their lives until they saw you . . .'

'Except yourself,' interjected Penelope. But Lady Kenyon ignored the interjection, and went on as if Penelope had not spoken.

'No, my dear, if your revenge is to be worth anything, it must be practised on someone worthy of your mettle. The Bishop of Glastonbury, whose clergy you have been leading along the primrose path, is worthy of your steel. I should not wonder if in him you were to meet your match. I will arrange a tournament between you and him, and I myself will "rain influence and judge the prize" – with complete impartiality I assure you, for, though I greatly admire the Bishop, I cannot but enjoy your adventurous spirit.'

IV

The Bishop of Glastonbury was a man of considerable scholastic eminence, which had enabled him to rise in the clerical profession in spite of what some considered a regrettable frivolity. Although no real scandal had ever been fastened upon him, he was known to be fond of the society of charming ladies and not always wholly serious in his converse with them. Lady Kenyon, who knew him well, told him all that she had gathered about Penelope and the havoc that she was wreaking on his clergy.

'The girl,' she said, 'is not really bad, but only very angry. And it must be admitted that she has cause for anger. I was unable to exert a good influence upon her, partly, I think, because her story amused me and I could not find it in my heart to scold her. But you, my dear Bishop, will, I am convinced, succeed where I have failed. If you are willing, I will get her to meet you here, and we shall see what we shall see.'

The Bishop agreed; and Penelope was duly invited to meet him at Mendip Place. Recent experience had given her confidence, and she did not doubt that she would be able to turn the Bishop round her little finger. She duly told him her tale, but was somewhat disconcerted by the fact that he smiled at the most pathetic parts. And when she looked up at him with adoring eyes, such as no vicar or Rural Dean could resist, to her horror he merely winked. The wink made her change her tone, and she became simple and sincere. The Bishop elicited from her that, in spite of furious anger, she still loved Philip, but pride would not allow her to admit it to him.

'My dear,' said the Bishop, who was treating her affectionately but not seriously, 'I don't think your present course is likely to bring you much satisfaction. The world is full of silly men ready to fall in love with you, but you cannot love a silly man. And no man who is not silly can fail to see that your husband holds your heart. He has, of course, played an all but unforgivable trick upon you, and I do not suggest that you should behave as if nothing had happened. But I think that if you are ever to achieve any happiness, you must find something better to do than bemusing foolish parsons. What you should do is for you to decide, but it should be something more positive and satisfying than revenge.' With that he patted her hand and said, 'Think it over, my dear, and in due course let me know your decision.'

She went home somewhat deflated, and realizing for the first time that a noble wrath is in the long run an unsatisfying diet. There were difficult practical decisions to be made if she altered

267

her way of life. She was not prepared to surrender to the point of becoming the submissive wife of a country curate, still less was she prepared to go back to her father. She must therefore find some way of earning a living. In a long letter to Mrs Menteith, she related what had happened to her since her marriage, ending with the Bishop's friendly admonition.

> *From you* [she ended] *I have had so much kindness that I hesitate to ask even more. But I feel that perhaps you could help me to find my feet. Would you be willing to meet me in London to talk things over?*

They met and, in consequence, Mrs Menteith persuaded her own dressmaker to take on Penelope as a mannequin. When she moved to London, she ceased to have any communication with her husband. Poppleton forgot her. And no one missed her except Mrs Quigley – and possibly her husband, though his feelings were never expressed. Her beauty made her an asset to the dressmaker, and it was gradually discovered that she had great talent as a dress designer. She rose rapidly, and within three years was earning a very comfortable salary. She was about to be taken into partnership, when she received a doleful letter from her father saying that he was very unwell and feared he was dying:

> *You have behaved very ill* [he said] *both to me and to your worthy husband. But I wish all ill-feeling to end before I die, and for this reason I shall be glad if you will return for however brief a space to your old home.*
>   *In all Christian love,*
>
>   YOUR FATHER

With a heavy heart she went to Liverpool Street. As she was looking for a seat, she saw – but could it be? – her husband, not in clerical dress, looking very prosperous and about to get into a first-class carriage. For a moment they stared at each other. Then she exclaimed, 'Philip!' And at the very same moment he exclaimed, 'Penelope!'

'My dear, you are lovelier than ever,' he said.

'Philip,' she replied, 'what has become of those clothes that caused our rupture?'

'They are left to the care of moth-balls,' he replied. 'I discovered that I have talent as an inventor, so I gave up the Church. I have a very good income, and am on my way to visit the Cambridge Scientific Instrument Makers about a new patent. But how about you? You don't look exactly poverty-stricken.'

'No,' she said, 'I, too, have prospered.' And she related her successful career.

'I always thought you were no fool,' he said.

'And I always thought you were a knave,' she replied, 'but now I no longer mind.' With that they fell into each other's arms on the platform.

'Jump in, Sir and Madam,' said the guard. And they lived happy ever after.

Acknowledgements

John Galsworthy, 'A Fisher of Men' from *Caravan*, reprinted by permission of the Society of Authors as the Literary Representative of the Estate of John Galsworthy

Christopher Park, 'The Vicarage Clock', reprinted by permission of the author

T. F. Powys, 'The Rival Pastors' from *The White Paternoster*, reprinted by permission of Gerald Pollinger Ltd and the Estate of T. F. Powys

Bertrand Russell, 'Benefit of Clergy' from *Satan in the Suburbs and Other Stories*, reprinted by permission of Routledge Ltd and the Bertrand Russell Peace Foundation

Dylan Thomas, 'The Enemies' from *Miscellany Three*, reprinted by permission of David Higham Associates

William Trevor, 'Autumn Sunshine' from *Beyond the Pale and Other Stories*, reprinted by permission of the Peters Fraser & Dunlop Group Ltd

Every effort has been made to contact copyright-holders. However, the editor and publishers would be pleased to hear from any that they have been unable to trace and due acknowledgment will be made in future editions.